Empire Night

On Union Station

Also by the author:

Book Eighteen of EarthCent Ambassador

Empire Night
On Union Station

Foner Books

978-1-948691-25-3

Northampton, Massachusetts

One

"In conclusion, it is the view of Union Station Embassy that the unexpected royalty stream from the All Species Cookbook should be used to start a rainy day fund, but between the upcoming Conference of Sovereign Human Communities trade show and my less-than-stellar track record dealing with finances, I would like to request the addition of an investment officer to my embassy staff to handle the day-to-day—what's the word I'm thinking of?"

"Management," the Stryx station librarian suggested.

"Management," Kelly concluded. "Could you splice that onto the end so I don't have to repeat the whole thing, Libby? If I start over I'll probably just forget something else."

"Done and sent. If you're that bothered by these little memory slips you should start writing things down."

"You mean on paper?" the ambassador asked incredulously.

"EarthCent Intelligence can provide you with pencils, or you could use the pen that M793qK gave you."

"I'd feel funny pulling out a solid gold pen every time I needed to write something down. What comes next? A jewel-encrusted notebook?"

"A pencil and a small diary to carry in your purse would serve as well."

"But I'm not forgetting about appointments or things on my mental to-do list, or at least, I don't think I am. It's just that sometimes when I'm talking I can't come up with common words. Do you think I have dysphasia?"

"Anybody who can use dysphasia in a sentence doesn't have it," Libby replied.

"Isn't there a test you can give me? When my father was having problems towards the end and my mother took him to the doctor, she said they showed him a bunch of cards with inkblots and asked him what he saw."

"You're confusing the subjective Rorschach test with an objective neuropsychological assessment tool. Problems coming up with words can be quantified with a naming test."

"All right, then." The EarthCent ambassador straightened up in her chair and gripped the edge of her display desk as if to brace herself. "Hit me with a naming test."

"I don't have to, Ambassador. We speak at length every day and I'd notice if you were experiencing a sudden cognitive decline."

"Thank goodness," Kelly said, letting out her breath. "Wait. What if it's not sudden? What if I'm slowly going downhill?"

"Then you better get started investing the cookbook windfall while you're still capable of learning something new," Libby replied. "We've been making an exception by allowing you to carry excess funds on the embassy's programmable cred, but it's been a full year now."

"I know. Donna's husband explained to me a long time ago that programmable creds can't be used to hoard money because they have something like a half-life or a built-in tax."

"Above one million creds of old money, the balance begins to decay at an accelerating rate. We created our currency to encourage trade, not to serve as a galactic safe deposit box."

"Isn't our cookbook income new money?" Kelly asked.

"The amounts received over five cycles ago are now old. We base the accounting on a first-in, first-out basis, so as long as you keep the creds moving, you won't run into a problem even if the balance goes much higher. Why don't you keep track of the flows in your new diary?"

"What's the sudden enthusiasm for me writing things down? Did you invest in a paper factory?"

"Taking notes will help you form stronger memories," the Stryx station librarian explained. "In addition to the extra effort that goes into editing your thoughts, the time available to impress new information on your brain is stretched out by the writing process."

"Where am I going to find a paper diary on Union Station?" Kelly asked. "And it sounds like you're suggesting I should start looking into investing opportunities by myself. Maybe I'll just ask Blythe."

"That's a good idea. She could print one of her translated alien romances for you and substitute a file of blank pages, though perhaps you should ask for lines."

"I meant I could ask her help with investing, though then she might wonder why she's continuing to subsidize EarthCent Intelligence and Eccentric Enterprises if we're rolling in money here."

"Blythe and Chastity are entrepreneurs, not investors."

"Is there a difference?"

"Entrepreneurs create new businesses," Libby explained. "Investors seek returns on existing wealth."

"We have an unexpected guest from Flower and it sounds like there's a potential problem with CoSHC," Donna's voice announced from Kelly's display desk. "Daniel just got off a conference call and he wants to meet Flower's emissary in the conference room if you're not running home to cook."

"The timing works out perfectly because Samuel said he could join us for supper this evening if we pushed it back," the EarthCent ambassador told the embassy manager, her best friend of over thirty years. "Joe is going to handle the cooking on the grill so I'm free for another hour. I'll be out in a sec."

Kelly grabbed her purse from the deep file drawer before going over to her office door and waving open the security lock that she always engaged while making her weekly report to EarthCent. Donna was just disappearing into the conference room with a tall stranger, and the door to her associate ambassador's office was open, but the room was empty, so Daniel must have gone ahead.

"Do you know what this is all about, Libby?" Kelly subvoced as she followed the others.

"You're going to find out in less than a minute," the Stryx librarian responded. "Patience is a virtue."

"So it's bad news," Kelly said, fishing for a reaction, but none was forthcoming. She entered the conference room and was immediately struck by the rugged immersive-star looks of their unexpected guest. Nobody had taken a seat yet, and Donna made the formal introductions.

"Dewey, this is Ambassador McAllister," the embassy manager said, and then gestured to Daniel, who was coming out of the kitchenette with a fresh mug of coffee, "and the caffeine addict is Associate Ambassador Cohan. Dewey is a special emissary from Flower," she concluded.

4

"Pleased to meet you," the handsome man said, shaking hands with Kelly and Daniel in turn. "I'm sorry for showing up without any notice, but it's all very hush-hush and Flower doesn't trust your communications security."

"Can I get you something to drink?" Daniel offered.

"If you have high-proof alcohol, I can always store it in a holding tank for my backup micro-turbine, but as an artificial person, I require neither food nor drink."

"Oh, I thought you looked a little too good to be human," Kelly said. "I was thinking Vergallian, though."

Dewey smiled, and then removed a device from his shoulder bag that looked remarkably like the Farling version of an external translator. He held a finger up to his lips for a moment, then flipped the device over and slid open a panel on the back before pressing a button. The air in the conference room began to shimmer, and the little background noises that were always present in the embassy suddenly sounded muffled or flat.

"Please forgive my caution, but Flower insisted I borrow a jammer from M793qK," the artificial person said. "The Farling random molecular vibration shell is proof against the eavesdropping technology of any tunnel network species, though I'm told the Stryx could reconstruct what we say without any difficulty."

"Not to mention that the station librarian is always listening through my implant," Kelly added.

"Flower knows better than to try keeping secrets from the Stryx," Dewey said, and then returned to the matter at hand. "As you know, our ship hosts intelligence agents from several of the tunnel network species in cooperation with EarthCent Intelligence. While these agents are officially in competition with one another, Flower has fostered a collegial approach to the whole business. Putting together tidbits from various sources, she's concluded that the Stryx are about to offer empire status to the Conference of Sovereign Human Communities."

"Empire status?" Kelly repeated.

"The Human Empire," Dewey confirmed. "EarthCent Intelligence recently completed their first census of humans living on CoSHC worlds and the number has passed one billion."

"But I thought that empire status required at least twenty sovereign worlds or colonies," Daniel protested. "Not to mention a fleet."

"The recent addition of the Traders Guild to CoSHC has given you a fleet of over a million small ships, even if none of them are jump-capable, and you're way past the bar with sovereign human communities."

"The requirement was for communities, not worlds?"

"A sovereign presence on at least twenty different worlds," Dewey said. "The latest version of the tunnel network treaty doesn't stipulate that you must own the world or be the only sovereign entity in residence."

"How come we haven't heard the results of the census yet?" Donna asked. "EarthCent Intelligence would have informed us immediately."

"I believe Flower's information in this case comes from the intelligence services of some of the other species tapping into your secure communications for the raw data. Your intelligence analysts are no doubt busy writing up a report that you'll receive in the near future."

"Doesn't Flower work for EarthCent Intelligence?" Kelly asked pointedly.

"Yes and no," Daniel replied before Dewey could speak. "I'm in regular contact with Captain Pyun and Lynx, and they've been reporting for some time that their relationship with Flower has grown fluid. They believe that she's acting in our best interests," he added hastily, with a glance at the artificial person, "but she has her own ideas as to where those interests lay. And she recently applied to register as a sovereign human community herself."

"But she's a twenty-thousand-year-old sentient Dollnick colony ship," Kelly protested. "How can she become a member of CoSHC?"

"Kute's Rule," Dewey supplied the answer. "Flower claims that her presence has been sufficiently diluted by the nearly three-quarters of a million humans living on board to meet the legal requirements."

"But surely the Stryx will notify us as soon as all of the qualifications for empire are met," Daniel said. "Why did Flower think it necessary for you to rush here and warn us?"

"Speaking on my own account, I'm sure the idea of impressing you with her utility as a potential member of CoSHC, and by extension, the future Human Empire, crossed her mind," the artificial person said. "But the official reason is to make sure that the other species don't catch you off guard with their reactions."

"She thinks they'll feel threatened by a Human Empire?" Kelly asked. "As long as Earth remains a Stryx protectorate, I don't see how that changes anything."

"Flower isn't worried that the other species will suddenly find you threatening," Dewey said with a smile. "How do you think the Grenouthians will react to CoSHC becoming an empire?"

"I better ping Walter," Daniel said, referring to his brother-in-law, who was the managing editor of the Galactic Free Press. "Donna, can you get your daughter up to speed at the same time?"

"Which one?" the embassy manager asked.

After a moment's thought, the associate ambassador said, "Chastity first, then Blythe. This is more about spin control than an intelligence emergency. Chastity knows all of the top Grenouthians at the network, and maybe she can persuade them that it's not that funny."

"What isn't that fun—oh," Kelly said, as Daniel and Donna both pointed at their ears and began carrying on subvoced conversations over their implants. "So Flower thinks that the Grenouthians are going to treat this whole thing like a joke," she said to the artificial person.

"It's pretty low hanging fruit, making fun of a Human Empire," Dewey said. "A fleet that consists of pre-owned trade ships, most of them obsolete Sharf models, and all of the qualifying sovereign communities being located on worlds or space structures that belong to other species."

"I wonder if that's a first. Libby?"

"It seems congratulations are in order," Libby replied dryly. If Dewey was surprised by the Stryx librarian's ability to project coherent sound waves through the Farling isolation technology, he didn't show it.

"And you couldn't have warned me earlier?" Kelly followed up.

"Declaring a Human Empire will have wide-reaching effects on your business relations with the tunnel network species," Libby explained. "Alerting you to the possibility would have created an unfair competitive advantage. Everything you need to know is in the tunnel network treaty if you read the fine print."

"The tunnel network treaty is even longer than the end user license agreements for our implants," the EarthCent ambassador protested. "Nobody could possibly read the whole thing."

"Flower did," Dewey said. "She also thought that the Grenouthians would be amused by CoSHC's lack of a formal governing structure. Daniel is the closest thing the sovereign human communities have to an emperor, and the annual tradeshow is run by an ad hoc council. They aren't even bothering with a full conference this year."

"The membership just isn't that interested in building governmental institutions," Kelly told Flower's special emissary. "They're all happy concentrating on business and buying whatever services they need from their host species."

"Chastity is on her way to gather Walter and then they're both going to the Grenouthian studios," Donna said, dropping her hand.

"I'm surprised Chastity is taking it so seriously," Kelly said. "The Grenouthians have made fun of us before and they'll make fun of us again. I doubt they'll even give the story much play because the visuals will be so boring. Are they going to show a bunch of sales reps making deals at the last tradeshow? Their viewers would fall asleep."

"Chastity was planning to surprise everybody with this but she decided to just tell us now," Donna said. "The Galactic Free Press has been fighting a losing battle against demands to increase their video content, and the result has been that their subscribers just go elsewhere for it. So they're doing a trial hookup with the Grenouthian Network to cover the tradeshow jointly. The paper will provide in-depth analysis and the bunnies will do the holographic recordings."

"Based on my experience with network coverage at Flower's first con, I could see that going wrong in spectacular ways," Dewey said. "Sales reps aren't professional politicians. If they have any experience speaking on camera, it would be through their local Children's News Network affiliate."

"Chastity said the tradeshow was supposed to be a beta test," Donna told them. "The Grenouthians actually do some decent journalism if you ignore all of the snark about primitive species and video of things blowing up. I'm going to ping Blythe now," she added, and pointed at her ear again.

"So we'll try not to blow anything up at the tradeshow and the Grenouthians won't have a reason to run the video on their network," Kelly said. "Was Flower aware of any immediate obligations that CoSHC will have to deal with when the official census numbers are released, Dewey?"

"There are a number of things, mainly procedural in nature, but the one that you'll want to get a jump on is preparing for alien observers. According to the tunnel network treaty, CoSHC's decision on whether to accept or reject empire status must be made in a transparent nature, and that includes hosting official observers from any alien species that cares to send them."

"Walter just told me he heard the same from one of his sources," Daniel said, lowering his hand. "Apparently he's been hearing rumblings about the empire thing for some time, but everybody thought we were still years away. I'm not sure how CoSHC can be expected to host alien observers, but I guess it will fall to me to make the effort."

"As long as our embassy is cosponsoring the tradeshow, I suppose that we can be front-and-center on dealing with any alien observers," Kelly said. "Aabina's royal training has made her a walking encyclopedia of alien protocol, so I'll ask her if she's willing to take the lead."

"Blythe tells me they'll be burning the midnight oil at EarthCent Intelligence all weekend and should have a briefing ready for us on Monday morning," Donna reported. "She and Clive are in a meeting with their senior analysts as we speak, and they're all mortified that they missed this. Since the cat's already out of the bag, Clive wants to take the time to put together an accurate assessment of our options rather than just adding to the confusion."

"According to Flower, the first thing we have to do is to issue an open invitation for alien governments to send observers as CoSHC decides whether or not to begin the empire process," Daniel recapped what Donna had missed. "The process needs to be transparent, and our embassy is going to take responsibility for the observers who will probably expect diplomatic attention."

"So at this point, we're basically waiting to hear how Chastity and Walter do with the Grenouthians," Kelly said. "I have a question for the three of you while we're waiting. I underestimated the cash-flow from the All Species Cookbook royalties and subsidiary rights, and the president agrees that we should save a substantial portion of the money rather than rushing to spend every last cred. Do any of you have any investing experience?"

"Does casino gambling count?" Daniel asked.

"My husband is the money manager in our family, and the girls keep Stanley busy handling the finances for InstaSitter," Donna said. "I'm sure he'll be willing to give you all the advice you want for the price of dinner."

"This body is the only significant investment I've made in my life," Dewey informed the ambassador. "It took all of my savings."

"I'm sure there will be plenty of opportunities to talk about investments at the tradeshow," Daniel said. "Businesses in our sovereign communities are always looking for capital."

"That reminds me," Kelly said. "Who's doing the keynote for the tradeshow?"

"It's on my to-do list to ask you."

"It will be my pleasure, and I know that Aabina likes to keep her speechwriting skills sharp."

"Where is your special assistant?" Daniel asked. "She's usually the last of us to leave on Fridays. Is there some special event at the Vergallian embassy she needed to attend?"

"She's with my son on the travel concourse seeing her mother off," Kelly said. "Samuel wanted to travel with the Vergallian ambassador, of course, but Aainda said he needs to stay on Union Station to represent her embassy at the trade-show. Until then, she's loaned him to EarthCent as a goodwill gesture."

"If Samuel is going to be working here, who's going to be left at the Vergallian embassy?" Daniel asked. "We aren't losing Aabina, are we?"

"We need Aabina more than her mother does, and I didn't offer her in trade," Kelly said with a laugh. "The Vergallian embassy is basically on standby during Jubilee since their whole empire practically shuts down for three months. Dorothy's friend Affie, the princess under contract to handle Alt affairs on Union Station, will fill in for their ambassador if the need arises."

"So Aabina will be back at the embassy this evening?" the associate ambassador asked hopefully.

"I invited her to come eat with us," Kelly said. "That's why I'm still here after five on a Friday evening. The ambassador's ship leaves at six, and then Samuel will be able to join us for dinner for the first time in weeks. You shouldn't be working late either, Daniel. You have a wife and two children at home."

"No, I have a wife and two children spending the afternoon at Libbyland with Aisha for the *Let's Make Friends* cast rotation get-together, which included a banquet at the medieval castle."

"Was that today? How old is Grace now?"

"Eight. This will be her last season."

"Anyway, it looks like I know how I'll be spending my weekend," Kelly said mournfully. "I'll try to arrange an emergency meeting with my Intelligence Steering Committee on Sunday to get the input of the president and the other senior ambassadors. Do you have somewhere to stay, Dewey? We have plenty of room at home."

"Flower wanted me to return and report after delivering her message," the artificial person said, and pressed the button on the back of the Farling device. The shimmer in the air disappeared. "It was very nice meeting you all, and I suspect Flower will send me back to talk again after you reach a decision on accepting empire status."

"Thank you for coming," Daniel said, offering Dewey another handshake. "I think I'll stop by EarthCent Intelligence and see what they've come up with so far. Maybe Clive has an analyst available who has actually read the tunnel network treaty."

"It's a good thing I invited Aabina tonight for dinner," Kelly said brightly. "She probably knows the treaty by heart."

Two

"Wow, it feels like forever since I've been back here," Dorothy told Flazint while removing a backpack from the shelf. "I'd almost forgotten that my idea for designing cross-species apparel came from working in the lost-and-found while I was studying fashion at the Open University."

"You and Chance searched through the lost hats accumulated over thousands of years trying to spot how fashions repeat themselves," the Frunge girl said. "Eventually the two of you realized that different species were actually copying from each other. I was working that day. Remember?"

"I do, and I had a dream about it last month when Kevin and I got home from chaperoning your date at four in the morning on our time. I've been meaning to bring it up ever since."

"I'm sorry about the time difference, but you're the one who insisted we alternate inconveniences."

"Not that," Dorothy said. "My dream was more like a flashback. It started with the first time we met, when you had that big hair-vine trellis that forced you to walk sideways behind the lost-and-found counter, and ended with the guy who bought you a grow lamp for your birthday. How is it that you were dating left and right

14

while you were in school, and then all of a sudden it became this serious thing with contracts and chaperones?"

"You mean my practice dating?" Flazint asked. "That doesn't count."

"What do you mean it doesn't count?"

"It's just kid stuff. Did you take it seriously when your little brother and Vivian began practicing ballroom dancing three hours a day?"

"Actually, everybody who saw them dance was sure they would end up together. That is, if my brother ever got over Ailia, the little Vergallian orphan who Aisha brought home when the girl's nurse abandoned her on set."

"Oh. Well, it's not like that with us. When our hair vines begin budding, our ancestors give us permission to start practice dating so we can learn how to behave in mixed company. It's highly choreographed and we're graded on the results."

"You never told me that!"

"It's kind of embarrassing," Flazint admitted. "The Drazens have practice dating too, but they start later than we do, and they don't have to fill out exercise books."

"You mean there's a physical element, like you have to wrestle with the boys or something?"

The Frunge girl's hair vines flushed dark green and she pretended to take an interest in a Huktra egg-carrier with a long shoulder strap before replying. "I wish you wouldn't say such things, Dorothy. I meant an exercise book like the ones you showed me from when you went to the station librarian's experimental school."

"You spent your practice dates doing story problems?"

"Not exactly, but sort of. Like when that boy gave me the grow lamp, he was learning how to purchase an expensive gift and I was learning how to receive one. I had

15

to return the grow lamp when we completed that set of lessons."

"And all those hours you spent training your hair vines on new trellises for big dates, that was just make-believe?" Dorothy asked.

"Not make-believe, practice. I never understood how you could just start dating that David boy who came into the lost-and-found when you never had any formal training. Affie and I were terribly worried that it would end badly."

"It did end badly—he eloped with that woman my Mom brought back from Earth. I was always suspicious that was Libby's doing, getting him out of the way so I'd be free when Kevin returned to Union Station."

"Tzachan really enjoys hanging out with your husband on our dates. Sometimes I'm jealous. Kevin didn't mind taking off work in his chandlery to watch your baby today?"

"It's Sunday on our calendar, my whole family is watching Margie. Kevin says we better hurry up and give her a younger sibling or she'll grow up spoiled."

"But she's only two! How close together can you make babies?"

"You don't want to know," Dorothy said, pulling a strapless soft-sided case from the shelf. It looked like it might have been intended as a screen protector for an oversized tab, and there was some alien branding with a logo embossed on the side. "What do you think of this one?"

"Didn't we agree that handles are a must," the Frunge girl said. "You know how many free samples there are at tradeshows."

"If you ask me, designing a swag bag is beneath the dignity of SBJ Fashions," the EarthCent ambassador's daughter said, tossing the case back on the shelf. "I wouldn't be surprised if Affie claimed she had to meet an Alt delegation in the Vergallian embassy today just to get out of it."

"I know. Swag bags don't even have clasp hardware. I mean, CoSHC could hand out shopping bags at the tradeshow and nobody would know the difference."

"Are you planning on showing your latest puzzle clasps at the tradeshow?"

Flazint grimaced. "Shaina and Brinda say that they're too hard for Humans to solve. I guess there have been some issues with customers not being able to get their purses open again after putting in all of their stuff."

"But you always include a cheat sheet!"

"It seems that some buyers thought that the safest place to keep the cheat sheet was in their purse. I don't even know if Jeeves is going to pay for a booth this year. Stick hasn't mentioned anything."

"Just because Stick's the sales manager doesn't mean he knows everything that's going on," Dorothy said. "I just wish that we had something new to show. Sometimes I wonder where the last year went."

"It's just not the same with Affie out so often, and you know that little Margie keeps you too busy to take work home the way you used to," Flazint said.

"Maybe we should just—what's this?"

"What's what?"

"This," Dorothy said, pulling from the shelf an attractive tote with a message embroidered in Horten script. "What's it say?"

"I only know a few thousand words in Horten and I don't recognize those," Flazint said apologetically. "The color scheme is very attractive."

"Libby?" Dorothy asked, holding out the bag with a hand underneath to present the embroidered side to the ceiling. "Can you read this?"

"Better safe than sorry," the Stryx librarian translated the words. "It's in the Old Tongue, which is why you didn't recognize any words, Flazint."

"How about the printing around the outside of the circle with the—what is that—a beckoning hand?" Dorothy asked.

"It says 'Come home to Gortunda.' That's the official trademarked logo of the Horten religious revival that's been running on Stryx stations for over four hundred thousand years."

"That's a really good logo," Flazint said. "I wonder what they did to the fabric to give the bag that full look. It would work well for a tradeshow because the visitors coming in would think that the ones leaving had found all sorts of great stuff to take home."

"It doesn't look full, it is full," Dorothy said. "Somebody probably set it down in a corridor and a maintenance bot grabbed it as abandoned. You know how they are."

"What's in there?"

"Don't make a mess," Libby warned them. "You have to keep it all together in case the owner returns to claim it."

"How long has it been here?" Dorothy asked.

"That shelving unit was last stocked fifty-four hundred years ago."

"I don't think Hortens live that long, Libby."

"Perhaps the bag belonged to a longer-lived visitor. Gortunda welcomes all comers."

"Look," Flazint said, drawing a small case out of the swag bag. "It's a grooming kit, with scissors, a razor, nail clippers, and a file."

"What a waste," Dorothy sighed. "I could use a file."

"And a thermos," the Frunge girl continued, shaking the container. "It's still full."

"I wonder if the liquid is still warm."

"After fifty-four hundred years?"

"Libby?" Dorothy asked.

"Horten travel thermoses are only rated to retain ninety percent of their content's heat for three cycles," the Stryx librarian replied.

"What's that printed on the thermos?" Flazint asked.

"Fifty percent tithing reduction for aliens, this week only," Libby translated for them.

"Is that a fifty percent reduction for life, or fifty percent for the week?"

"The message leaves that open to interpretation," the Stryx librarian explained. "The Old Tongue isn't the most precise language for commercial offerings but it works well for prophecy."

"I don't know," Dorothy said, holding the bag open for Flazint to replace the ancient freebies. "I think something more modern looking is what we want. Is there another example of a revival swag bag in the lost-and-found, Libby? Maybe something with metallic thread?"

"Oh, yes. Metallic thread is the best," the Frunge girl enthused.

"I shouldn't do your work for you, but in the interest of limiting the mess you make in here, try the shelving unit at 1 SM 10/22," the station librarian advised.

"It must be old with that prefix number," Dorothy said. "I'm not sure I remember how the system works."

"It's easy," Flazint said, running her finger along the shelves. "Look, we're in 2 SM now, so it's that way."

"Are you sure?" Dorothy called back after turning the corner. "This unit starts with 1 KGS."

"Oops, then it's somewhere in between."

The former lost-and-found employees navigated to the end of the row where the Frunge girl quickly found the location that the Stryx librarian had suggested.

"Wow! That's a serious piece of baggage," Dorothy said, admiring the suitcase Flazint pulled off the shelf. "You could hide a person in there, but it's a bit much for a convention giveaway."

"Behind it," Libby instructed.

"This?" Dorothy pulled out a dull black blob of cloth. "It looks like a dishrag."

"Shake it open. It's been crumpled up for over five millennia."

"I like it," Flazint said immediately. "See how the corners hold their shape even though there's nothing in the bag? And the Gortunda trademark is just an iron-on patch, which means if we can find a supplier, all we have to do is supply the artwork."

"I hate the color, but the fabric is interesting," Dorothy said, crumpling it up, and then snapping it open again by jerking on the handles. "It doesn't weigh any more than it would if it was made out of silk, and it's pretty useful to have a tote bag that you can ball up and stick in a pocket or a corner of your purse."

"It must be a variation on Verlock memory metal, but in a weave," the Frunge girl said, rubbing the fabric between her thumb and forefinger. "I've never seen it before, though. Do they still manufacture it, Librarian?"

"There's a distributor on the Verlock deck with over a hundred thousand units left over from an order that was never picked up. I'm sure they would have gotten rid of the bags by now if not for the fact that they take up so little storage space when you put them under compression. And you can change the color by running the bags through an electromagnetic field of the proper frequency. It was considered quite a fashion engineering feat around twenty thousand years ago."

"I don't understand how fabric that combines color programmability with shape memory could ever go out of fashion," Dorothy said. "I've got to get Jeeves to buy me some."

"There was a minor problem with the color programming that the inventors never quite overcame."

"Does it fade with time or in the wash?"

"Nothing as crude as that," Libby said. "The Frunge Metallic Fibers Manufacturing Association wasn't happy about losing business to the Verlocks, so they put their scientists to work on countermeasures and developed a low-cost disposable color programming unit."

"How come I never heard about this?" Flazint demanded.

"It happened some time ago, and I don't think your ancestors were particularly proud of their solution."

"I don't understand," Dorothy said. "Wouldn't a low-cost color programming unit make the fabric even more attractive?"

"The color of the crystalline metallic fibers is controlled by the frequency of the applied electromagnetic field," the station librarian explained. "A prankster with a small parabolic dish antenna could reprogram the color from across a large room. After the Frunge scientists figured out the frequency combination to turn the fabric transparent, it was relegated to uses like packaging, or swag bags."

"What a tragic waste of a wonderful material," Dorothy said mournfully. "Couldn't the Verlocks come up with a version where the color could only be changed by an authorized user?"

"I'm afraid that changing colors under an applied electromagnetic field is an inherent property of the crystalline metallic molecules."

"I guess it will work fine for a swag bag if the Verlocks give us a good price," Flazint said. "As long as we're here, are there any other examples of chameleon materials you could show us, Librarian? Maybe something that was just too expensive for everyday use?"

"Jeeves isn't going to like this," Libby said as if to herself. "Check the shelves at GN 37/3."

Dorothy stuffed the Gortunda revival swag bag back on the shelf and raced Flazint around a series of switchback turns in the shelving until they reached the proper section. The Frunge girl got to the unit first and pulled out the only item at that designation, a black sash.

"Is this it?" Flazint asked. "It looks like something a Grenouthian might wear, but it's heavier than I'd expect for the length."

"The sash is woven from Gem nanofibers and was a luxury item in their old empire."

"How do we change the colors?" Dorothy asked, feeling the fabric. "Oooh, it's softer than the Verlock crystalline metallic cloth."

"The feel is also programmable to a large extent," the station librarian informed them, "but the nanobots are currently quiescent, so the first step in making alterations is to recharge their power with ultraviolet light."

"Will the grow lamp I use for my hair vines do it?" the Frunge girl asked.

"Set the frequency to the Lyman-alpha line of hydrogen and leave it for a few days."

"You're letting us take it?" Dorothy asked eagerly.

"Not to keep," Libby said. "The Gem are trying to rebuild their pre-cloning economy. They've submitted an official request to station librarians across the tunnel network asking us to check our lost-and-founds for potentially viable technology that the previous Gem government abandoned as having no dual-use applications."

"Dual use?"

"Cloning or military. After confirming that the nanofabric is still functional you'll have to deliver it to the Gem ambassador."

"Will they be able to start manufacturing it again?" Flazint asked. "You know that I studied traditional metallurgy at the Open University rather than anything high-tech, but I was taught that manufacturing process secrets are often lost to the passage of time. Regaining them depends on the availability of good documentation."

"That's generally true, but nanobot technology is the one area other than cloning where the Gem haven't gone backward," Libby told her. "In this case, a sample of the functional fabric would be enough for their scientists to reverse engineer the material and manufacture identical nanobots."

"You mean they'll clone them," Dorothy said. Then she grabbed Flazint's upper arm and exclaimed, "Do you know what this means? We can have a monopoly."

"How do you figure that?" the Frunge girl asked.

"My mother told me last week that the current Gem Ambassador is stepping down because Gwendolyn and Myst are returning."

"Myst?" Flazint closed her eyes for a moment to consult her long-term memory. "Oh, your clone friend who left the station to go into stasis right after you started working with me at the lost-and-found. But wasn't she going to sleep long enough for them to grow her a boy?"

"She has. We were both sixteen when she went to sleep, and that was over twelve years ago. I was ten when Metoo fixed the election to get my mom elected Carnival Queen, and that's when the Gem started cloning baby boys from the genetic samples they bought from the Farlings with Myst's prize money. So the first boys are eighteen years old now."

"You're talking about Human years," the Frunge girl reminded her. "Even though they're clones, the Gem are an advanced species with normal, I mean, extended lifespans."

"But unlike the rest of you, they mature at almost the same speed as humans do until they're grown," Dorothy told her. "I asked Dring about it, and he said that the Gem were obsessed with efficiency even before they reduced their civilization to a single individual. Altering their DNA to speed up maturation was actually their first species-wide genetic experiment."

"So why didn't they choose to mature even faster than Humans?"

"The speed of Human maturation is already near the theoretical maximum to allow for the development of higher cognitive functions in the humanoid form factor," the station librarian informed them.

24

"And you think that the new, I mean, the original Gem ambassador will give us a monopoly because they believe your mother sparked their revolution?" Flazint conjectured.

"We can ask, anyway. Besides, I already sent Myst a message telling her all about SBJ Fashions and inviting her to come work with us. We were always designing make-believe clothes for princesses when we were girls."

"But she's been in stasis this whole time. If the Gem mature at the same rate as Humans, isn't she too young to start working? Maybe she'll want to go to the Open University next year."

"I hadn't thought of that," Dorothy admitted. "I hope she doesn't feel like I'm pushing her."

"Let's take this sash to my apartment and start recharging the nanobots. Is there anything else we need to know about it, Librarian? Like, if I drape it right over the lamp, could it catch fire?"

"For best results, the fabric should be far enough from the lamp to avoid excessive heating. An arm's length would be fine. You'll have to contract directly with a Gem nanotechnology expert for reprogramming information."

"So unlike the Verlock technology, if we use the nanofabric in our fashions, the color will only be changeable by the owner?" Dorothy asked.

"The fabric is woven from threads of millions of identical nanobots," Libby said. "Gem encryption is rudimentary, but reprogramming requires physical contact, so I believe you could call it secure for practical fashion applications."

"And just so I know how much I need to butter up Jeeves, what will it cost to manufacture?"

"You know I can't share that kind of competitive information with you, Dorothy."

"Can you tell us what it cost at retail back when this was made and adjust for inflation and the exchange rate of Gem currency?" Flazint asked.

"I could, but I would just be leading you down the garden path. The cost structure of Gem nano-manufacturing is not a constant, and their new government's goal of growing interspecies trade will have more impact on the price than the raw materials and engineering effort."

"Just a hint?" Dorothy pleaded. "You don't even have to give us a number, just a range. Like, will it be more expensive by measure than the Frunge micro-weave designer pack I bought at the last CoSHC tradeshow?"

"Appreciably so," Libby replied.

"Ooh," Flazint said. "Jeeves isn't going to be happy."

Three

"Why did you want to meet so early?" Samuel asked his mother's special assistant. "I was awake anyway because I'm still on the Vergallian clock, but the EarthCent embassy doesn't open for another hour."

"I wanted us to get here before Donna and Daniel come in," Aabina said. "Ambassador McAllister asked me to show you how everything works, and we'll just get in the way if we wait until later."

"Do you have to call my mom 'Ambassador McAllister' while you're talking to me?"

"It's only proper while we're in the embassy," the Vergallian girl replied. "First, let's get you authorized for the locks."

"Can you do that?"

"Sure, that's just basic admin-level stuff. Ambassador McAllister wanted to give me the top security clearance, but I had to decline since I'm an alien and it's against EarthCent Intelligence guidelines. Besides, the embassy contracts out to the Stryx librarian for all of our information technology needs. Libby?"

"Yes, Aabina?" the Stryx librarian replied immediately.

"Can you authorize Samuel for all of the embassy locks and display desks at my security level?"

"Done. Welcome to the EarthCent embassy, Samuel. Please let me know if you need anything."

"How can you tell Libby to grant me access to the display desks when my real job is working at the Vergallian embassy?" Samuel asked Aabina. "We all joke about EarthCent not having any secrets worth stealing, but I don't have your royal training in compartmentalization."

"Firstly, I know that Ambassador McAllister talks about work at home, so unless you're ready to move out with Vivian, you'll be dealing with a conflict of interest until you leave the Vergallian embassy. Secondly, access to a display desk means that you can use it for your own work, not that you can look at what other people have been doing."

"If you say so, but I don't know how much use I'll be to anyone around here. You know that half of my job at your mother's embassy was dancing at dinner parties, and the EarthCent embassy doesn't even have a ballroom."

"But the other half of your job was acting as a filter for all of the problem cases who showed up at the Vergallian embassy, and we both know you excelled in that role. I'm good at helping people with legitimate questions but you have a gift for dealing with the crazies. Now, let's sit down at Donna's display desk and I'll take you through everything on the calendar for the next half-cycle."

"Is that everything?" Samuel asked forty-five minutes later. "Aside from the upcoming tradeshow stuff, I handle more appointments in a slow week at the Vergallian embassy than you get in a month here."

"But there are at least five times as many Vergallians as Humans living on Union Station, and I don't know how many more passing through."

"Well, I could take over orientation for new immigrants," Samuel offered, running his finger through a list of appointments in the holographic calendar. "I went along on a few of those with my mom during school vacations as a kid."

"That will be very helpful because I didn't know where I was going to find the time. We used to get around one request a month for a station tour, but recently the number has increased by more than tenfold. I probably shouldn't have added it to the list of embassy services in our last Galactic Free Press ad."

"EarthCent advertises the embassy? Since when?"

"It's been a few cycles now. The idea grew out of my customer satisfaction field survey."

"Did you stand around in the Little Apple or the Shuk with a tab asking strangers questions about the service they received from EarthCent?" Samuel teased.

"Yes, actually, that's exactly how I went about it. I didn't want to limit the results to the self-selecting audience we'd get if I only interviewed people who came into the embassy looking for help," Aabina explained. "One of my most interesting findings was that among new immigrants, which I defined as Humans living on Union Station for less than a year, only eighteen percent even knew that EarthCent had an embassy here."

"Just eighteen percent? Did you ask how many knew that EarthCent even exists?"

"Not as a direct question, but I'd estimate that at least half the people I talked to were pretty hazy on the concept. It's not that surprising given that the original purpose of EarthCent was to serve as humanity's point of contact with the other species. Almost everybody I interviewed had heard of the Conference of Sovereign Human Communities, though some of them didn't recognize the CoSHC acronym. It will be much simpler if they change it to the Human Empire."

"So you talked my mom into advertising?"

"She was getting a bit desperate to find things to do with all of the cookbook money coming in. That was one of my survey questions, by the way. I asked people who was responsible for publishing the All Species Cookbook, and every last person was sure it was the Galactic Free Press. Humans living on the station don't understand how much Ambassador McAllister has accomplished for them."

"Morning," Daniel said, entering the embassy with a large cup of take-out coffee and a box of donuts. "The two of you are here early."

"I wanted to show Sam how everything works without getting in the way," Aabina explained. "The meeting starts in ten minutes, so don't get stuck on a holo-conference."

"I'm just going to straighten up my office a bit before my wife gets here," the associate ambassador told them. "Shaina volunteered to take a few weeks off from SBJ Fashions to come in and help until the tradeshow is over. This empire business is going to make life complicated."

"We'll get the conference room ready," Aabina said, taking the box of donuts from the associate ambassador. "Do you need me to teach you how to make coffee, Sam, or do you already know?"

"Of course I can make coffee, it's coded in our genes," the EarthCent ambassador's son replied, and started for the conference room. "Do you have the briefing packs and the minutes from the last meeting prepared and ready to zap to people's tabs as they come in? Your mother taught me the basic version of the Imperial Rules of Order, so I can manage discussions for groups up to a hundred."

"We don't do things so formally here," the Vergallian girl said, looking somewhat embarrassed. "Ambassador

McAllister likes to encourage the free flow of ideas in her meetings."

"Sounds like chaos," Samuel muttered, but he went into the kitchenette and started the coffee brewing. He checked the fridge, and then called through the open door to Aabina, "Where are the vegetable platters?"

"It's just caffeine and sweets for morning meetings," she replied. "Come help me with the chairs."

Together they quickly rearranged the conference room, moving the custom chairs intended for bulky or tall aliens against the wall and replacing them with the human-sized spares.

"Leave that one," Aabina instructed Samuel as he began to move the Verlock-sized chair used by Ambassador Srythlan away from the table. "Clive promoted Wrylenth to be his personal assistant at EarthCent Intelligence and brings him to all of the meetings."

"Who else will be here?"

"Daniel and Donna, of course, and hopefully Daniel's wife will be here in time to start getting up to speed. You, me, and Ambassador McAllister."

"Why don't you say 'Associate Ambassador Cohan' all the time?"

"Daniel asked Libby for the names of my mother, grandmother, great-grandmother, and great-great-grandmother, and then he kept on addressing me formally until I agreed to use his first name," Aabina admitted.

"Good morning," Donna said, passing by on her way to the kitchenette, and reappearing a few seconds later with the coffee pot and a tray of mugs. "Does anybody take cream in their coffee?"

31

"Me," Shaina said, entering a step ahead of her husband. "Don't ask me any more questions until I finish the first cup."

"I gather she's as bad as you, Daniel," Donna said.

"Where do you think I got the habit from?" the associate ambassador retorted. "Where's Kelly?"

"I hope she isn't buying more donuts," Aabina said. "The box you brought—" she stopped and pointed at her ear.

"Good morning, everybody," Clive said, entering the conference room with his Verlock assistant.

"There's been a minor change in plans," the Vergallian girl announced, dropping her hand. "I just heard from Ambassador McAllister and she's going to be late. Samuel, your father is fine and she told you not to come, but he dropped a keg on his foot and was trying to walk it off when your mother saw him. She was afraid he wouldn't go to the doctor unless she took him herself."

"All right then, let's get started, and you can fill the ambassador in on what she misses, Aabina," Daniel said, taking his seat. "The purpose of this meeting is to make last-minute adjustments to our program for the CoSHC tradeshow in light of the pending empire tender from the Stryx. I spent the weekend on tunneling conference calls with mayors, governors, and managers from our member communities, and the only thing they all agreed on was that we should defer any serious decisions until we have a chance to meet in person."

"So they aren't in any hurry to declare the Human Empire," Clive surmised.

"Correct, and thank you for sending me that executive summary of our options. It's good to know that we can reject the whole thing and just continue on as we have, and the timeline for the steps to officially declare empire was especially useful. I only glanced at the treaty text and I didn't realize there was a whole body of precedent-based law supporting it. How did you pull everything together so quickly?"

"Wrylenth had the plan prepared in his contingency files," the director of EarthCent Intelligence said, and turned to his Verlock assistant. "Why don't you explain it to them?

"Director Oxford insists that I spend twenty-five percent of my office time on independently conceived projects," the bulky alien said at his best talking pace. "I identified a lack of contingency planning for high-probability events that are bound to affect humanity. Given the growth trajectory of CoSHC's member community populations, it was clear that the triggering of the empire clause was imminent, so I researched the consequences and prepared a brief on possible responses."

"Lucky for us you did," Daniel said. "How long have you known about this, Clive?"

"I found out Friday evening, about ten minutes after you dropped by the office. Wrylenth didn't feel that his underlying mathematical proofs were sufficiently rigorous to show me his plans before events caught up with us."

"Are there any other just-a-matter-of-time events we should know about?" Daniel asked the Verlock.

"Many. My mistake was giving equal priority to all events with at least a one in ten chance of occurring in the next five hundred years, which is the minimum planning period Verlock civil servants normally take into account. I've since been informed that five years is considered extreme by Human planning standards."

"How about events likely to occur in the next year?"

"CoSHC making the empire cut-off was the only one with a probability of greater than five percent," Wrylenth said.

"How can you make such concise predictions?" Samuel asked him. "When we took that required business course together at the Open University, I remember you telling me that forecasting the future is considered black magic by the Verlocks."

"You're forgetting the context—I was talking about business trends in retail and entertainment. For example, nobody knew that professional LARPing was going to become the next big thing on the tunnel network until it had already happened, and your sister could tell you that it's impossible to predict the next hot fashion. Forecasting that CoSHC would reach a billion members was just a matter of extrapolation."

"So this was basically an educated guess on your part, and you didn't want to disturb your boss?" Daniel followed up on his earlier question.

"My last calculation put the probability at above ninety-eight percent, but still not what I would call a sure thing," Wrylenth said apologetically.

"What would you call a sure thing?"

"One hundred percent, by definition."

The associate ambassador exchanged a look with the director of EarthCent Intelligence, who could only smile at the Verlock's conservative approach. "We'll have to wait until Kelly arrives to hear what happened with the Intelligence Steering Committee yesterday," Daniel continued and turned to the ambassador's special assistant. "I know that you have a number of points prepared, Aabina, so why don't you take us through those while we're waiting."

"Ambassador McAllister asked me to summarize the Steering Committee meeting for you since I attended as well," Aabina said. "The ambassadors and the president agreed that we, I mean, EarthCent, doesn't have jurisdiction in this matter since the communities involved are sovereign. Everyone agreed that we should do whatever we can to support decision-makers in CoSHC, including making available any intelligence and analysis we can provide."

"But I thought you sort of ran CoSHC," Samuel said to Daniel. "Do you really need to consult with all of the communities, or is the final decision up to you?"

"I'm more of a referee than an executive," the associate ambassador replied. "I'm authorized to make decisions related to the tradeshow, but nothing like this has ever come up before, and we don't have a true governing structure in place. To the extent that CoSHC has official leadership, it's an ad hoc committee, but the biggest single decision they've taken to date was extending a membership invitation to the Traders Guild."

"This is why everything works better with queens," the EarthCent ambassador's son said in frustration. "How can humanity expect to make any progress when everything goes to committees and votes?"

"We're not Vergallians, Sam, other than myself," Aabina reminded him. "Why don't we start with the checklist on the last page of Wrylenth's contingency plan?" She swiped and tapped her tab, which brought the conference room display system to life. An image of the checklist appeared on the large display mounted on the wall that separated the conference room from the kitchen.

"It looks like it's in shorthand," Donna commented. "What does it mean, Wrylenth?"

"Decision," the Verlock read off the top item. "The first step for CoSHC is deciding whether or not to start the empire certification process that will eventually lead to being recognized as a full tunnel network member with all of the privileges and responsibilities that entails."

"I asked the ad hoc committee members to try to get here a week before the tradeshow starts so we can at least decide how to decide," Daniel said. "How long do we have to make up our minds?"

"One cycle. As long as you've reached a decision by the end of the tradeshow, you'll have ample time to fill out the required forms."

"So a little under two months," Daniel said, missing the Verlock's pained look at the crudity of the associate ambassador's calendar-unit conversion. "Does this mean that our decision to get out in front of the Grenouthians by using the Human Empire label ourselves first was a mistake?"

"We got lucky on that front," Clive said. "I talked to Chastity first thing this morning. The executive producer of the Grenouthian news channel woke her up in the middle of the night to compliment her strategy. They can't run the Human Empire story as breaking news since it's already been out on a dozen other networks and in the Galactic Free Press. Even better, their analytics group is standing by the conclusion that reporting on the tradeshow as straight business news will match their advertiser requirements better than a satire. We'll take our licks from some of the news anchors who can't pass up a good joke, but as long as the visitors don't get into a brawl, coverage should remain positive."

"Are you awake enough for a question, Shaina?" Daniel asked his wife.

"Who made the coffee?" she asked.

"Me," Samuel said.

"Make it stronger next time," Shaina instructed him. "What's the question?"

"The branding we talked about when you got home from the Libbyland party Friday night," her husband said.

"Good news there," she said. "I was able to drag two members from our design team in to SBJ Fashions on Saturday morning and asked them to volunteer a little time to help out. Dorothy and Flazint worked their magic and came up with a very inexpensive Verlock-made bag that meets all of your needs. All we have to do is settle on the branding and have stickers printed locally."

"That's all right for attendees, but going by what Aabina told me, any alien observers who show up will expect something that looks expensive," Daniel said. "Kelly has authorized us to spend cookbook money supporting the Human Empire tender, so funding won't be a problem."

"If we decide on the design today, we could get embroidered patches with sticky backs for the bags," Shaina offered. "Or depending on how many observers you're expecting, I could ask the girls to hand-stitch something for them."

"So we'll run with the Human Empire for the tradeshow, and if our members decide against it in the end, the bags and tablecloths will become collector's items."

"For a brand, you want something catchy that evokes the idea in a fun way."

"Crossed swords?" Clive suggested.

"Too martial," Daniel said immediately. "The bunnies would have a field day with it."

"There's always the globe," Donna said, pointing up at Dring's lacquer-on-copper construction that was suspended over the table.

"Too close to EarthCent's trademark symbol. It would get confusing."

"This may be a one-time thing, and we have no time left to build brand recognition," Shaina said. "Leveraging somebody else's brand might be the best way to create a meme for viral marketing."

"We're not trying to sell the bags," Daniel said. "They're free for tradeshow visitors." His wife gave him a look, and he added, "Okay. I'll be quiet now."

"I've got an idea," Samuel said. "The whole event is taking place at the Empire Convention Center, right?"

"And I came in yesterday to make provisional reservations on a block of premiere suites with all-species facilities in the attached hotel to host the observers," Donna told them.

"Empire@Empire," Samuel said confidently. "I mean with the 'at' sign from those old Earth character sets, not the word."

"Empire@Empire," Shaina repeated. "I like it. I'll check with our Frunge intellectual property attorney."

"What for?" Daniel asked.

"It really is piggy-backing on the Empire Convention Center brand, but I doubt they'll object since it will be good marketing for them too."

The door to the corridor slid open and Kelly entered, slightly out of breath. "Sorry I'm late," she said. "The doctor at the travel concourse said that nothing was broken, and now I'm never going to hear the end of it from Joe. Are you working through Wrylenth's checklist?"

"I was about to start on the administrative options for empires without a sovereign ruler or royalty," Aabina said. "The next step is to establish a transparent mechanism for making the decision whether or not to begin the process."

"Wouldn't a vote by the ad hoc committee be sufficient?" Clive asked.

"Since they've never claimed to be the official leadership of CoSHC, you would have to do something to establish their authority," Wrylenth explained. "I would suggest transparently repeating the process by which the current ad hoc committee was selected, but I couldn't find any information about how that was done."

"Here we go with committees again," the EarthCent ambassador's son muttered to Aabina.

"To the best of my recollection, the ad hoc committee is self-appointed," Daniel said. "Nobody wanted to be in charge so I got stuck as the central point of contact. When issues arose that I thought required buy-in from our member communities, I would invite their representatives onto Stryxnet conference calls, and the ones who showed up most often eventually evolved into the ad hoc committee."

"Too opaque," Wrylenth said.

"But the community leaders are all elected," Shaina pointed out.

"Not necessarily," Daniel said. "In some instances, communities elect or otherwise appoint a mayor or governor. In other cases, I'm dealing with the manager of the communal business enterprise or the winner of a beauty contest."

"Beauty contests?"

"Or singing competitions. You know how humans living on open worlds tend to go native, so they generally appoint leaders in imitation of their alien hosts. For example, on Verlock and Grenouthian worlds, everybody has to take a civil service test, and they rotate the high scorers through office."

"But the Verlocks have an emperor," Samuel protested.

"Only because there's no provision for abdication," Wrylenth said. "On the local level, everybody is appointed through competitive testing."

"The Human Empire could adopt EarthCent's civil service exam," Kelly suggested.

"That's an idea, but there isn't time to announce it and arrange for testing across the tunnel network before the tradeshow," Daniel said. "We have two weeks to work something out before the ad hoc committee members start arriving. I suppose if all else fails, we can just hold an election by show of hands after the keynote address. That's pretty transparent."

"But CoSHC represents a billion people living in over a thousand communities spread over more than a hundred worlds and orbitals. Less than one percent will attend the convention and trade show."

"Less than one-hundredth of one percent," Aabina corrected the ambassador.

"I'm just saying it doesn't meet the requirement for a transparent and democratic process," Kelly said.

"If the currently appointed community leaders do the voting, it would be a form of representative democracy," Daniel countered.

"Excuse me," Wrylenth spoke up. "You're reading something into the transparency requirement that isn't there. You can choose your leadership through a lottery or a wrestling contest as long as the process is transparent.

When the Hortens became an empire, they sold imperial offices to raise money for a new sports stadium."

"Everybody think about it," Daniel said. "We don't have to decide today."

Four

"Are you sure you're okay to come along?" Kelly asked her husband for the third time. "It's only been a week and you're still limping."

"It's just a bruised foot," Joe said. "Beowulf dragged me around the whole perimeter of Mac's Bones this morning, and you know he wouldn't have done that if he thought I was injured. Besides, I like the Thark ambassador. He's the funniest alien diplomat I've met."

"He must have a sense of humor to co-locate his embassy with the off-world betting parlor, but I suppose that there's some sort of nepotism involved."

"I gave up trying to work out their family relations," Joe said. "I think the ambassador's nephew is the one who provides the optional insurance for our ship rentals, and they're both related to the Thark who rescued us from the Vergallians in time for Dring's ball. They're like the Grenouthians with clans that extend out to fifth cousins five times removed."

"Wouldn't that include pretty much the whole species?" Kelly asked as they exited the lift tube.

"Maybe it does. Have you been here since the Carnival election?"

"Oh, don't remind me," the EarthCent ambassador said as they entered the cavernous off-world betting parlor. "I can still picture Metoo draped in a wall-hanging from our living room floating next to the tote board and rigging the results to make me Carnival Queen."

"Isn't that the ambassador at the fourth window from the left?" Joe asked, pointing at the row of cashier windows along the wall.

"I think so," Kelly said, altering her course to intercept. "He looks cheerful enough."

"Maybe he just won."

"You don't think the Thark ambassador gambles, do you?"

"I'd be shocked if he didn't," Joe replied.

The Thark diplomat spotted the EarthCent ambassador and her husband and waved them in the direction of the giant tote board where he had apparently reserved a front-row table. When Kelly and Joe caught up with the wrinkly-skinned alien, he was already perched on a chair and working a device that looked like a marriage between a Dollnick tab and a Grenouthian abacus.

"Sit, sit," the Thark said without looking up. "I just need to finish a quick calculation and get my bet in before—there," he concluded, sliding all of the beads to the top of the abacus and giving the screen a final tap. "I'm honored that you thought of consulting me about your little money problem, Ambassador. My sister manages our loan operations, but given your request for privacy, I decided to handle your account personally."

"I think you misunderstood my message," Kelly said. "I don't need money, I have too much. I'm seeking advice on what to do with it, but the station librarian wouldn't help me because—"

"The Stryx consider it competitive information and don't want to give you an unfair advantage over the other species," the Thark ambassador interrupted. "Very interesting. And the station librarian recommended you consult with me?"

"Actually, I tried Dring for advice next, and he suggested talking to you since your species runs so much of the financial industry."

"The Maker recommended me? Then I'll have to do my best to give you honest advice."

"What if the Maker hadn't recommended you?" Joe asked.

"Then it would be caveat emptor," the Thark ambassador replied with a jolly grin. "Well, let's see. The betting is already closed for the fifth race on Horten Prime, which is a shame because I could have put you on a very good thing." He looked up at the tote board and rapidly scanned the odds. "Nothing else is jumping out at me in the next few minutes. Do you have a particular preference?"

"What do you mean?" Kelly asked.

"Races, fights, political events. You might be interested in the prop bets relating to your new Human Empire. My nephew just posted the odds of CoSHC going through with the process within the next cycle, though I think he's just throwing a dart at the board and waiting to see how the money comes in."

"I'm afraid you've misunderstood me again," Kelly said. "I don't want to gamble with my money."

"You want to gamble with somebody else's money?" The Thark ambassador shook his head disapprovingly. "It's considered very bad form."

"I'm not interested in gambling at all. I want to invest the extra money the embassy is bringing in from the All Species Cookbook. Didn't I make that clear in the message I left you?"

"I may not have listened past the first thirty seconds. So you came to me for help in starting a new business?"

"Joe, you explain it to him," the EarthCent ambassador said in frustration.

"The Stryx told Kelly that if she lets the cookbook income keep piling up on the embassy's programmable cred the balance will start to decay," Joe told the Thark. "She's looking for a risk-free alternative so the principal will grow until EarthCent needs it."

The Thark ambassador listened intently to Joe's speech and then broke out laughing. "Funny one, Joe. You had me going there for a minute. I'll have to incorporate that into one of the stories I tell about the Aurillians. Everybody will believe it about them."

"But we're serious," Kelly protested. "What's so funny about wanting to invest for the future?"

"Maybe there's a translation issue," the Thark said, tapping the side of his skull above the spot where his implant was located. "You tell me. How do you differentiate between investing and gambling?"

"Well, investing is where you put your money to work for a guaranteed return, while gambling is just betting on stuff."

"Betting on stuff?" The alien ambassador laughed again. "Give me an example of a guaranteed return. I'd like to get in on that bet, I mean, that *investment*, myself."

"Bonds," Kelly said, glancing at Joe to see if she had guessed right. Her husband shrugged.

"You mean promissory notes that allow the borrower to defer paying back the principal to a future date in return for regular payments?" the Thark asked.

"Yes, that sort of thing."

"Many species issue bonds, but there's always a risk. I should know as we often make book on them, though some customers insist on calling it insurance. Governments fall, businesses fail, currencies fluctuate, and poorly managed ones have inflation. More often than not you'll come out ahead, but buying bonds isn't what I would call investing. The closest thing to a risk-free asset I'm aware of is the Stryx cred, but the Stryx don't allow anybody to stash large sums of money on programmable creds to prevent the wealth of the tunnel network from concentrating in just a few hands."

"That's what Libby told me," Kelly said. "But if I can't buy bonds or invest through a brokerage..."

"A brokerage? You want to put your money in commodities like Dollnick Tan tubers or ice harvesting futures? We handle those bets on the tote board as well, though the odds aren't anything special."

"How did we get back to gambling? My mother used to be in an investment club on Earth, and she did very well doing—what did she do, Joe?"

"Purchased shares, mostly," the ambassador's husband replied, and then added for the Thark's benefit, "Large businesses on Earth are usually organized as corporations, and many of them have publicly traded stocks so that anybody can own shares in the company."

"Like a Drazen consortium?" the alien ambassador asked.

"I thought to invest in a Drazen consortium you have to become a partner of sorts and work there."

"Of course. Do you mean Humans buy shares in these corporations without having any say in how the business is run?"

"They get to vote for a board of directors that oversees the management, though in most cases, the votes don't mean anything," Joe explained.

"But say I bought stock in a corporation that built apartments," the Thark ambassador posited. "Would I always have a place to live? Or if the corporation built furniture, could I stop in once a year and pick out a nice chair?"

"No, but they pay dividends, sometimes. That's the excess earnings divided over the number of shares after the management decides how much they want to distribute."

"It sounds to me like the management does pretty much whatever it wants, and the only thing you get in exchange for your money is an entry in the bookkeeping system as a fractional owner. I suppose if they went bankrupt you could always try to repossess your share of the equipment and sell that, though divvying up the real estate and goodwill would be tricky."

"I just remembered something Mom told me," Kelly said. "Most of these corporations issue bonds and run credit lines at banks to finance their business. If they go bankrupt, the debt holders get paid first and the stockholders usually get nothing. She dabbled in buying stocks in failing companies a few times because the valuations seemed attractive, but in the end all she got was a tax loss."

"So you're saying that you buy shares in these corporations, hope that the management pays dividends, and count on a greater fool coming along and buying the shares from you at a higher price if you need the money back," the Thark summarized.

"That sounds about right," Joe said.

"And you call that investing?"

Kelly nodded.

"So I was right—we were having translation issues," the Thark said with a smile. "Based on your definition, every proposition on our tote board is an investment, and I would be happy to help you with handicapping."

"That's not what I want at all," the EarthCent ambassador said. "Betting on the races and things on your tote board is pure gambling, while buying shares in companies is—I don't know. Responsible?"

"Wait a second, Kel," Joe said. "Does that offer to help with handicapping extend to me? I like to stop in from time to time to play the ponies. I used to bring the kids, but we never had that much luck."

"You bet on horse racing?" the alien ambassador asked. "Human or Vergallian?"

"Vergallian," Joe answered quickly. "Human horse races are all fixed."

"If you come back in three days the first in the Jubilee series is starting. I'm not usually a big fan of quadruped racing myself, but the recordkeeping in the Empire of a Hundred Worlds is both detailed and trustworthy. I dip my toe in during the Jubilee celebrations, because with a trillion Vergallians betting to uphold the honor of this or that queen's stables, there are bound to be mispriced bets."

"How does your nephew go about setting the odds for alien horse races happening halfway across the galaxy?" Kelly found herself asking.

"The first step for establishing any betting line is to determine the true odds," the Thark said, his voice taking on the tone of a professor who had given this particular lecture more times than he could remember. "By that I mean we start by trying to assess the probability of any given outcome occurring, including draws in the case of competitions that can end in tie scores."

"So you're going to spend the next several days watching immersives of recent Vergallian horse races?"

"No, that's where the reliable recordkeeping comes in. And the Vergallian veterinarians publish examination results as soon as they do them, so everybody with a Stryxnet connection has access to the same information. Of course, there are local factors like the weather that are difficult to take into account before the race, but over the aeons, we've established a network of sources." The ambassador paused a moment, trying to remember where he was in the explanation. "Next we make a minor downward adjustment to the true odds, which gives us our basic profit margin. The bookmaker further adjusts the odds as needed to balance our liability."

"I don't understand what that means."

"Let's say you and Joe want to bet on the flip of a coin," the Thark said. He removed a five-cred piece from his pocket, flipped it in the air, caught it, and slapped it down on the back of his other hand. "I can tell you from experience that the true odds of it coming up stations are one-in-two. If the off-world-betting parlor was a public service rather than a business, we would let you bet at those odds, but in order to make a profit, we need to change them a little. What do you say to one-point-one the coin is stations-up, Joe?"

"I guess I can bet eleven creds to keep the math easy."

"What does that mean, one-point-one?" Kelly asked.

"It's the Thark version of moneyline odds," her husband explained. "It means to win one cred, I have to bet one-point-one creds, or a hundred and ten percent of what I'll make. The ten percent is the bookmaker's vigorish."

"Thank you," the Thark said. "And how much will you bet on the opposite outcome, Ambassador McAllister?"

"I play a little poker to be sociable, but this is just gambling," Kelly protested. "Besides, we're married, so betting against Joe is just a guarantee that we'll lose ten percent however the coin comes up."

"Think of it as an education in the risks of bookmaking," the alien ambassador said. "How much?"

"One cred," Kelly offered reluctantly. "I better start writing this down if I'm going to remember anything." She reached in her purse and drew out a paperback with blank lined pages Blythe had printed for her, and then removed a pencil from the special sleeve Dorothy had sewn on the underside of the purse's flap. "Ready."

"Why are you writing in a book with a picture of a bare-chested Dollnick flexing on the cover?" the Thark asked.

"I couldn't find a diary for sale and I wanted lined pages in a binding. My embassy manager's daughter runs a publishing house and she was able to have it printed for me."

"It looks like a rather clever security solution for a low-tech species. At your level of development, anything else you might use to take notes could be easily hacked by any number of advanced species, but as long as you maintain physical custody of your diary, the information will remain safe. Are you employing a code as well?"

"Scribble encryption," Joe answered for his wife. "We've been married for thirty years and I can't read her writing."

"You were about to explain how taking a bet with a guaranteed profit is risky for you," Kelly reminded the Thark.

"First let me ask you a question," the alien ambassador said. "Let's say everybody else in here wants to bet on the coin flip. Do you think I'll offer them the same odds?"

"Sure. The outcome will always be fifty-fifty, and you know you'll make a profit eventually."

"That's only true if everybody is willing to keep betting on coin flips until I come out ahead," the Thark said. "But most of the money we handle comes in on events where the true odds can only be estimated and the exact proposition never repeats, like CoSHC becoming the Human Empire."

"Like CoSHC becoming the Human Empire," Kelly wrote industriously. "Go on."

The Thark ambassador removed the hand covering the coin, the visible face of which displayed a Stryx station. He sighed, dug in his pocket again, and handed Joe a ten-cred piece. "Now, what just happened?" he asked the EarthCent ambassador.

"You lost ten creds," she said. "Let's do it again."

"You're missing the point. The true odds were fifty/fifty, and I lost nine creds. That's the bookmaker's risk."

"How do you figure nine creds instead of ten?" Kelly asked.

"You owe me the one cred you bet against your husband," the Thark ambassador explained. "If I had allowed everybody else in here to participate in the bet, I would have adjusted the odds to reduce my risk as more money came in. In other words, even though I know the true odds of a coin flip are fifty/fifty, if ninety percent of the bets are coming in on stations and only ten percent of the bets are coming in on digits, the bookmaker will keep lowering the payout on stations and raising it on digits."

"The people who place bets before the odds change get to keep their original odds," Joe added.

"But in the end, if everybody keeps betting stations, you could still lose a lot of money," Kelly said. "Why don't you just stop taking bets?"

"If we think the fix is in, we do stop taking bets, but changing the odds encourages gamblers to lay their money on the other side of the proposition to bring the book into balance," the Thark said.

"The fix?"

"You know, if the game is rigged, like your Carnival election."

"I never knew that gambling was so complicated," Kelly said, setting down her pencil. "But I really don't want to take unnecessary risks with the cookbook money. Isn't there something else I can do with it?"

"Invest," the Thark ambassador advised her.

"But you just said there's no difference between investing and gambling!"

"No, I said that everything entails risk, and that the activities that you think of as investing, I think of as gambling. The way most of the advanced species approach financial management—write this down—is that the difference between investing and gambling lies in the degree of control you have over the outcome."

"Degree of control you have over the outcome," Kelly repeated as she wrote. "But what does that mean?"

"Unless I am cheating, I have no control over the outcome of a coin flip or a horse race," the Thark ambassador explained. "The same is true for your purchases of bonds or shares in large corporations. In those cases, you are simply hoping for the best and trusting that some regulator is watching out for your interests. On the other hand, if you opened a chocolate store, the risk that you lose all of your money may be higher than if you bought stocks or bonds, but I would call the new business an investment because you have a large degree of control over the outcome."

"That makes sense, sort of, but I'll have to think about it," Kelly said. "Hypothetically speaking, would I actually have to work in the chocolate store, or could I just own it?"

"The farther you distance yourself from day-to-day operations, the more I would consider it a gamble rather than an investment."

"How about if I went in twice a day and bought something?"

"You'd regret it, Kel," Joe said, and then addressed the Thark ambassador. "Now that you know what my wife is looking for and she knows that there's no such thing as risk-free, do you have any recommendations for what she can do with the money short of starting a business?"

"Advice like that will cost you," the Thark said, eyeing the ten-cred piece which Joe had left lying on the table in front of him. The EarthCent ambassador's husband used his forefinger to move the coin over in front of their host. "Excellent. My advice would be to speak to the other ambassadors whose commercial activities aren't as concentrated in the financial services industry as mine are."

"I have another question," Kelly said. "When you talk about having control over outcomes, how about the bets you accept on political events related to EarthCent? I'm not saying that I would try to influence CoSHC's choice of whether or not to become an empire, but isn't it risky for you to accept bets from humans who could be involved in the process?"

"We take all of that into account when trying to establish the true odds, and of course, we adjust those odds based on how the money comes in," the Thark said. "But I like the way your mind works, Ambassador. Perhaps you have a future as a gambler after all."

Five

"Are we chaperoning a date for Flazint and Tzachan, or are we moving your office?" Kevin demanded, though his voice was muffled by the mound of heavy fabric samples his wife had just piled on his extended arms.

"It doesn't count as a date because we're working," Dorothy replied. "Just put those samples on the mulebot and help me with these patterns. Later we'll all get something to eat."

"And then that counts for a date?"

"No, because it's—I forgot the legal term. Tzachan?" the ambassador's daughter called to the Frunge attorney. "Why did you say that lunch won't count against your dating quota?"

"Jeeves is paying for the meal, and that makes it a regular and necessary part of Flazint's employment at SBJ Fashions," the alien said. "If anybody from the matchmaker's office comes around asking, I volunteered to help with the move in order to maintain a positive relationship with a valuable client."

"That explains why Flazint is tying you up to keep you from running off."

"I am not tying him up!" the Frunge girl protested, her hair vines flushing with chlorophyll. "I've been meaning to straighten out this tangle of metallic yarn for years, but you always had something better to do when I asked you to sit for me and hold out your arms."

"I don't remember that," Dorothy said disingenuously. "In fact, I would have sworn that I looked under your bench last week and all of the metallic yarn was wrapped in nice, tight balls."

"You would have sworn falsely," Flazint declared, rising to the bait. "My suppliers deliver the yarn in either hanks or skeins, and the only time I end up with balls of it is when I unravel something for reuse."

"Professional point of interest," Kevin said over his shoulder, while Dorothy stacked patterns on his own outstretched arms. "My implant translated your words to say that Frunge suppliers deliver yarn in hanks or skeins, but I deal with a lot of twine in my chandlery business, and I thought the words meant the same thing."

"With us, it depends on how the yarn will be used," Flazint explained. "If you wind yarn in a ball, you draw from the outside, but a factory-wound skein draws from the center, and a hank is a skein that's been twisted and folded for shipping."

"This is why we use holographic images in court filings whenever possible," Tzachan added. "Seemingly precise words can mean different things in different trades, not to mention cross-species misunderstandings, but it's tough to argue with a hologram."

"Especially if it's trying to sell you something," Stick contributed from the doorway, where he was struggling to maneuver a large floating bin into the room. "I made the mistake of subscribing to the new LARPing channel under my real name, and now advertising holograms follow me all over the station trying to sell me enchanted weapons from some Verlock mage."

"I'm surprised they don't give up when you never buy anything," Dorothy said to Affie's boyfriend. "I've tried to get Jeeves to run some of those interactive holographic ads for our fashions, but he says they're too expensive."

"I might have bought a couple of ensorcelled throwing stars and a demon whip, but I was planning on getting those anyway. Speaking of weapons, just how many pairs of scissors do you have on that table?"

"One less than I need, always. Are you cleaning out Affie's workstation yourself?"

"She's stuck at the embassy," Stick said.

"But Jubilee has already started," Dorothy pointed out. "Samuel is on loan to my mom's embassy until the Vergallian ambassador returns."

"Affie isn't at the embassy substituting for the ambassador today. She went in because there's a large group of Alt tourists and businessmen visiting and she's their contract-queen on Union Station. That's your fault, if you've already forgotten."

"My fault? Your ambassador is the one who bribed Baa to hijack my Cinderella shoe campaign. She did it to manipulate Affie into accepting the contract-queen gig and you into joining SBJ Fashions as our sales manager."

"Whatever," Stick grumbled, deploying one of his favorite human borrow-words. "So is your brother going to work for your mom all through Jubilee?"

"No. Samuel still has to work at the Vergallian booth at the tradeshow," Dorothy said, and then pivoted to her husband. "Be careful with that magnifier, Kevin. Baa enchanted it for me to show the exact location of the needle under the fabric."

"Where is Baa anyway?" Stick asked, and then failed to pick up on the jerking head movements of his co-workers who tried to clue him in to her presence. "I'm not moving that Terragram's stuff unless she helps. Half of it is probably cursed."

"Luckily for you, I'm right here, and if you want to complain about cursed items, complain about your throwing stars and the demon whip," Baa announced from behind the curtain where she was working.

"You wouldn't."

"I already did. You're the sales manager for the only fashion business in the galaxy with a Terragram mage on staff. Show some brand loyalty."

"I was only buying samples to check on the competition," Stick protested, and this time he missed Dorothy's attempt to use body language to tell him that their boss had just floated in. "I even put them on my company cred."

"You've only been working here a year and you're on track to spend as much as Dorothy," Jeeves said. "If I wasn't related to the station management, it would have cost me a fortune to break the lease on this place just to move down the corridor into a bigger office with two bathrooms."

"He always leaves the seat up," Dorothy told their Stryx employer. "And poor Flazint was losing leaves from her hair vines worrying about Stick walking in on her."

"That's what locks are for," Stick said. "Besides, it's in the basic Vergallian employment code that facilities for male employees will include a standing urinal. I only waited a year to complain because I planned on being fired by now."

"You're not getting out of your contract that easy," Jeeves told him. "I considered your first year to be training, but this coming year I'm counting on you to double our sales."

"Then you have to let me fix your business model," the Vergallian said stubbornly. "It's been clear since my first day that none of your designers are interested in men's fashions. If we're going to double sales without expanding distribution beyond the tunnel network station boutiques and the LARPing shops, we need to start offering fashions for the other half of the biological population."

"I'm not working in the same room with male designers," Flazint said. "It wouldn't be proper."

"Ergo, the larger and more expensive office," Jeeves said. "In addition to his and hers bathrooms, we'll now have space for his and hers design rooms. I have no doubt that one day you'll all force me to hire a Fillinduck trio, and then we'll need three bathrooms and a cuddling pod."

"Is that what the locked door in the new office is?" Dorothy asked. "A third bathroom that you're keeping in reserve?"

"That information is on a need-to-know basis," the young Stryx replied.

"So why don't you expand distribution beyond the tunnel network stations?" Kevin asked. "You could open boutiques—"

"Too expensive," Jeeves cut him off. "SBJ Fashions hasn't achieved the production scale that would justify investing in our own stores on stations, much less on tunnel network worlds. Now, where's this miracle Gem fabric that Dorothy claims is going to change the galaxy?"

"I already packed it away, but I'll get it out," Flazint said, abandoning Tzachan with his forearms wrapped in metallic yarn. "Let me see. I put it in the exotic fabrics box, and it's either on the mulebot or—right here," she concluded, lifting the lid off the only bin remaining on her workbench.

Jeeves floated over and took the black sash in his pincer. "Interesting," he said, and the lights on his casing began flashing in a rhythmic pattern. "The nanobots are fully charged, but the programming is protected by the same encryption the Gem military used for their doomsday weapons."

"Oh," Dorothy said in disappointment. "So we'll have to wait for Gwendolyn and Myst to arrive and ask—"

"Cracked it," Jeeves declared. "Was anybody timing me?"

"Are you serious? Can you make it change colors?"

"Is that what Libby told you it does?" Jeeves began rotating his pincer, spinning the sash like a lasso, and then tossed it to Dorothy.

"It's still black," she said, catching the mass of silky fabric. "Does it take the nanobots time to—are you doing sleight-of-pincer again? Where did this T-shirt come from?"

"Do you mean the nanobots can be programmed to reconfigure the fabric?" Flazint asked. "That changes everything. It could be the most popular cloth in history!"

"I almost forgot," Jeeves said, and extended his pincer to touch the T-shirt, which abruptly turned white. "So, why do you think the Gem only used this nanofabric in luxury goods rather than for all of their clothes?"

"To maintain exclusivity," Dorothy said immediately.

"Does anybody else care to guess?"

"Because after you sell somebody a fully reprogrammable garment they never need to buy another," Flazint suggested.

"That's a good point for all of you to remember, but it's not the reason the Gem treasured this material."

"It must be expensive to make," Stick ventured.

"But nanobots are mass-produced by other nanobots in nanobot factories," Kevin said. "I know that the Farling doctor uses medical nanobots that he buys from the Gem, but I thought the main cost was in the programming."

"You're both right," Jeeves said. "General purpose nanobots are inexpensive to construct in nanobot factories after you get the sunk costs out of the way, but in this particular case, the combination of properties the fabric needs to embody requires expensive feedstocks. You could run that T-shirt through an atomizer and sell the raw elements for over a hundred creds, and that's before they're processed into the molecules required for nanobot construction."

"So how much can I buy?" Dorothy asked.

"With your money or mine?"

"For work."

"None, unless you come up with a business model where we can sell dresses for five thousand creds, or convince the Gem to provide the fabric at a loss."

"How about if they recover the technology and then reduce the features?" Dorothy pleaded. "Like, just a chameleon version without the shape-shifting?"

"It's also proof against most projectiles and thermally stable," Jeeves told her.

"You mean it maintains the same temperature?"

"Until the nanobots run out of juice. I'm saying this in front of witnesses just so there won't be any misunderstandings. You are forbidden to purchase Gem nanofabric for SBJ Fashions without my prior approval. Now finish up moving what you can and I'll have the maintenance bots take care of the furniture and equipment. Attendance at the company lunch is mandatory, so I'll see you at noon on Universal Human Time in Pub Haggis."

"That only gives us a half-hour to finish up," Kevin said. "What are you doing, Dorothy?"

"You heard him," she replied as Jeeves floated out the exit. "He's sending maintenance bots to move the furniture. Put those patterns back in the drawers. I was only emptying them out to save weight."

"That gives me an idea," Baa said. She yanked down the curtain she had insisted on hanging to keep her spell-casting private and threw it over her cluttered workbench. A look of concentration came over her face, the lights in the design room dimmed momentarily, and then her bench had been replaced by a giant cabinet.

"Really?" Flazint asked. "Is an illusion going to fool a bot?"

"The maintenance bots have difficulty discriminating between platinum necklaces and chains folded out of the foil wrappers from sticks of chewing gum," the mage said dismissively. "I'm done here, so I'll see you all at the restaurant."

"Wait," Stick said, putting on his most charming smile. "Can you do the same for Affie's stuff? I was going to just throw it all in this bin and let her arrange it in the new design room when she gets the chance, but you know how artists are."

"I know how sales managers are too, especially the kind that buys discount enchanted LARPing weapons from a Verlock hack, even though he works with the most powerful mage on the station."

"I'll bring the stuff to you to have it re-enchanted," Stick offered. "And there are some other players in my raid party who have bought weapons from the Verlock. I'll persuade them to do the same."

"I might be interested if you invited me to come along on your next raid," Baa insinuated.

"But you always—all right," he conceded, recognizing that the Terragram was in no mood to be lectured over her in-game conduct. "Just try to leave some of the treasure for the rest of us, and no reviving our party members as zombie slaves."

"We'll see," Baa said. She turned her attention to Affie's workbench, which was easily the messiest corner of the design room, and wiggled her fingers while chanting something in an untranslatable tongue. There was a theatrical puff of smoke, and the sculptor's collection of tools and materials were transformed into a concert grand piano. "I needed to choose something with the appropriate weight or the bots will get confused," the mage explained on her way to the exit.

"I'm going to go finish cleaning out the sales office," Stick said. "Keep the floating bin. I'll see you guys at the restaurant."

"If the maintenance bots are going to do all the heavy lifting, aren't we finished here?" Kevin asked.

"You could untie Tzachan and take him to unload the mulebot at the new office," Dorothy said. "I'll just finish stuffing everything else back into drawers."

"He is NOT tied up," Flazint said, pulling the finished skein of metallic yarn off her boyfriend's forearms and twisting it into a hank. "You can go with him and I'll help Dorothy," she told Tzachan. "Some of us who keep our workplaces organized don't have any packing left to do."

Less than a half an hour later, the couples reunited at Pub Haggis, and to Dorothy's surprise, the Hadad sisters arrived with Jeeves.

"I asked Ian to give us a few minutes to get the business part of this meeting out of the way before taking your orders," Jeeves began. "Starting tomorrow, we'll be working out of our new offices, and my expectation is that the increased overhead will be met with an even larger increase in productivity. Unfortunately, you'll have to settle into the new space without adult supervision."

"Where will the two of you be?" Dorothy asked the Hadads, intentionally not including Jeeves in the adult group.

"I took a leave of absence to help my husband with the Human Empire trade show," Shaina replied.

"And our sentient resources officer informed me that I have five weeks of vacation to use by the end of the cycle or it goes away," Brinda said.

"Aren't you our sentient resources officer?" Stick asked.

"That's why I thought I'd better do what I say," the younger Hadad sister replied. "Besides, Walter is going to be working overtime for the foreseeable future, and I've got a growing child and a lonely Cayl hound at home."

"Don't worry about a thing," Stick said. "I'll make sure nobody goofs off."

"Who put you in charge?" Dorothy demanded.

The Vergallian slid his plastic business card across the table. "What does that say?"

"SBJ Fashions. Dietro. Sales Manager."

"Does anybody else have a card with 'manager' on it?"

"Children, children," Baa chided them. "There's no need to fight with each other over who will be in charge when that responsibility obviously falls to me. I'll go over your daily goals with you each morning and correct your behavior as needed."

Dorothy and Stick turned to the three owners and asked simultaneously, "You're leaving HER in charge?"

"I graciously acceded to the request of my partners to fill in for them as long as required," Baa answered for them.

"Partners?" Flazint squeaked.

"Baa insisted on an equity share when her enchanted handbags became our leading product line," Jeeves said. "That was over a year ago, and I'm sure you'll all agree that it hasn't gone to her head."

"She does work three times as many hours as the rest of us, but that's because she doesn't need sleep," Dorothy said grudgingly. "I guess we all know our jobs by now anyway."

"Which brings us to our booth at the tradeshow," Jeeves said. "All of the attention right now is on the political implications of a Human Empire, but from the perspective of SBJ Fashions, it's an opportunity to make inroads while everybody else is focused on the headlines. Stick will be responsible for building a male customer list with our Shadow Dancer product, Dorothy and Flazint, you'll be pushing women's fashions and looking for new retail relationships, and Baa will handle the LARPing line."

"You want all four of us to work the booth together?" Dorothy asked. "The office will be empty during the tradeshow."

"It won't hurt the business a bit for all of you to take a week off from thinking up new ways to spend my money and try to make some for a change. Affie should be available a few hours here and there to help, but between contract-queening for the Alts and filling in for the

Vergallian ambassador as required, I wouldn't count on her too heavily. If you have too much time on your hands, you can always get started prototyping formalwear for men."

"I don't know anything about making men's suits," Flazint protested.

"But you know plenty about zippers and magnetic sealing strips," Jeeves pointed out. "That's at least half of the battle. I'll be away the next three weeks on Stryx business, so try not to bankrupt me. And don't stint on the bespoke swag bags, EarthCent is paying for your time."

"What bespoke swag bags?" Baa asked. "I'm not enchanting throwaways for a hundred thousand trade-show attendees even if Gryph gives me free access to the station power grid."

"We only need the special bags for the alien observers," Shaina said. "We don't even know how many are attending yet, but Daniel thinks it won't be more than a couple of dozen."

"So you want me to hand-embroider Empire@Empire on them?" Dorothy asked.

"And the names of the observers, so they don't steal each other's swag. I already checked with Libby and she can provide you with templates so you don't have to look up all the alien characters."

Six

"What's wrong with that alien?" a little boy asked, pointing at a Horten whose skin was bright blue.

"Don't point," the boy's mother scolded, pushing down her son's hand. "He's probably having a bad makeup day."

"You're not that far from the truth," Samuel told them. "The Hortens accidentally altered the DNA of their entire species with a badly engineered cosmetic product back before they joined the tunnel network, and as a result, their skin changes color with their emotions. One time my friend Marilla turned bright blue and got stuck that way until I embarrassed her so much that her blush response triggered again and cleared it."

"You're friends with an alien?" the teenage daughter of the family asked.

"Sure. I must have more alien friends than human friends." Seeing the shocked reaction of the parents, Samuel hastened to add, "My mother is the EarthCent ambassador so I grew up seeing aliens all of the time."

"And you went to school with robots?" the boy asked excitedly.

"With young Stryx who inhabit robot bodies for the sake of interacting with the other species. Our station librarian runs an experimental school for children, and the offspring of Stryx from all over the galaxy attend."

"We've already registered the children in a school on the human deck," the father said. "I suppose it was interesting for a diplomat's son to attend classes with aliens and artificial intelligence, but it's not for us. The main reason we decided to move to Union Station is we want the children to spend more time around their own kind, especially now that Jenna is old enough to start dating."

"You always embarrass me!" the teenage daughter exclaimed, turning bright red.

"Look, now Jenna's a Horten," the son said, pointing at his sister.

"What did I just tell you about pointing," the mother scolded him, again pushing his hand down.

It seemed to Samuel that the family had played this exact scene three times already during the short orientation tour, but as a graduate of Libby's school, he felt duty-bound to give recruiting one more try.

"There aren't any aliens attending the experimental school, Mr. Johnson. Just humans and young Stryx. We had a Gem for a while when my sister was going, but she's in stasis now."

"Your sister is in stasis? Does she have an incurable disease?" the father asked.

"My husband is a plain-spoken man," the mother said apologetically. "I'm sorry about your sister."

"My sister is fine. It's her Gem friend who's been in stasis for over a decade, though they're in the process of waking her up now. You probably know that the Gem started cloning boys to restore their species, and Myst decided to sleep until they had a few males for her to choose from."

"That's, uh, very nice to know," the mother said, and her teenage daughter blushed even brighter than she had before, "and your Shuk is very, er, cosmopolitan, but is there a shopping area where we might see more humans? Not that there's anything wrong with aliens," she concluded in a rush.

"Oh, I just thought that you'd want to see the areas of Union Station where all the oxygen-breathing species come together," the ambassador's son said. "Let's just hop back in the lift tube and I'll show you around the human deck. Since our numbers have been increasing, there's a whole corridor of shops and boutiques extending from the Little Apple towards the embassy."

"Little Apple?" the boy asked. "Is that like a fruit store?"

"My mom told me it's named after a famous city on Earth, or maybe it was a state," Samuel replied, ushering the family into the lift tube.

"It's a city-state now," the father told his son. "That's where your mother and I caught the space elevator up to orbit when we left Earth before you were born."

"Little Apple," Samuel instructed the lift tube, and then asked the father, "So did you leave Earth on an alien contract?"

"Yes, but we never saw them," the man said. "I put in fifteen years doing repairs on an ice harvesting fleet owned by the Grenouthians, but the ships were all operated by humans. Our only complaint was the lack of a social life for the children. My wife home-schooled them with the help of their teacher bots, and the habitat was spun up so that we weighed almost the same as on Earth on the residential deck. But the population was only a few thousand, and families with children didn't stay long."

"Except us," the teenage girl groused.

"Here we are," Samuel said as the lift tube door slid open. "While the Little Apple is officially open around the clock, the food stalls mainly run on Universal Human Time, which means we're between breakfast and lunch right now. The pizza places are just starting to warm up their ovens. I'll show you the shops and boutiques in the corridor first if that sounds good."

"Yes," the mother and daughter said simultaneously. The boy rolled his eyes and dropped back with his father, and the ambassador's son found himself primarily addressing the two women.

"All of these shops are leased directly from the Stryx, but on some of the alien decks that have been occupied much, much longer than ours, the majority of the properties are sublet from families whose roots on the station go way back. The Stryx don't sell station real estate outright, but once somebody leases a space, the Stryx are inclined to let it stay in the family as long as the payments are made on time."

"Inclined?" the father asked, proving that he was paying attention after all.

"Well, there may be something about it in the lease agreement, but those contracts are so long that everybody signs them without reading the details. Besides, the Stryx always include a clause saying they can make unilateral changes. My dad leases a large space right on the station core that used to be a junkyard, and I grew up in a scrapped ice-harvester crew module."

"Oh, it's a wedding boutique," the mother said, stopping to look at the elegant gowns in the display window. "I can just imagine how beautiful you would be in that one, Jenna."

The teenager turned red again, and Samuel began to wonder if she really did have some Horten blood in her. Then a Drazen girl came out of the boutique and motioned with her tentacle.

"Excuse me a minute," the ambassador's son said and went over to talk with his fiancée. "Have you finally started looking for a dress? I'm working right now so I can't talk long."

"You know that Dorothy would kill me if I didn't let her make my wedding dress," Vivian said. "I asked Libby where you were so I could see you in person before I leave."

"You're going somewhere?"

"Echo Station, it's my first solo field mission. There's a Horten immersive festival, and my handler wants me to circulate and see if I can pick up any leads about their upcoming season."

"Why you?"

"Because I can pass as human."

"That's because you are human, Vivian. Sometimes I worry that you're spending too much time wearing the prosthetic tentacle and that custom facial overlay."

"And you think I don't worry about you waltzing at work with upper-caste Vergallian women who are just waiting for a chance to dose you with their pheromones? Anyway, I'll be gone for twelve days, and I just stopped to see you on my way to the travel concourse."

"How could an assignment spying on an immersive festival come up all of a sudden?"

"We had an agent in place, an entertainment critic from one of the Earth networks. Herl just found out that the guy is a double agent working for the Hortens. You can't trust humans."

"If you say so." Samuel bent a little to give her a good-bye kiss, and Vivian wrapped her prosthetic tentacle around the back of his neck. When she finally released him and ran for the lift tubes, the EarthCent ambassador's son was as red-faced as Jenna.

"You're dating an alien?" the round-eyed teenager asked him.

"She's my fiancée," Samuel said, and then realized that the family may take it the wrong way. "I mean, she's not a Drazen if that's what you're thinking. The tentacle is fake, and she's wearing a facial overlay to—"

"I think we've seen enough for today," the father interrupted. "Come on, kids. Let's get something to eat, and then we'll stop by the travel agency and see about tickets to Earth. I don't think this place is going to work for us after all."

The EarthCent ambassador's son watched helplessly as his charges cut short the orientation tour and most likely their stay on Union Station as well. Then he remembered his mother's advice about dealing with diplomatic disappointment. After a quick stop in Hole Universe for a triple-chocolate donut, he felt appreciably better about the morning. He was considering going back for seconds when his implant chimed with an incoming ping from Aabina.

"Accept," he said. "Did my group already report me for inappropriate behavior?"

"I haven't heard anything," his mother's special assistant replied. "I was pinging to ask if you'd meet me at the Empire Convention Center after the tour."

"The tour is over, they dumped me," Samuel said. "Where will you be at the Empire?"

"The Galaxy Room. I'll leave the embassy now and meet you on the lower level, under the stadium seating at the Andromeda entry."

"Andromeda. Got it." Recalling his mother's warning about how the universe maintained balance by punishing donut lovers with excess weight, he ran back to the lift tube, and then continued jogging to his meeting, arriving before the Vergallian girl. Just to be safe, he did a set of push-ups while he was waiting.

"What's with you?" Aabina asked. "First you lose your orientation group, and now you're in training for the professional LARPing league?"

"Humans don't have the caloric intake regulation options that Vergallians do," he said as he straightened up. "Stick told me you can just increase your body temperature to burn off excess fat."

"I've never resorted to such a thing in my life," Aabina said indignantly. "And how did you scare off that nice family you were showing around?"

"Vivian dropped by in full Drazen disguise for a good-bye kiss before leaving the station on an urgent mission. She'll be gone until the tradeshow."

"Your loss is the EarthCent embassy's gain," the Vergallian girl said. "It means I can schedule you for more hours. Are you sure you want to go back to work in my mother's embassy when she returns?"

"If she'll have me. I've been thinking about some of the things she said when we saw her off, and I'm beginning to suspect she's easing me out."

"My mother wants what's best for you," Aabina said. "She's talked to me about your situation and she knows there isn't a meaningful career path for a Human in the Vergallian diplomatic service. She can keep you employed as long as she's the Union Station ambassador, but what happens when she leaves?"

"I just thought that was a long way off."

"Mom has already accomplished everything she wanted to achieve as ambassador. The only reason for her to return after Jubilee is that it gives her an excuse to let my aunts take turns at playing queen at home."

"Oh," Samuel said and was silent for a minute. "So why are we meeting here?"

"The Dollnick who manages the convention center was so pleased with our Empire@Empire campaign that he offered us early access to the galleries under the seating. We have so many vendors signed up for the tradeshow that we're splitting them between the Nebulae Room and the space down here. The other species are beginning to realize that Humans aren't the only ones who come to these tradeshows."

"How do you choose what vendor goes where? I'd think everybody would want to be in the Nebulae Room."

"That's true for the small stuff, but we saw a big jump in heavy equipment last year. We're offering the vendors who reserve space down here the bonus of rotating turns on the Galaxy Room stage for demonstrations."

"You mean like heavy equipment, or will you have salesmen showing off juicers and other fun stuff?"

"It's primarily construction and mining equipment on the schedule so far. The delegation from Chianga is even going to stage a floater race, with the audience on the stage, and the drivers using the upper seating sections as a velodrome."

"Like the time that nutty alien stole a demonstration floater and the Cayl emperor chased him down?"

"I wasn't on Union Station when the Cayl visited," Aabina reminded him. "Donna and I have worked up a map of the vendor spaces on my tab, and since the Empire is letting us load in early, we need to get the partitions straightened out. I didn't want to ask the Dollnick manager to assign the work to his facility staff because he's already doing us a huge favor."

Samuel walked over and gave one of the partition walls a shove. For a temporary divider, it didn't show any sign of wanting to move. "Have you ever done this before?" he asked.

"No, but Donna said that she and her daughters used to move these walls around when the girls were still in school. Supposedly a twelve-year-old can rearrange the room without help."

"So if we can't figure it out, you can ping Daniel and ask him to send us his son Mike, or I could check with Aisha and see if Fenna is available."

"Very funny. There has to be some kind of control mechanism somewhere. Check near the corners. That's where I'd put the locks if I were designing partitions."

Samuel approached the outer corner of a room and ran his hands over the surface as if he were looking for invisible hardware. He crouched down to inspect the bottom of the partition, but the wall was flush with the floor. Finally, he gave up and walked over to where Aabina was having no better luck.

"The problem, as I see it, is that we have to think like twelve-year-olds," he said.

"So what would you have done when you were twelve?"

"Kicked something? But now that you mention it, I kind of remember Vivian was always asking questions at that age. If I didn't know the answer, she'd talk to the station librarian."

"Asking the Stryx for help moving a partition seems a little frivolous," Aabina said.

"But it gives me an idea," Samuel said. He walked back to the corner where he had started and addressed himself to the wall. "Move."

A little panel popped open showing a control pad. "I cannot comply without authorization and a grid destination," a mechanical voice reported in oddly accented English. "Please identify yourself."

"I'm Samuel McAllister, with the EarthCent embassy. I'm here doing setup for CoSHC."

"Identity not confirmed," the wall said, and the access panel snapped shut.

"Let me try," Aabina suggested. "You probably don't show up in the public database as working for EarthCent, and the Dollnick was very enthusiastic about the branding for the tradeshow. "Wall," she said in English. "I am Aabina, special assistant to Ambassador McAllister at the EarthCent embassy, and Samuel is with me today. We wish to reconfigure the partitions for our upcoming Human Empire tradeshow."

The panel snapped open again, and this time the voice intoned, "Identity confirmed. Grid destination required to carry out your request."

"I have a map but it doesn't have any grid coordinates," Aabina said. "Can we—"

"Look up," the voice interrupted, and Samuel and Aabina both complied without thinking. A grid showing a double set of numbers was now displayed on the translucent drop-ceiling which diffused the light from hidden fixtures above.

"Thank you," the Vergallian girl said. "Samuel, can you take a quick run around the perimeter and make a note of the coordinates at each entrance? I'll use those to calibrate the map on my tab, overlay a grid, and then the job is practically done."

"That wasn't some pre-programmed routine telling us to look up," the EarthCent ambassador's son muttered. "There's a Dolly sitting in a control room somewhere laughing at us."

"He who laughs first laughs longest," the wall quoted. "You Humans have the expression wrong, as usual. Now run along and note the coordinates for Aabina so we can get the partitions moved and I can go back to my nap."

Samuel began to jog around the perimeter of the space, which, unlike the amphitheater above, was square rather than round. At the exact midpoint of each wall was an over-sized sliding door, large enough to allow a piece of heavy equipment to drive through. He paused at the centerline of the first door and looked up to check the grid coordinates, which made him scowl. Just to be safe, he ran around the rest of the perimeter before returning to Aabina.

"The closest door to us is at zero/one," he told her, pointing it out on her tab. "The next one is at one/two, after that is two/one—"

"And the fourth door is at one/zero," Aabina surmised. "Of course, they used a simple grid and the center of the stage is at one/one. It is so simple that a twelve-year-old could figure it out. The grid locations we see looking up are all decimals, they just divided the coordinates by a thousand."

"A thousand whats?"

"Princely hands," the Dollnick informed them. "It's our foundational measurement unit. The space you're renting is two thousand hands on a side, or four million square hands, and the radius of the Galaxy amphitheater is one thousand hands."

Aabina used the four points to calibrate her tab, and the locations where she and Donna wanted to place partitions were now shown in Dollnick coordinates.

"So we have to go around talking to every partition and give it the grid locations for both ends?" Samuel asked.

"That would work," the wall informed him.

"Is there another option?" Aabina asked, putting a restraining hand on Samuel's arm. "Could I just send you my drawing?"

"That would work too," the Dollnick admitted in a whistle that came out like a sigh. "Just hold your tab up near the closest control panel and select share, but be prepared to run."

"Run?" Samuel repeated.

Aabina held her tab up near the control panel and shared the map. The partition began to retreat soundlessly, at the same time changing its angle relative to their position. Then something shoved Samuel from behind, and it was only the balance and coordination he'd acquired in fifteen years of ballroom dancing that saved him from falling on his face.

"Run!" Aabina cried. "All of the partitions are moving at the same time!"

The two of them dodged around the partition wall that had run into Samuel, and the EarthCent ambassador's son guided Aabina to the nearest exit. For a fraction of a second, he thought the door was going to refuse to budge, but then it slid back into the wall, and the pair escaped into the corridor. The door hissed closed behind them.

"I knew he was going to be a joker the minute I saw the coordinates over the entrance," Samuel said. "He could have just told you, but he wanted to make me run a lap."

"Dollnicks do have an interesting sense of humor," the Vergallian ambassador's daughter agreed. "I wonder how long it will take the partitions to sort themselves out?"

"I wonder what the controller will do with all the extra ones. Your layout couldn't have used half as many partitions as were in there."

"My guess is that they'll just go double-width, or place them against the outside walls. I didn't see any wheels, so the driving force was probably inset magnets getting moved around by coils embedded in the deck. It's impressive how quiet the system is."

The door slid open again, and both of the young people reflexively jerked back, as if they were afraid that the partitions were coming in pursuit. But all motion had ceased in the room, and a quick check proved that the walls now corresponded exactly with the map that Donna and Aabina had drawn up.

"You're welcome," a booming Dollnick whistle assailed them. "Don't they teach manners in the Human Empire?"

"Thank you," Aabina said to the nearest partition.

Seven

Daniel was in the reception area waiting for Kelly when she arrived at the embassy. "Did you see the new Grenouthian documentary?" he asked.

"That's why I'm a little late," the ambassador said. "I stayed up last night to watch it with Joe, and then I couldn't fall asleep because I was worried about investing our cookbook money."

"I can see how it would have that effect, but the important thing is that they didn't make any Human Empire jokes."

"No, they just made fun of Earth's pre-Stryx financial system. It's the first time I've seen a Grenouthian documentary use so much content from the Children's News Network. That interview the girl did with the Swiss insurance executive was an eye-opener."

"The Grenouthians broadcast that last year, and the ratings on reruns were probably what drove the bunnies to go deeper into the subject," Daniel said. "They made a whole series of documentaries about Earth's financial system decades ago, but those focused primarily on Ponzi schemes and stock markets. This might have been the first documentary that was entirely about government-issued bonds."

"I understand why it was beneficial to the Swiss government to sell a hundred-year bond with a negative coupon, but I still don't get why anybody purchased them."

"The documentary implied that we just aren't too bright as a species. But I watched it with Shaina, and she assumed that most of the buyers were practicing a form of asset allocation which forced them to choose the best of the worst. If they were committed to investing in bonds, and everything else looked riskier than paying the Swiss government a small amount every year for the privilege of loaning it money, it makes a certain sort of sense, relatively speaking."

"That's not what the Thark ambassador would call investing," Kelly said. She fished her paperback diary out of her purse and checked her notes. "He says that investors have to exercise some sort of control over their money or it's the same as gambling. I doubt that the Swiss government took administrative advice from people just because they bought bonds."

"Probably not," the associate ambassador agreed. "How's your schedule looking this morning? Shaina arranged a meeting with a Verlock expert on the tunnel network treaty if you want to sit in. He's going to demonstrate a mathematical proof for the transparent decision-making process."

"I think I'm free," Kelly said, flipping her paperback around in her hand and opening it from the back. "I've started jotting down my appointments so I don't have to rely on Libby to be my memory, and, oops—it looks like I'm expecting Bork."

"His embassy manager pinged me fifteen minutes ago to confirm," Donna spoke up from her desk. "He wanted me to tell you that he'll be bringing Glunk, his friend who runs Drazen Foods."

"I haven't seen Glunk since I toured his factory on Earth with Joe and Samuel. I'll meet them in my office so that Daniel can use the conference room. Please send Aabina in when she arrives."

"Sorry, I'm borrowing her," the associate ambassador said. "Just in case Shaina and I can't figure out what the Verlock is talking about."

"I suppose it can't be helped. Where is Aabina now?"

"With your son, shopping for party favors," Daniel said. "I think they were going to split up to cover the Horten and Frunge decks this morning. Donna let them raid petty cash."

"And I expect you to pay me back with cookbook money," the embassy manager said. "Petty cash pays for our dance mixers."

"What party favors?" Kelly asked Donna after Daniel headed into the conference room to brew an extra-strong pot of coffee in preparation for the Verlock expert's presentation. "Are we hosting something at the embassy that nobody bothered telling me about?"

"Party favors are what I call the extras for the alien observers who are coming to witness the birth of the Human Empire," Donna explained. "We're expecting a pair from each of the tunnel network species, and there have been a few reservations coming in from off-network empires as well. Aabina said that species-specific cosmetics and grooming products are the minimum they'll expect, and Shaina has the design staff at SBJ Fashions hand-embroidering Verlock swag bags with the names of the observers as we get their reservations."

"But I thought the swag bags were for freebies from the tradeshow."

"Apparently the observers travel light and expect more. Samuel and Aabina are filling the bags with as many of the comforts from home as they can dig up for each species. We're expecting a couple of dozen observers in the end."

"This is getting too complicated," Kelly said, drawing a sympathetic smile from the embassy manager. "I'll leave my door open so you can send Bork and Glunk in as soon as they arrive."

"If Samuel returns with Aabina, should I tell him to join you or Daniel?"

"Daniel," the ambassador said, and turned back guiltily to explain. "It's not that I don't appreciate Samuel's help, but he keeps trying to get me to do things the way he learned in the Vergallian embassy. I should be used to it by now, but I don't need our discussion about investing getting sidetracked into the superior returns available in the Empire of a Hundred Worlds."

"I take it you aren't interested in producing immersive dramas about palace intrigues," Donna said with a smile.

"Absolutely not. And with Bork bringing Glunk, I'm hoping they'll be able to tell me something about putting money in the alien businesses that are operating on Earth. We're going to have to send some money back home for the sake of appearances if nothing else, and alien business-es just seem like a safer bet than—you know."

"We watched that documentary last night too. Stanley got so angry that I had to make him a glass of warm milk with honey."

"I wish I could remember what Glunk liked to drink," Kelly said, not noticing that the two Drazens had just entered the embassy. "Bork claims to have developed a taste for all of our watered-down beverages, as he puts it, but Glunk spends most of his time on Earth, and he must be sick of making do by now."

"Not true," the principal stakeholder in Drazen Foods joined the conversation in fluent English. "I have the final word on every product we export, and I've come to appreciate the subtle differences in flavor that are associated with the various growing regions on your homeworld. I can identify over a hundred strains of coffee beans just by the aroma and—what's that I smell?" Glunk broke off, sniffing the air and turning in the direction of Daniel, who had just emerged from the conference room with a steaming mug of black coffee. "I detect a hint of caramel with nutty overtones, but there's a fruity component that I don't recognize from any roast I've ever encountered."

"Can I get anybody a cup?" Daniel offered. "I made it strong for my wife, but I can add a bit of water."

"I'm sure it's fine as is," Bork said, and turned to his friend. "Why don't you and Associate Ambassador Cohan get acquainted and I'll be back in a minute with a couple of cups."

"Glunk," the Drazen introduced himself to Daniel and offered a handshake in perfect Earth fashion. "Can you tell me the brand of that coffee?"

"I'm afraid I didn't notice," Daniel said. "Donna?"

"It's Flower's special roast," the embassy manager informed them. "She gifted us with a three-month supply when she stopped here for MultiCon. I don't know if she's planning to make the coffee commercially available, but from what Lynx told us, Flower started growing the beans as a proof-of-concept for some low-gravity agricultural theories she's working on."

"Don't scare me," Glunk said. "Competition from the Dollnicks is the last thing I need. Before you know it they'll be terraforming an ag world to mimic Earth's growing conditions, and there goes my lovely monopoly."

"I wouldn't worry," Kelly told him. "I'm sure that Flower is just as concerned about competition from Dollnick ag worlds as you are. She's heavily invested in growing the ingredients listed in the All Species Cookbook for her packaged foods business. And she's still on the outs with her makers, even though they're probably her biggest market for alcohol-infused baked goods."

"Here," Bork said on his return, handing Glunk a mug of coffee. "Shall we grab ourselves chairs, Ambassador?"

"I have three in the office," Kelly told him and waved her door open. "After you."

The two Drazens preceded the EarthCent ambassador into her office, where Kelly was relieved to see that nobody had borrowed the two extra chairs by her display desk. She took her seat, stored her purse in the file drawer, and then fished out the notebook and pencil.

"Is that a shirtless picture of Ambassador Crute?" Bork asked, looking at the cover which was upside-down to him from the other side of the desk. "It seems like a rather odd thing for you to have around."

"The Dollnick is one of Blythe's cover models. I think she said he lives on Flower."

"Interesting choice of reading material," Glunk said. "I've noticed the growing popularity of alien romance novels among our female employees who read during their lunch hour, and I've been thinking of bringing in an author for our weekly lecture series."

"You have weekly lectures at the factory?" Kelly asked.

"Workers do not live by pay alone. I've modeled my business after the standard Drazen factory, though I substituted quiet time for choral practice after the dogs working in perfume quality control went on strike. Our employee retention rate is nearly a hundred percent, even if they complain about the stretching in the morning."

"You should talk to Flower. The two of you would get along like a house on fire."

"So I understand you have a little problem with your cookbook windfall, Ambassador," Bork said. "You mentioned being up against the limit on your programmable cred?"

"Right. If I don't start spending the old money, the value will begin to decay on its own. Libby tells me that the Stryx have actually been cutting me some slack the last few cycles."

"I happened to be here visiting, and Bork requested I come along to give you my impressions of the investing environment on your homeworld," Glunk said, and then smacked his lips. "This really is extraordinary coffee. I'll have to visit Flower myself when she stops at Earth and see if we can work something out. Do you have any prior experience with investing, Ambassador McAllister?"

"I was in hock before I got married and my husband has always handled our finances," Kelly told the Drazen. "But I've been trying to educate myself, and according to the Thark ambassador, I should be looking for opportunities where I'll have some control over what happens." She hesitated before adding, "The truth is, I'm less worried about control than finding partners I can trust."

"I work with many Human suppliers, some of whom are looking for capital to expand their businesses," Glunk said. "I can give you their contact information if you want to write it down."

"Actually, I was hoping to find alien partners." The EarthCent ambassador flinched under the look both

Drazens gave her. "It's not that I don't trust my own people, but I just saw a Grenouthian documentary that suggests we aren't the most rational species, at least when it comes to money."

"Did the Thark ambassador tell you about the Copper Rule?"

"Is that related to the Golden Rule?"

"I'm not sure," Glunk said. "I've never heard of that one. The Copper Rule dates back to the Verlock's Copper Age, perhaps eight million years ago. It postulates that the risk of investing in an enterprise is inversely proportional to its need for outside funding."

"Just a moment," Kelly said as she diligently copied the Copper Rule into her notebook. Then she frowned. "Does this mean that I should only invest in businesses that don't want my money?"

"It's a quick way to quantify risk—the Verlocks are a very conservative culture."

"I'll wager that Drazen Foods is in a very strong financial position," Bork hinted broadly.

"That's exactly the kind of investment I'm looking for," Kelly said.

"Unfortunately, you run into the other side of the Copper Rule," Glunk said. "As you yourself postulated, our strong financial position means we have no need for outside funding. I've heard that there's a tradition on Earth of large corporations borrowing money whether or not they need it and then using the funds they raise to increase payouts to the shareholders and executives. But I'm afraid that goes against basic bookkeeping rules for a Drazen consortium, so I can't take your money."

"If you can't, you can't," Kelly said in disappointment. "I guess it won't hurt to write down the contact information for the human-owned businesses you work with, and maybe I can convince somebody in our president's office to look into the details."

Glunk reeled off a list of names and best contact information from memory, and the EarthCent ambassador diligently recorded them all. Then the entrepreneur gave her a quick rundown of business trends on Earth, and the meeting came to an end. Kelly escorted the two Drazens out of the embassy, and as they parted, Bork puzzled her by offering his services as an imperial mentor should the need arise.

As the EarthCent ambassador turned to reenter the embassy, a distinctive voice behind her proclaimed, "Rinty bubbles."

"Ptew?" Kelly guessed and turned to see that it was in fact the Fillinduck ambassador. "Were you coming to see me?"

"If you have a few minutes to spare," the alien said, gesturing for the EarthCent ambassador to precede him into the embassy. "I just came from a meeting with our Thark colleague, and he happened to mention your embarrassing problem."

"Embarrassing?" Kelly asked, leading the Fillinduck into her office.

"Excess wealth always comes as an embarrassment to those who least expect it. Given my friend's humorous description of your financial acumen, I thought I would drop by and offer some plain-spoken advice from my own area of expertise."

"I appreciate that, especially in light of the decades in which our relationship was, if I can use the word, nonexistent."

"Before we talk creds and centees, have you pledged anything to the Colony One movement?" Ptew asked, ignoring the EarthCent ambassador's usual attempt to fish for the reason the Fillinduck had boycotted every meeting she attended for nearly thirty years.

"The group that's raising funds to outfit a human colony ship? No."

"That's a relief. Philanthropy is a bottomless pit full of broken dreams."

"If it's bottomless, how can it be full?" Kelly asked, even as she jotted down the ambassador's words in her notebook.

"I never really analyzed the saying, it's just something we're taught in school," the Fillinduck said. "Is that the book everybody is talking about?"

"My diary?" the EarthCent ambassador asked. "The cover was just a spare. It's not like I dream about trillionaire Dollnick—"

"We're all adults here," Ptew cut short her disclaimer with a wave. "I just find it fascinating that you can do scribal work. It's a specialty in our society."

"You don't practice handwriting?"

"Me? I learned as a child, of course, but now I dictate to my tab, and I have a signet ring for signing contracts." He tapped his ring on the ambassador's display desk and smiled at some private memory. "Returning to the purpose of my visit, how much do you know about Rinty bubbles?"

"Just that they take a long time to grow, and maybe I've heard they have some, uh, special cultural significance for your people. I was impressed by the number I saw growing in your embassy the one time I was invited."

"Then you'll have to return for a closer look," Ptew said graciously. "Rinty bubbles play a key role in our mating practices. They take forever to grow and they can only be used one time. Popping them is required to release the payload, which acts as an aphrodisiac on all three members of a trio. Do you know what that makes them?"

"Dangerous?" Kelly guessed.

"Valuable,' the Fillinduck said. "You can double your money every hundred years, and I'm talking about Stryx creds, not some inflation-riddled currency."

"But a hundred years is an awfully long time," the EarthCent ambassador said doubtfully. "I'm sure we'll need the money for something before then. Do partially grown Rinty bubbles have any value?"

"It's an issue," Ptew admitted. "They can't be moved without the risk of breakage, and to put it bluntly, anybody selling early is obviously in financial distress, so you couldn't expect to get the best price. I suppose if your investment window is less than a hundred years, Rinty bubbles wouldn't be the best option. Perhaps you could start growing a crop for your children?"

"That would still be a little optimistic on the hundred-year window, but for the grandchildren, maybe. Joe keeps telling me we need to work on our estate planning, but somehow I never seem to have the time."

"It couldn't be too hard to add the disposition of a few Rinty bubbles to your will," the Fillinduck encouraged her. "It happens I could let you have some starter crystals at— you don't have a will?" he concluded in disbelief when Kelly started shaking her head.

"We've talked about it enough times. It's just a matter of sitting down with the children and getting their input. I know Joe plans on leaving the lease to Mac's Bones to his adopted son since Paul has always been the one most involved in the ship repair business. And with her share of

InstaSitter, Vivian will be one of the wealthiest women on the tunnel network, so unless she breaks off her engagement with Samuel, he'll never want for money. What?" she asked, noting the pained expression on Ptew's alien features.

"Is this really how your species does estate planning?" the Fillinduck asked. "Don't you have any traditions or laws to tell you how to proceed?"

"I guess we figure it's up to the individual to decide how to dispose of their assets," Kelly said. "In olden times, some of our cultures used to practice primogeniture, but these days, most people just do what they want, unless they die intestate."

"You mean there are people even less prepared than you who die with no plans in place?"

"More than you might think, but then it just goes according to the local laws, though that means the lawyers get a larger share."

"Why don't you ask the Stryx to handle it for you?" Ptew suggested facetiously. "I understand you're on intimate terms with the station librarian."

"That's right," Kelly said. "I forgot that Joe and I asked her years ago to take care of the children if anything happened to us. But we didn't really have any assets to dispose of, other than the lease to Mac's Bones and all of the junk. Libby? What would happen if I died suddenly?"

"We would all be greatly saddened," the Stryx replied in a somber voice.

"I meant, what would happen to my stuff and my EarthCent pension?"

"In the absence of a will, the assets of a married person on a Stryx station go to the spouse. If Joe predeceased you, your assets would be divided equally among your children."

"We want the lease for Mac's Bones to go to Paul," Kelly said.

"Then you should sit down and make a will," the station librarian said. "As to the pension, once you reach retirement age, you can elect to reduce your payment by a third in exchange for Joe receiving half of the amount should you go first, but it doesn't make sense from an actuarial standpoint."

Ptew couldn't contain himself any longer and broke out laughing, though it sounded more like an owl hooting. "You asked the Stryx to take care of your children if anything happened!" he chortled when he regained his composure. "I'm not saying they aren't capable of the task, but I would have thought you'd have somebody closer. Perhaps what you need is a mentor."

"Are you volunteering?" Kelly asked.

"Is that an official request?" Ptew said, and something in his tone made the EarthCent ambassador pause.

"I appreciate the offer, but not at this time."

Eight

"The new office is too cold," Dorothy complained, setting aside her embroidery needle. "Don't you think so, Flaz?"

"I'm fine with the temperature but the air is too dry," the Frunge girl said. "It's a good thing my day is over so I can go home and mist my hair vines. Don't forget you're chaperoning for us later."

"How could I forget? It's programmed into the dating calendar I had to buy."

"Try talking to Baa about the climate controls again," Flazint suggested. "She should be back in a few minutes. I've got to run."

As soon as her friend left the office, Dorothy pinged her husband. "We're chaperoning after work today. I forgot all about it."

"What time?" Kevin asked.

"I don't have the calendar with me, you'll have to check."

"Why didn't you ask Flazint?"

"Because then she'd know that I forgot. Are you at home or at the chandlery?"

"At the chandlery, but I may as well close the counter for the next couple weeks and help Paul and Joe."

"Why's that? Has something happened?"

"It's all the sales reps coming in for the tradeshow. Your dad and Paul started moving their project ships out to Gryph's long-term parking this morning just to make room because it looks like every Tunnel Trips rental ship on the network is going to end up parked here in the next week. Marilla even brought in her younger sister to help her start cleaning them all."

"Is Margie with you?"

"Last time I checked," Kevin said. "We never should have taught her to walk."

"You have the gate up, don't you?" Dorothy asked.

"She figured out the latch. I think Alexander coached her."

"We must be the only parents on Union Station who have to worry about their Cayl hound teaching their toddler how to get in trouble."

"At least Alexander never takes his eyes off of her. Assuming I can find them, are we bringing Margie tonight?"

"I don't even know where we're going," Dorothy said. "Check the shelf where you keep the dates and figs, and if it's not there, it must be at home."

"I'll bite," Kevin said. "Why would the calendar be with the dried fruit?"

"Dates and calendars go together. I'm trying to get more organized. Besides, I think we stopped in the chandlery on the way back from bowling that last time."

"Found it," Kevin said, pulling out the Frunge device and powering it on. "Tonight at quarter past seven we're Live Action Role Playing. I wonder why it counts as a date? I thought Flazint and Tzachan could get away with treating LARPs as work-related activity."

"She doesn't want their matchmaker getting suspicious, and they just used the work excuse for that lunch we had

94

after moving the office," Dorothy explained. "Kiss Margie for me if you can find her. She's way too young for LARPing so we'll leave her with my parents. I have to get back to work if I'm going to finish these swag bags today."

"See you in a few hours."

The EarthCent ambassador's daughter checked the tension screw of the metal embroidery hoop SBJ Fashions had standardized on in deference to Flazint's sensitivity about wood. She quickly finished the gold part of the observer's name, and then began outlining the alien characters with small stitches in royal blue. She didn't hear the Terragram mage return.

"Vishmiat," Baa read over Dorothy's shoulder. "There should be an accent over the 'shmi.'"

"If it's not on the pattern, it doesn't go on the bag. These spellings are all from Libby."

"Your Stryx librarian doesn't know everything. The Binderfall always add an accent over the 'shmi' unless..."

"Unless the bearer of the name carries the Winter Stigma," Libby completed the sentence. "Going by the length of her tail, it's obvious Vishmiat has had a run-in with frostbite."

"Why would the Binderfall have any interest in whether or not the Humans choose to establish an empire?" Baa demanded. "Inviting unaffiliated species with no vested interest in the tunnel network to observe the diplomatic process just creates headaches for the hosts."

"I don't mind the embroidery," Dorothy said. "I was getting out of practice."

"But while you're busy producing bespoke swag bags nothing else is getting done around here. What happened to Flazint?"

"It's already early evening on her clock and she went home to mist her hair vines for a couple of hours before her date."

"A love-sick Frunge, a Vergallian royal who's busy substitute queening for the Alts, and a Human who spends more time playing with her toddler than working on new designs. It's no wonder your team hasn't produced a new lineup in over a year."

"Every time I have a great idea, Jeeves says it's too expensive," Dorothy protested. "Besides, Stick has everybody convinced that the catalog is unbalanced and we need to add male fashions. Personally, I don't see the point."

"So we finally agree on something," the mage said. "I refuse to put my Baa's Bags logo on the military rucksacks Stick keeps bringing me to enchant as bags of holding. I don't know why males even bother picking up treasure in LARPs if they're just going to stuff it in some shapeless sack. It's a waste of my magic."

"I wish I could do magic. Not any of the fighting stuff," the EarthCent ambassador's daughter qualified her statement, "but if I'm going to go on a quest, I want my seamstress character to be able to do something special."

"You chose to pursue crafting in a league that's based on combat," Baa pointed out. "I can teach you magic, but the only—"

"You can teach me magic?" Dorothy interrupted.

"I can teach anybody magic in a LARP. Out here in what you call the real world, a modicum of aptitude is required. The Verlocks are the only tunnel network species in which the trait is widespread, and even then, just one in a hundred thousand has what it takes to become even a poor excuse for a mage."

"And you're saying I don't have any aptitude."

"I would have noticed by now," Baa said. "Do you think I would spend twelve hours a day enchanting purses if I could train you to do it?"

"I guess not. But what if you taught me how to create bags of holding inside a LARPing studio?"

"Ah, now you're getting into game mechanics. The magic I can teach you to cast inside a LARP will only work in that instance."

"Instance?"

"For example, a season of the professional LARPing league that SBJ Fashions sponsors is a single instance for the players in that league. But if you enchanted a cloak to be arrow-proof in that instance and then wore it in a LARPing studio for any other action, it would just be a piece of cloth."

"I thought that the magical weapons players can win or buy work everywhere," Dorothy said. "And how about all of the bonus rings and scrolls?"

"You have to read the fine print," Baa told her. "My bags-of-holding work in all LARPing studios, as do items and weapons enchanted by other mages or generated by the game engine, which on Stryx stations means you-know-who. But if I taught you magic during a LARP, your enchantments would only work in that instance because you aren't a real mage."

"I'd still like to try it."

"You'll get your chance tonight," Baa said. "I made Stick invite me to his party."

"Oh," Dorothy said. "Are you going to force us all to buy stuff from you again?"

"A modest fee will help you take your magical studies seriously. Just bring what you have."

"Baa, Dorothy," Stick called from the door. "Do you have a minute?"

"We're busy," the mage answered irritably. "What do you want?"

"I've got a few ideas for men's suits that we should talk about. Jeeves told me to push you while he's gone."

"If Jeeves wants to push me, he'll have to show up and do it himself," Dorothy said. "If you ask me, men's fashion is an oxymoron."

"So work up some designs that will get people to take men's fashion seriously," Stick said. "I'll expect to see something before the tradeshow is over."

"Look who's acting like he's in charge," the mage grumbled after the Vergallian ducked back out of the room.

"Speaking of being in charge, Flazint wanted me to ask you to turn up the heat, plus she says it's a little dry in here."

"One more thing," Stick said, leaning back into the room. "Turn down the heat. It's too hot in here, and some of us have to wear suits when we have clients."

Five hours later, against the advice of all and sundry, Stick and Baa agreed to split the party. The sales manager took most of the group on a raid, while the mage set up school next to a broken fountain in the courtyard of a tumbled-down castle.

"Tuition will be one gold," she announced. "Each."

"I've got this," Dorothy told her friends, handing over half of the coins her seamstress character had earned in years of repairing garments for other players in LARPs. "Put your gold away, Affie."

"But you never play, and I'm loaded from going on raids with Dietro," the Vergallian girl said. Her friends looked over in surprise on hearing her use Stick's real name. "There's something about working in the embassy all the time that makes me feel funny about dating a guy called Stick. Besides, he stopped selling Kraaken sticks, and he doesn't even burn it himself anymore."

"I knew there was something different about him," Baa said. "He's getting more motivated and proactive with each passing cycle. Next thing you know he'll be going into business for himself."

"I can't believe he talked Tzachan into going on the raid," Flazint complained to Dorothy. "You and Kevin better agree to chaperone us out for ice cream later or this date will be a complete waste."

"You could have gone with them," the EarthCent ambassador's daughter pointed out.

"I thought Affie would go on the raid and I didn't want to abandon you with Baa."

"And I was sure Flazint would go with Tzachan," Affie said.

"You realize I'm standing right here and I can do magic," Baa growled at them, putting an end to the discussion. "Now, I can guess what Dorothy wants to learn, but how about the two of you?"

"Can you teach me to cast fireballs?" the Vergallian asked.

"Do Stryx like math?"

"And I'd like to be able to put spells on my arrows," Flazint said. "Something so I could shoot the monsters without having to look them in the eye."

"Tell me again why you LARP?" the mage asked, and then launched into her lesson without waiting for an answer. "There are three ways you can acquire magic in this space. The first way is through instruction and practice, the second way is by acquiring and reading a spellbook, and the third way is to be gifted a spell. It's your gold, Dorothy, so you choose."

"I guess being gifted a spell would be the quickest," Dorothy said, thinking that the other two girls would still have time to catch up with their boyfriends for the raid.

"Unfortunately, since the 'Rain of Toads' incident, the station management has requested that I no longer gift magic to unprepared recipients."

"How about spellbooks, then?"

"Don't happen to have any with me. Do you?"

"Why did you say I have three choices if you knew all along that two of them weren't options?"

"If you were better at choosing, it never would have come up," Baa said. "Let's see. Flazint, your lesson is easiest. Do you see that tree over there with the sign nailed to it?"

"The 'no archery' sign?"

"Exactly. I want you to meditate on that sign to fix the image in your mind while I take care of these two. Affie?"

"I don't have a lighter if that's what you were going to ask."

"Very funny," the mage said. "Casting fire is just like casting ice, but you twist the flow to the right rather than the left."

"You know I can't cast ice."

"You girls have excuses for everything. Do you have a lighter?"

"We already covered that," Affie gritted out between her teeth.

"No sense of humor," Baa said. "All right then, we'll do it the old-fashioned way. Try to imagine a candle burning in the dark with nothing else around. You'll have to close your eyes to start. When you can see the flame with your eyes open, tell me."

"Give me a second," the Vergallian girl said. She sat cross-legged on the ground, closed her eyes, and then frowned as the task turned out to be harder than she imagined.

"That will take care of those two for a few minutes," Baa told Dorothy. "Now what will it be? Do you want to cast protective spells on clothing, or magically produce new materials to work with?"

"I can make my own fabric? Like turning cotton into gold?"

"Transmuting elements is an advanced spell that is beyond your capacity to learn. What I can teach you is how to magically craft new materials, like this." The mage waved her hand at a tall clump of grass, and the blades wove themselves into a crude mat. "No, that didn't come out very well," Baa critiqued her own work. She gestured again, and the mat reformed itself into a broad-brimmed hat. "There. Would that spell be worth a gold to you?"

"Making grass hats?" Dorothy asked doubtfully. "It's kind of limited, and most players already have hats. Besides, I'd rather have a new fabric than the ability to create finished products."

"Really? But then you're just making more work for yourself."

"I like work. I mean, I'd get bored sewing the same thing over and over again all day, but I love designing new clothes, and working with my hands makes me feel good."

"And what do you call what I'm doing?" Baa demanded, performing an intricate spell casting that reminded the ambassador's daughter of the hand motions from a dance move she'd seen in a Grenouthian documentary about the history of human mating rituals.

"I'm not sure. Is something happening that I can't see?"

"I'm weaving with invisible thread. Here," the mage told her, and then made a tossing motion in Dorothy's direction. The ambassador's daughter felt something as light as a silk veil settle over her head and hang down to her shoulders.

"It feels nice, but if it's invisible, nobody can see it," Dorothy pointed out.

"Obviously."

"But I'm a designer and I want people to see my creations."

"You don't want to learn the spell?"

"Could you teach me, but without the invisible part?"

"Ready," Affie declared and opened her eyes. She looked around and let out a shriek. "Where's Dorothy's head?"

"Right on her shoulders beneath the shawl of invisibility," the Terragram mage said. "I offered to teach her to weave the invisible fabric and she turned me down."

"Wait!" Dorothy cried. She pulled the piece of fabric off her head by feel and then stared at where her forearm now ended in an invisible wrist and hand. "You didn't tell me the cloth could make clothing that granted invisibility. I thought you meant it was see-through."

"What would the point of that be?" Baa asked. "Just hold onto it while I finish teaching the substitute queen here how to cast fire, because if you drop that shawl, we'll never find it. You isolated the candle flame, Affie?"

"It got easier the longer I tried. Now I can do it with my eyes open."

"Perfect. Now blow the candle out."

Affie pursed her lips to blow out the flame that only she could see. A stream of fire shot from her mouth and dissipated over the mage's magical shield.

"Not at me," Baa said in irritation. "Try casting up in the air to see how far you can reach."

"The flames are coming out of my mouth," the Vergallian complained. "I wanted to cast from my hands."

"That comes with the next level. First, you have to master Dragon's Breath."

"But I must look like a carnival performer. Everybody will laugh at me!"

"Not the monsters you incinerate. Go and practice behind those rocks or you might get an arrow in the back," Baa instructed her. "Flazint? Do you have the sign firmly fixed in your mind?"

"I think I'm ready," the Frunge girl said.

"Now shoot an arrow directly at me."

"How about if I aim over your shoulder?"

"Aim wherever you want, just keep that sign in mind. And you better stand behind me, Dorothy."

The ambassador's daughter didn't need a second invitation, and she resisted peeking over the mage's shoulder to watch Flazint nock and fire the arrow. The projectile whizzed past the pair and thunked into a sapling.

"You let the image of the sign slip from your mind," Baa accused Flazint.

"It's my training," the Frunge girl apologized. "I did archery in school and they were very stringent about picking a target and keeping your eyes on it. I thought this was going to work like the magic bow and arrows you gave me to use in our booth exhibition that time."

"I was directly controlling your arrows with my magic during the noodle weapon demonstration. And there's

103

nothing wrong with your training to keep your eye on the target, but the whole point of this exercise is to see that target through your mind's eye. This time, close your eyes before you release, and concentrate on that sign."

Flazint nocked another arrow, pointed in the general direction of the tree line, closed her eyes, and released. The arrow flew in a straight line for about half the distance, and then it made a hard turn and buried itself in the 'No archery' sign.

"Good," Baa said. "Keep practicing, but point in the other direction if you don't mind. Have you lost that shawl yet, Dorothy?"

"No, I've got it right here. But if I had dropped it, wouldn't we be able to see it because the ground would become invisible?"

"It only works on players," the mage said. "Players and their mounts, if you weave a big enough piece. Are you ready to learn?"

"It's not really what I had in mind," Dorothy said. "I mean, I can tell that it's powerful magic, and garments of invisibility would be valuable in LARPing, but part of being a fashion designer, maybe most of it, is seeing the clothes I make. Invisible fabric is kind of self-defeating."

"Then you tell me what you want," Baa said, crossing her arms and tapping her foot. "You're on the clock."

"I guess I have the Gem nanofabric stuck in my head. It's such a brilliant idea. Programmable cloth that can take on different forms and fill different functions is a designer's dream. Can I learn something like that?"

"Spells don't work for complex mechanisms," the mage said. "You can do this or you can do that, but you can't do everything at the same time. I could work a number of enchantments on a piece of cloth that would layer together

104

to give it similar properties to the Gem nanofabric, but the amount of my time involved would make it prohibitively expensive, even in LARPing space. It's unlikely you'd ever find a single player with enough gold to purchase whatever you made from it."

Dorothy's eyes began to shine so brightly that for a moment the mage thought they were going to shoot out beams of light. "Baa!" the EarthCent ambassador's daughter shouted, distracting both Flazint and Affie in the midst of their releases, and forcing the mage to intercept the arrow and the ball of fire that headed her direction as a result. "You just gave me the greatest idea ever. The only question is how to manipulate Jeeves into going along."

Nine

"I know I said we would convene this meeting of the ad hoc committee exactly on the hour, but maybe we should wait a few more minutes to give the alien observers a chance to find the embassy," Daniel said. "Shaina? Are you sure you pinged them all?"

"More than once, thanks to our back-office support," his wife replied. "Libby?"

"The alien observers who are already on Union Station were alerted to this meeting when it was scheduled," the Stryx librarian replied. "I sent updates this morning, and again ten minutes ago."

"That's curious," Daniel said. "Maybe they just aren't that interested in the organizational aspects of empire building. In any case, I'm sure you all recognize Maker Dring, who is here to record the birth of the Human Empire for history. And if you've never met my wife, this is Shaina."

"Hi," Shaina said, giving the ad hoc committee members a quick wave.

"You all know Aabina from our holoconference calls, and sitting next to her is our ambassador's son, Samuel, who is on loan from the Vergallian embassy. Maker Dring requested that I ask everybody who participates in the discussion to introduce themselves the first time they speak so he gets your names right for the record. In that

106

spirit, I'm Associate Ambassador Daniel Cohan, the acting chair of the Human Empire ad hoc committee, and we're here today to come up with a transitional framework that meets the tunnel network treaty requirements. Yes, Bob?"

"Bob Winder, Mayor of Floaters on Chianga, a Dollnick open world. All of our technology is manufactured under license from Prince Drume. I just want to state for the record that Chiangans are happy with the current state of affairs and we view the idea of humanity starting an empire to be as useless as a fifth arm. Our main concern is what impact it could have on current relations between the sovereign communities on Chianga and our prince."

"Joan Powell. I'm the designated stakeholder for the human consortium operating mines on the Drazen open world of Two Mountains. I agree one hundred percent with Bob, substituting a second tentacle for a fifth arm, of course."

"Of course," Daniel said. "Did you have something to add, Tac?"

"Tac, from the Verlock open world of Fyndal, representing the academy," said an athletically built woman of around thirty. "I just wanted to remind everybody else that I'm only here as a substitute for our academy head, Hep, who is leading the effort on Earth to reverse engineer a Drazen jump drive."

"Any word of the progress on that?" Bob asked her.

"Hep is hoping to test our prototype later this year," Tac replied. "He said that parts of the theory of operation still elude our team of scientists, but he's confident that the copy they're making will operate the same way as the original."

"Interesting," Dring muttered to himself. "I must arrange to be in the neighborhood to see that."

"I suppose I don't really need to do this, but can I get a show of hands on how many of the committee members are happy with the status quo?" Daniel asked. Every hand went up. "Right. We met with a Verlock tunnel treaty expert to go over our options, and it turns out that there's a never-been-used-before middle path between accepting and rejecting empire status. Aabina?"

"It's called the Thousand Cycle Option," Kelly's special assistant explained. "Choosing it will give the Human Empire approximately a hundred and fifty years to comply with the requirements, and there's no penalty for dropping out."

"So why would anybody ever agree to empire status right away and not take advantage of the wiggle-room?" Samuel asked.

"There is one downside," Aabina said, "The Thousand Cycle option is predicated on our admitting that we lack the institutional knowledge to proceed, and therefore mandates the selection of a Stryx-approved mentor to guide the process of empire-building."

"What's the problem with that?" Tac asked. "There's no shame in accepting mentoring."

"It could be tricky picking a mentor without offending allies. After all, the ad hoc committee represents communities on worlds owned by a half-dozen different species."

"I think it's obvious we should choose the Vergallians," Samuel said. "They're the most populous empire on the tunnel network and they already provide the Alts with contract-queens. I'm sure the Stryx would approve you as our mentor."

"Me?" Aabina said. "I'm too young for that kind of responsibility."

"I think asking the Drazens would make more sense," the woman from Two Mountains said. "Everybody knows that Drazen Intelligence already acts as a mentor for EarthCent Intelligence."

"The Verlocks—" Tac began.

"The Dollnicks—" Bob said at the same time.

"Let's postpone selecting a mentor until we get through the process of establishing a preliminary framework for decision making," Daniel said quickly. "Any ideas there?"

"Annie, I'm the official secretary for the Break Rock mining cooperative. The executive committee of our cooperative is so dysfunctional that they try to pass off all of the decision making to me, and over the years, I've learned to delegate as much as possible to experts in the area. A mining habitat is a bit like a world in miniature, but despite the politics, everybody understands that we need an engineer in charge of air circulation and a police chief in charge of security. Maybe we could define vital sectors or interests for an empire and then assign working groups."

"I like it," Daniel said. "Just looking around this table I see potential working group heads for manufacturing, education, mining, health, and agriculture. Did I leave anybody out?"

"Trade," a man said, raising his hand. "I'm Larry, the council head of the Traders Guild, and though I've visited some of the open worlds the committee members hail from, this is the first time I'm meeting most of you in person. I'm not sure I quite understand what we'd be delegating in this case."

"We're not sure either, but I understand that the Thousand Cycle option requires us to begin the process of building an imperial infrastructure," Daniel said. "I'm hoping it's like taking an advanced math class where the instructor gives partial credit for showing your work when you can't completely solve the problem."

"Excellent analogy," Dring said, writing rapidly on the scroll he had brought to record the proceedings. He dipped his quill in the inkwell to recharge it, and then added, "I didn't mean to interrupt. Please continue."

"So you're saying that we're going to be graded on the process rather than the results," Bob surmised. "If that's the case, we should do something that will make the aliens stand up and take notice."

"I heard that the Vergallians on Aarden, where the independent traders held our last Rendezvous election, are still laughing at our guild's method of self-government," Larry said. "I don't think they're overly impressed by democratic processes."

"A general election is viewed by my people as a complete breakdown of royal leadership," Aabina informed him. "What's the point of having queens if you still have to sit through political campaigning?"

"Point taken," Daniel said.

"Evie, I'm actually from the human community on Aarden," a woman spoke up. "Maybe we could choose a queen from among our own people. Would that meet the tunnel network treaty requirements?"

"Why not a prince, or a council of princes?" the mayor from the Dollnick open world suggested.

"Or we could organize as a consortium and hold a singing competition," Joan said. "That's how we settle everything on Two Mountains."

"I certainly understand where you're all coming from, but I'm afraid that your suggestions would only resonate with the populations of the open worlds you call home,"

Daniel said diplomatically. "We want a process that all of our communities will see as fair and transparent."

"Like an open outcry auction," Larry suggested. "It's how traders handle pricing when a bunch of us are competing for the same wholesale merchandise."

"An auction!" Shaina cried, grabbing her husband's wrist. "How could I not have thought of that? We can sell the seats for the working groups to oversee the creation of various government departments, and the communities that have a vested interest in the outcome can make their priorities clear through their bids. It's the best discovery mechanism for true market value."

Dring's quill scratched furiously across the parchment as he took down Shaina's words, his reptilian lips pulled back to show blunt teeth in a happy smile.

"But you wouldn't want to end up with working groups that represent just a single interest," Samuel said. "What's to stop a rich community from buying all of the seats and driving the outcome for the whole empire?"

"Auction bylaws," Shaina said. "Listen. We'll limit each community to one seat per working group, or maybe to participating in one working group overall, since that will force them to choose carefully. We'll want an odd number of spots on every working group so there won't be any tie votes, let's say five seats, and the chairman for each could be the high bidder. After that, we could offer the remaining open seats at the second-highest bid, and if they don't fill, we could go to the third-highest bid."

"There should be some accounting for the size of the community," Larry said. "I represent millions of independent traders, but the way you're talking, I could end up having the same weight on a working group as a member from an ice-harvesting habitat with a few thousand transient residents."

"But you could bid enough to be chairman," Daniel pointed out.

"I can't claim any experience with direct elections," Aabina said, "but I've read about your representative democracies on Earth, and there was usually some kind of adjustment for population. Maybe you could weight the votes of working group members in accordance with the population they represent, but give them all the same amount of time to talk."

"It might work better to give them all the same voting weight, but apportion their talking time by the number of people they represent," Daniel said. "Don't forget that the first task for the working groups will be deciding whether or not to go ahead with the Thousand Cycle option, after which they might disband without doing anything else. We're just looking for a method that will meet the transparency requirement and let people feel like their concerns are being heard."

"How long would it take you to set up an auction?" Bob asked. "The tradeshow opens in just five days, and I'd really like to put this whole empire issue behind us before we go home."

"I can do this in my sleep," Shaina said confidently. "I ran an auction business with my sister and Stryx Jeeves for years. All I need is an audience, a space, and something to sell."

"Was that you who did the Kasilian auction around twenty years ago?" the woman from the human community on Aarden asked. "I was glued to our entertainment system for the whole week. Where was it held?"

"In the Galaxy Room of the Empire Convention Center, which we've already reserved for the tradeshow. We could hold the auction right after the opening ceremony and the keynote address."

"I don't have any objections, but we'll have to finalize the auction rules and get them out to all of our members in a hurry," Daniel said. "What do we have so far?"

"If you'll allow me," Dring said, looking down at his scroll. "For each working group, you will auction five seats, with the highest bidder becoming chairperson. The amount of speaking time in the working group allocated to each member is to be proportional to the population of the community they represent. After the winning bidder becomes chairperson, the second-highest bidder is seated, and other participants get the chance to buy in at the same bid."

"What if there are more than four people interested at that price?" Samuel asked.

"First come, first serve?" Shaina suggested. "We could use InstaSitters for spotters, just like we did at all of our auctions on Stryx stations, and if there's an argument, the station librarian could check the security video."

"All in favor?" Daniel asked. Every hand went up.

"Splendid," Dring muttered as he moved his quill across the parchment at a breakneck pace.

"How many working groups in all do we want?" Daniel asked, glancing down at the limited notes he'd taken on his tab. "I have six so far, including trade."

"Phillip, President of the Actors Guild, representing the sovereign human community on Timble, a Grenouthian orbital," a man with a goatee spoke up for the first time. "Entertainment is a must."

"Entertainment," Daniel repeated. "That makes seven. I'd say transportation, but the Traders Guild has a corner on human-owned spaceships. And there are tens of millions of humans working as mercenaries, but they aren't living in sovereign communities, so we don't need a military committee. Aabina?"

"Gaming," the Vergallian girl suggested. "Several CoSHC members are involved in the industry, and this may be a good time to bring the ad hoc committee up to date on Flower's request."

"Funny old bird," Bob said. "I never miss the chance to visit when she stops at Chianga."

"Flower has expressed an interest in joining CoSHC and then the Human Empire," Daniel said.

"But she's Dollnick to the core!"

"Flower claims that the human population she has living on board deserves representation and that she's the one in the best position to represent them."

"Personally, I like Flower, but if you let her join, she'll take everything over before the year is out," Samuel cautioned them. "A Drazen friend of mine lives on board and we visit every time Flower stops at Union Station. Nothing would make her happier than being appointed Empress of the Human Empire."

"She'd make an interesting mentor," Bob said.

"I don't see how we can exclude Flower's population, or that we would even want to," Daniel said. "We just need a rule stating that representatives on the working groups must be humans."

"Can't do it," Aabina said. "The tunnel network treaty prohibits limiting committee participation by species."

"It does? I've never heard of humans sitting on alien committees."

"There are plenty of ways to achieve exclusivity without employing species-based language. For example, it's impossible to serve on a public working group in the Empire of a Hundred Worlds without pledging your loyalty to a queen."

"What's so hard about that?" Daniel asked.

"It's up to the queen whether or not to accept your pledge."

"I'm not comfortable with the idea of limiting our membership to humans-only," Phillip said. "There are a number of alien actors living in our community on Timble. In addition to enriching our acting traditions, they contribute to the Grenouthian pension fund that we all participate in. The bunnies weren't willing to cut separate deals with every individual alien who showed up, so we let them work under our contract. It wouldn't be fair to take away their voices as community members."

"I don't see what you're all so concerned about," Shaina said. "Just maintain the auction results after the empire decision is made and then Flower's influence would be limited to at most one governmental department."

"Clever," Dring said, underlining the last sentence he had recorded.

The door to the corridor slid open and a male Frunge stumbled in, followed by a female with a towering hair-vine construction on an elaborate trellis work. Both of the aliens carried Human Empire swag bags with custom embroidery.

"Is this the Human thing?" the male demanded. "Where's the bar?"

Aabina jumped up from her chair and approached the inebriated observers. "Pizzer, Klzmat," she greeted them.

"How good of you to come. Please take a seat and I'll get you a drink."

Daniel held up a hand to stop the Vergallian as she passed him on her way to the kitchen. "Are they really observers?" he whispered.

"Absolutely. I delivered their bags last night and gave them a personal invitation to this meeting."

"Welcome," the associate ambassador addressed himself to Klzmat, as Pizzer seemed to have fallen asleep in a chair against the wall. "Long night?"

"There was a little bar in our hotel room with miniature bottles," the Frunge woman said, holding her thumb and forefinger apart to illustrate the size. "Pizzer thought that the Human Empire put them there as a challenge so we had to drink them all. Then we went out clubbing."

"I'm glad you're enjoying yourselves. To get you current with what you've missed, we've just defined an auction system to—"

"Isn't that a type of shopping?" Klzmat interrupted, brandishing her swag bag. "Where? I've never been to an auction."

"Shaina?" Daniel nudged his wife.

"Is it your first time on Union Station?" Shaina asked.

"First time anywhere," Klzmat said. "We're newlyweds. I've barely been off my family's farm, except for school."

"Why don't I take our guests to the Shuk and show them around, and you can continue with the boring details of empire," Shaina said, giving Daniel a wink as she rose from her seat. "I'll take those, Aabina," she added, intercepting the Vergallian as Kelly's special assistant emerged from the kitchen with a bottle of wine and two glasses. "We're going to have a little wine-and-cheese tour of the Shuk."

116

"Lovely idea," Aabina said, gladly handing over her burden. She helped Klzmat get Pizzer back on his feet, and then Shaina ushered the two Frunge out of the conference room.

"Those were the observers?" Samuel asked. "I'm not great with alien ages, but she didn't look any older than Flazint."

"You never know who you're going to get with observers," Aabina explained. "It's entirely up to the species that send them, and they all have different selection methodologies. If there's an important event, the local ambassador usually makes the choice, but for something like this, I wouldn't be surprised if the Frunge picked a couple out of a line at the spaceport."

"The birth of the Human Empire isn't an important event?" Bob asked.

"Not to the Frunge, apparently."

"Well, if that's what all of the observers are going to be like, I guess we're lucky they didn't—Hello," Daniel cut himself off as the door slid open and a Verlock slowly shuffled in.

"Don't – mind – me," the bulky alien rumbled at a glacial pace. "A – custom – chair. How – thoughtful." He settled in the seat assigned to the Verlock ambassador at diplomatic meetings, folded his arms on the table, put his head down, and immediately began to snore.

Dring reached across the table and flipped over the fabric swag bag that dangled from the new arrival's wrist. He smoothed out the section Dorothy had embroidered.

"What are you doing, Dring?" Samuel asked.

"Getting his name," the Maker said, transcribing the Verlock characters onto his scroll. "The key to writing good history is to put everything in, including the drunks and tunnel-lagged statisticians."

"How can you tell he's a statistician?"

"That's the symbol embroidered after his name, the Verlock equivalent of a question mark. It's too bad he's sleeping because I'm sure he would have had something interesting to say about your auction proposal."

Ten

Vivian's twin brother Jonah looked up as the host of *Let's Make Friends* came into the improvised dressing room tent that the Grenouthians had set up in the food court of the Empire Convention Center for the on-location shoot.

"You look half-dead, Aisha," he said. "I mean, really tired. Was there a problem with the temporary set?"

"The set was fine, and they're changing it out for your kitchen as we speak," Aisha replied, sinking into a folding chair. "I'm just glad I don't have to do this all week."

"Did something go wrong?"

"It's the children. I never imagined that having an all-human cast could make such a difference. The little girl from a Horten open world said that axes are for sissies, so a little boy from the Drazen open world shoved her. Then she held her breath until she started changing color, and I was afraid she was going to pass out right on stage."

"So what happened next?"

"A boy from a Dollnick open world said something to a girl from a Sharf recycling orbital about sloppy engineering and I thought I was going to have a galactic war on my hands. I had to skip the rest of the introductions and go right to Storytellers."

"Well, that's always popular," Jonah said. "What was your opening?"

"Once upon a time, seven children from sovereign human communities visited Union Station with their parents for a tradeshow," Aisha repeated her starter line. "Then I pointed at the little boy from a Verlock academy world, and it took him thirty seconds to say that he wanted to go home where people are better behaved."

"Tough start."

"Then I pointed at the girl from Timble, a Grenouthian orbital that's dedicated to the entertainment industry, and instead of one sentence, she stood up and delivered the soliloquy from 'My Mother's Pouch.'"

"I've never heard of that one," Jonah admitted.

"It's a classic Grenouthian play about childhood, and the speech goes on for five minutes about how the galaxy looks friendlier from inside a mother's pouch. I wanted to stop her after the first few lines, but the director pinged me from the control booth and insisted that I let her finish. It's the first time he's contacted me during a live performance in years."

"What did the rest of the children think of it?"

"The child from the Frunge open world started snoring and it sounded like somebody was sawing logs. Then nobody else wanted to go after the girl from Timble because she was obviously a child actor. I don't know what I would have done if the assistant director hadn't called a commercial break because the Grenouthian cameramen were all in tears from the soliloquy and couldn't see what they were shooting."

"I hope I have better luck with the guest assistants they pick out for me," Jonah said. "I'm kind of nervous since it's the first time I'll be working with girls who I don't already know from the cooking class I teach for InstaSitter."

"It can't go any worse than my show did," Aisha said. "I was so desperate to just get them talking about something when we came back from commercial that I skipped right to what they wanted to be when they grow up."

"That's always fun."

"Except what they want to be when they grow up are aliens! I started with the little boy whose grandmother is the designated stakeholder for the humans from the Two Mountains consortium world because I overheard him telling her before we started that he wanted to be just like her. Do you know what he said when I asked?"

Jonah shook his head at the rhetorical question.

"He wants to be a Drazen when he grows up. The girl from the Sharf recycling orbital asked him how he could be Drazen without a tentacle or extra thumbs, and before I had time to think, the children were all discussing prosthetics like they were seventy years old rather than seven. Since they knew what they were talking about, and it's better than hitting each other, I let them go on, but the whole rest of the show ended up being a discussion of how humans can be more like aliens. The worst part of it is that the assistant director told me it was my best show of the season."

An excited Grenouthian intern stuck her head in the tent and caught Jonah's attention. "You're on in five," she told him before ducking back out.

"Did they at least know the song?" Jonah asked Aisha as he tied on his apron.

"Everybody in the galaxy knows the song," she said tiredly. "I'm just glad I left Stevie home with Fenna rather than letting her bring him here."

"I'm sure it will be better tomorrow," Jonah said.

"I know it will because I'll be back in the studio with my regular cast," Aisha said. "This was a one-time special for me. I hope it works out better for you because they told me you'll be here all week."

"The Grenouthians cut a deal with the Dollnicks to promote the Empire Convention Center in return for free use of the Galaxy Room for a network awards show. We got a huge banner with the Empire@Empire logo to hang over the set, and they even replaced my regular apron."

The tent flap pushed open, and the intern called, "In three," before disappearing again.

"I better get out there," Jonah said. "I'm sure your show went better than you remember. The Grenouthians run a delay, you know, and they're experts at live editing. I remember the time I forgot that I had a pot of oil heating up on the back burner for donuts and it burst into flames. When I got home and watched the recording Mom made, the editors had spliced in a scene from a previous show where I did one of those product placement ads for nut-crackers. The transition was so seamless that I wouldn't have known what really happened if I hadn't been there."

"Thank you for that, but I think I'd rather forget today altogether," Aisha said. "Good luck."

Jonah exited the tent, and the young intern, who was related in some way to the producer or the director, walked him onto the temporary set and showed him his mark.

"Testing, three point one four one five nine—"

"I got it," Jonah interrupted the voice coming over his implant. "Where's my first guest?"

"Minor change in plan," the assistant director informed him. "You're going to do the intro alone, talk up the product of the day, and then you'll bring on Sephia."

"Who?"

"Girl from Chianga, a Dollnick open world. When the manager of the Empire Convention Center found out that a Human from his homeworld was on the guestlist for today, he insisted that you do the whole show with her."

"Do we know anything about the girl? Has she ever been on camera before?"

"Don't worry. I checked with some Humans in the audience and they all said that she's a looker."

"That's not what I—" Jonah cut himself off as he saw the light on the front immersive camera go live and immediately launched into his intro. "Welcome to *Stone Soup*, coming to you live from the food court of the Empire Convention Center here on Union Station. We'll be here all week with guest assistants from the Human Empire tradeshow. It all kicks off tonight in the Galaxy Room with a keynote address from our ambassador and an auction to determine the future of our sovereign human communities. But first, I'd like to tell you about one of my favorite ingredients from the All Species Cookbook."

The light on the immersive camera winked out, and the space above the counter was suddenly filled with a pre-recorded hologram which Jonah knew was now being broadcast in immersive mode. He waited a moment for the light musical score to fade and then began reading the scripted commentary on his heads-up display in time with the projection.

"Mozzarella is made from buffalo milk in the Campania region of southern Italy on Earth. The cheesemakers start by separating the curd from the whey. Then they cut the curd into smaller pieces and place them in the cooker, which runs at a temperature just below the boiling point of water at sea level. The result is stretchy dough, which can be kneaded into shapes and soaked in saltwater to add flavor and help the curd form a smooth surface."

The music swelled again, and although Jonah couldn't see through the holographic projection to the front, he knew that ordering instructions for the cheese were superimposed over the hologram in the language of whoever was watching via a home immersive system. The last element to appear was the official, "Certified by the All Species Cookbook," logo, which meant the advertiser had paid a licensing fee to EarthCent, as there was no actual certification process.

"And we're back," Jonah said immediately after the light on the front immersive camera popped on. "Now I'd like to introduce today's guest assistant who has traveled all the way here from the Dollnick open world of Chianga. Sephia? Come on out."

A stunning girl in her early twenties wearing an outfit that reminded Jonah more of a swimsuit than kitchen attire climbed up the stairs to the temporary stage and slipped behind the counter. He felt his jaw drop, and for the first time in over a year of hosting the show, found himself at a loss for words.

"Give her the apron," the assistant director prompted over the young man's implant.

"Apron," Jonah repeated out loud, breaking the spell. "Right. Welcome to *Stone Soup*, Sephia. We provide all of our guests with an apron for the show that they can also take home, so let's cover up your—I mean, safety first in the kitchen," he stammered. The apron intended for the guest was folded neatly on the counter, but when he went to hand it to her, she stepped close and then turned her back, obviously intending for him to tie it on.

"Allow me," Jonah said, slipping the top loop over her head, and then reaching around for the dangling strings to tie a light bow behind her back. He felt the blood rushing to his face, and stepping away, he went to his standby line to buy time. "Have you ever watched our show, Sephia?"

The girl turned around, and her shining blue eyes looked to him as large as saucers. "I've never missed an episode," she said in a husky contralto. "You're not going to believe this, but I've had dreams about you."

"Jonah! Jonah!" the assistant director's voice cried in the host's head five seconds later. "Snap out of it. Get started on the recipe."

"Our first recipe today is from Ambassador McAllister's favorite section of the cookbook, and I'll bet you all know what that means," Jonah said in a rush.

"Chocolate," several audience members called out in a variety of languages.

"That's right, and this recipe for chocolate date balls comes from Sue, who lives on a Dollnick ag world, so my guest assistant may already be familiar with it."

"Is choosing this recipe your way of asking me for a date?" she asked, displaying a smile that could have competed with that of a Vergallian princess. "If so, I accept."

"Steady," the assistant director murmured in Jonah's head.

"The great thing about this recipe is that there's no cooking required, though if the dates are dried out, you may want to let them soak a bit in hot water to soften," Jonah said, fighting to control his breathing. "We'll use eight good-sized dates," he continued, pointing at the ingredients already set out on the sideboard, "a cup of old-fashioned oatmeal, a half a cup of All Species Cookbook brand almond butter exported by Drazen Foods, two tablespoons of unsweetened cocoa powder, and for that flavor explosion, a half-cup of dried Sheezle bug flakes."

"You're really going to use Sheezle bug flakes?" Sephia asked in surprise. "We always substitute."

"Just making sure you're paying attention," Jonah said, sounding a lot cockier than he felt. "We're substituting unsweetened coconut flakes, because as I'm sure you know, coconuts have become a popular crop on Dollnick ag worlds."

"Dollnicks like coconut milk," the girl confirmed.

"If you can combine the oatmeal, cocoa powder, and Sheezle-bug-flake substitutes in the mixing bowl, I'm going to throw these dates in the blender with a dash of warm water to puree."

Jonah followed his own instructions, pulsing the blender on and off, then stopping to scrape down the sides with a flexible spatula. Sephia combined the other ingredients he'd named in the bowl and mixed them Dollnick style.

"Can you remind our audience why we mix dry ingredients before putting everything together?" he asked the guest.

"To make sure that the ingredients are evenly dispersed," Sephia replied immediately. "My mother used to say that I was the worst cook on Chianga and nobody would ever want to marry me. Then I started watching *Stone Soup* and making all of the recipes, and now she says any man would be lucky to get me."

"Smart mother," Jonah said under his breath, giving the blender a final pulse. "This is looking a bit thick, so I'm going to add another drop of water and give it one more go. We're shooting for a creamy paste, not date juice, so those of you who accessed the recipes ahead of time on the

Grenouthian network and are following along at home, don't over-blend."

"Is there anything else I can do?" Sephia breathed over the host's shoulder, making him jump.

"Go ahead and add the All Species Cookbook brand almond butter to your bowl, and then hold it out so I can pour in the date puree," Jonah said, removing the blender jar from its base and setting aside the lid. "When you're working with a puree of this consistency, always have a soft spatula ready to help get it out of the jar or you'll lose a quarter of the product." He held the blender jar by its glass handle with one hand, and using the other hand to work the spatula, scraped the date puree out into the bowl held by the girl. "You can see where an extra pair of hands always come in handy in the kitchen."

"That's why Dollnick chefs win all of the big cooking competitions," Sephia said, as proudly as if she was a four-armed alien herself. "They can hold a bowl, add ingredients, and stir them in, all at the same time."

"And Dollnicks are famous across the galaxy for their hospitality industry," Jonah added, figuring it was as good a time as any to segue into the negotiated commercial plug. "If you've never visited an Empire Convention Center, the chain has locations on most of the Stryx stations, serving all species around every clock. Just mention *Stone Soup* and receive a ten percent discount on your first stay at the hotel."

"We've stayed at the Empire every time I've been to Union Station and the whole family loves it," the girl added.

"The last step is to stir the mixture into a dough, so put the mixing bowl on the table and—"

"I can just hold it," Sephia interrupted. "I trust you not to get it all over me."

"Uh, all right," Jonah said. He could feel his face redden again and hoped that the Grenouthians were running a color compensation filter. "If we were making enough for a banquet I'd use an industrial mixer, but for a small quantity like this, you can't beat a wooden spoon. Unless of course, you're Frunge, in which case a nonstick metal mixing spoon would work just as well."

"Do Frunge eat oatmeal?"

"It depends on how traditional they are. I see we're about to break for a commercial, so everybody following along at home, just keep mixing your dough, and we'll be back in ninety-four seconds."

"Perfect," the assistant director declared, hopping onto the stage immediately after the status light on the front immersive camera winked out. "Brilliant work, young lady. The cameras love you." He slapped a furry palm on Jonah's forehead and added, "No fever. You might want to have your circulatory system checked out after the show. Your capillaries keep opening wide and changing your skin color."

"So this isn't your first time on Union Station?" Jonah asked his guest, keeping up a steady stirring motion as the bunny headed back to his usual position.

"I come with my father to every tradeshow," Sephia said. "He's on the ad hoc Human Empire committee, but his real job is being the mayor of Floaters and managing outside sales. I race them."

"Floaters?"

"Yes. I turned sixteen the year the racing circuit started—that's the minimum age for competition drivers—and I've been in the top ten every season for all seven years of its existence. I also do the test driving for our factory's new models."

"So you're twenty-three?" Jonah asked.

"You say that like I'm ready for retirement. How old are you?"

"Nineteen, but I'll be twenty next month."

"If you prorate our ages for life expectancy, we're perfect for each other," Sephia said happily.

"Five. Four. Three. Two. One," the assistant director concluded his countdown, and the status light on the front immersive camera went hot. "That means you start talking, Jonah," he prompted via the young man's implant.

"Welcome back to *Stone Soup*, coming to you live from the food court of the Empire Convention Center on Union Station," the host managed to say. "Our dough is just about mixed, so why don't you put the bowl down on the counter here and we can hand-roll some balls."

"It's not sticky at all," Sephia said a minute later, rolling a dollop of dough between her palms. "Do they have to cool in the fridge?"

"Only if you aren't going to serve them immediately," Jonah told her. "They're ready to eat now."

The girl took a small nibble from the ball she had rolled, said, "Yummy," and then extended her arm to the host, holding the ball up in front of his mouth. "You try."

Jonah felt his ears burning as he tried to take a sample from the date ball without nuzzling her fingers. Years of working in employee training and management at InstaSitter should have made him immune to flirting, but Sephia had blown through his defenses like they were tissue paper. The rest of the show went by in a blur, and he hardly knew what he was doing or saying. When Jonah got to the final commercial break, the assistant director hopped back on stage and went right to the girl.

"Listen," the Grenouthian said to her. "Are you here for the whole week?"

"Yes," Sephia said. "I'm flying our demonstration floater around the Galaxy Room when it's our turn for the space, and I'll be in the race there on the last day."

"How about coming back on the show? I can give you the standard five-day guest contract and you won't be disappointed by the compensation."

"Oh, I'd love that. Is it okay with you, Jonah?" she asked, putting her hand on his forearm and fixing him with those bright blue eyes.

"Yes," he croaked.

"Great," the assistant director said. "Don't forget to mention the room discount again in your final plug, Jonah, and the producer wants you to stop in at the all-species doctor on the travel concourse for a quick checkup. You aren't yourself today, but Sephia made the whole thing work. Great chemistry you two."

Jonah got through the closing on autopilot, then reflexively folded up his apron and put it on the counter for the intern to collect for the laundry.

"So?" Sephia asked. "Do you have supper plans?"

"I usually eat with my parents," he said, and then realized how young that made him sound. "My twin sister is away, though, and my parents are pretty busy because of the whole Human Empire thing, so if you wanted—"

"Why do you think I was asking?" She put her own apron on the counter and took possession of his arm. "I can't eat in a restaurant dressed like this, so let's go up to my room and I'll get changed."

Eleven

"...and so it was determined that an auction would offer the best mechanism for discovering the true interests of the sovereign human communities," Kelly said, her amplified voice easily reaching the crowd of sales reps and buyers from the Conference of Sovereign Human Communities who were packed into the Galaxy Room for the keynote speech. "The procedures outlined by the ad hoc committee to staff departmental working groups by auctioning seats will enable us to reach a decision on the Human Empire issue by the conclusion of the tradeshow and to move forward with the Thousand Cycle option if that's approved. So without further ado, get ready to put your money where your mouth is, and I'll turn the lectern over to your auctioneer for this evening, Shaina Cohan."

Daniel's wife surprised the ambassador with a high-five as they passed each other on the stage. Kelly returned to the folding chair where she'd left her purse in the reserved section of the onstage seating set aside for the alien ambassadors and observers.

"We ended up with nine governmental departments for which I'll be auctioning seats," Shaina announced. "The rules are simple, with the high bidder for each department becoming the working group's chairperson, the second-highest bidder given the right of rejection to a seat at their last bid, followed by anybody else who's interested. If need be, we'll go to the third-highest bid, et cetera. Each community is limited to one working group seat, so choose the department that's most important to you. Any questions?"

"You expect us to bid to sit on committees?" a man with prosthetic second thumbs called out, drawing laughter from all over the amphitheater.

"If you don't, we'll have to come up with a different methodology for selecting representatives, which will undoubtedly be more expensive and time-consuming," Shaina warned them. "If the working groups vote against establishing the Human Empire, their work will be done, but if you think the aliens look down on you now, wait until you've rejected the opportunity to stand on your own feet."

There was a groan from the audience, and a different man called out in a reluctant voice, "How will the voting work?"

"Given nine governmental department working groups and five seats on each committee, the odd numbers preclude a tie. Those of you representing large populations will be allowed a proportionate amount of debate time on your working group which can be ceded back to the chair if you have nothing to say. We've tentatively scheduled the meetings for each evening after the tradeshow closes, and the EarthCent embassy will pay for your meals if you choose to meet in a restaurant."

There was a murmur of interest at this last statement as everybody began calculating how high of a bid a week of free dinners would justify. Shaina also heard somebody loudly pointing out that they were already on an expense account so it wasn't fair.

"And if we agree to go ahead with this Thousand Cycle plan, how long will the working group members be stuck in their seats?" a woman in the front row asked.

"We'll be leaving that decision to the collective wisdom of the new seat holders," Shaina said.

"How about proxies?" a man from a Frunge open world with a symbolic sprig of herbs on his lapel inquired. "Our factory manager isn't arriving until tomorrow. If I bid on a seat, can I pass it on to her?"

"The seat belongs to your sovereign community. As far as we're concerned you can change the individual attending the meeting every time the working group meets. And I want to remind you that with a total of just forty-five seats to divide amongst every community represented here, most of you will be watching from the sidelines," Shaina said. "But don't confuse not participating with a vote for the status quo. The ad hoc committee has bound itself to the collective decision of the working groups, so majority rules."

"And what happens to the money we bid?" a woman sitting higher up on the amphitheater seating called out.

"All of the creds raised tonight will go into the scholarship fund for children from sovereign human communities attending boarding school on Flower. Are there any further questions before we begin?"

"I'm glad you could make it," Kelly whispered to Bork, while Shaina took a question about how the bidding process would work from somebody who had never attended an auction.

"None of us knew you were going to invent a new form of election," the Drazen ambassador replied in his normal tone of voice. "If you had told us ahead of time, we might have sent serious observers."

133

"Don't worry about noise," Ambassador Crute added from behind Kelly. "An old friend of mine manages the convention center, and I had him activate a one-way audio suppression field for our section of the stage. We can talk without causing a disruption."

"—and we've hired InstaSitters to assist with bid spotting," Shaina concluded. "No other questions? Good. The first department we're auctioning off is trade. Let's start the bidding at one thousand, just to get warmed up. One thousand creds, give me one, one for fun, give me one. Come on people, the eyes of the galaxy are upon you. One thousand creds to chair the Department of Trade working group for the Human Empire."

Kelly felt a tap on her shoulder, and twisting around, she saw the Horten ambassador leaning in her direction.

"Can I bid?" Ortha asked.

"I don't think so, no," the EarthCent ambassador replied. "It's for sovereign human community representatives only."

"One, one, one," Shaina tried again. "I'd like to say if I don't get a thousand I'll just keep the seat for myself, but it doesn't work that way. How about it, Larry?" she asked, calling out the head of the Independent Traders Guild council by name. "Do you want to see somebody else win the chairpersonship?"

"I'm already on the ad hoc committee," he replied from the fourth row of the stadium seating.

"Nothing in the rules prevents you from sitting on both. We just can't seat a Traders Guild rep on two working groups."

"I don't have a budget," he countered. "Could you start at a hundred?"

"A hundred creds?" Shaina cast a pained look in her husband's direction, but Daniel just shrugged, so the auctioneer said, "Very well. I have one hundred creds," and pointed at Larry without waiting for him to raise his hand. "I have a hundred, give me two. Two hundred creds to make history. Give me two or I'll be blue. Two. Two. Two. Come on, think of the poor children in need of a scholarship. One-fifty. One Five-Oh. I've sold shoes at charity auctions for more than one-fifty. One twenty-five? One twenty-five? Listen, people. If we don't get another bid, it will screw up the whole system because there won't be a runner up."

"You should have started lower," somebody called out.

"Lower than a hundred? You'll save more than that on meals if you stretch the meetings out for the whole week. Oops, did I just say that out loud? One-ten. Come on, somebody bid one-ten and I'll add the ten myself."

"One-ten," a woman way up in the seating offered.

"I have one-ten. Let's go, Larry. Give me twenty. It's just money. Twenty. Twenty. Don't get funny. One twenty?"

"Will you reimburse me for the twenty?" he asked.

"I should have known better than to start with the Department of Trade," Shaina said in frustration. "You all know how to haggle. Very well. One twenty going once? One twenty going twice? The chairmanship for the Department of Trade working group is sold to Larry, representing the Independent Traders Guild."

There was a round of applause in the packed amphitheater, with the most enthusiastic clapping coming from the small section of ambassadors and observers seated on stage, though nobody outside the audio suppression field could hear it.

"Fascinating," the Frunge ambassador said to Kelly. "It appears that the members of your sovereign communities are in no hurry to grasp power."

"Daniel warned me it could go this way, Czeros," she replied. "The CoSHC membership has always been focused on business. Most of them live on worlds where government means collecting fees for utilities and services and that's the end of it."

"Dring is in seventh heaven," the Drazen ambassador commented, and gestured to where the Maker stood at a small folding table that Aabina had procured to give the reptilian shape-shifter a place to smooth out his scroll and write. "I'll have to ask him later if he's ever heard of somebody holding an auction for a government before."

"I'm just hoping it doesn't turn into a failed auction," Kelly said. "We should have arranged for shills to run up the bidding."

"Either shills or reserve bids," the Grenouthian ambassador said agreeably. "Assuming your offer to buy meals includes drinks, some of the lucky winners are going to come out ahead on the deal."

"Libby," Kelly subvoced. "Could you ping Shaina and tell her that drinks are included in the embassy's offer?"

Shaina made the announcement and the bids immediately jumped, turning Larry's seat as chairman into the bargain of the night. Then there was a commotion behind the ambassador, and Kelly turned to see a pair of alien observers arguing over a plastic bottle of Union Station Springs water, one of the gifts Aabina and Samuel had placed in all of the swag bags.

Ambassador Ortha, his skin blazing an angry red, got between the Horten and the Sharf before the observers could come to blows. "What's this all about?" he demanded.

"I set my water on the floor to check if there were any salty snacks left in my bag and Mr. Rainbow grabbed it," the Sharf hissed angrily.

If anybody outside of the seating section had noticed the disturbance, they were doing a good job ignoring it, and Shaina started the bidding for chairpersonship of the Department of Agriculture working group at five hundred creds.

"Look," the Horten said, getting down on his hands and knees and pointing at a rapidly fading circle of condensation on the deck. "He set the bottle down inside the boundary made by the legs of my chair. That's the same as giving it to me."

"Odds or evens," the Sharf observer issued the universal challenge.

"Evens," the Horten grunted and made a fist.

The Sharf did the same, and they each counted to three while pumping their forearms up and down. On the third move, both of them stuck out a number of fingers.

"Odds," the Sharf crowed triumphantly, snatching back the water bottle.

"Replay," the Horten protested to Ortha. "He stuck out an extra finger after he saw my count."

"Here," a Vergallian female seated in the third row said, offering the Union Station Springs bottle from her swag bag. "I don't drink out of plastic."

"Six-thirty-five, keep it alive, six-thirty-five," Shaina chanted from the lectern. "Six hundred and thirty-five creds to chair the working group for the Human Empire's Department of Agriculture. Loosen those purse strings—

the observers are laughing at us," she added, pointing in the direction of the reserved seating section.

"Enough of that," Crute admonished the pair of Dollnick observers. They had started an eight-handed game of cat's cradle and gotten themselves so tangled up in the string that the other observers were dissolving in laughter. "If you aren't interested in watching history unfold, you're excused."

"The tradeshow better be more fun than this or I want my money back," the Drazen observer said, and then he pointed at his ear and his tentacle went up. "Showtime," he told his female companion. "The Humans set up an open bar in the lobby for after the keynote and I tipped a bellboy to ping me when they started serving."

Folding chairs scraped back as the observers all made a beeline for the nearest exit tunnel that went under the stadium seating. The two Dollnick observers still had half of their arms connected by a tangle of string, but it didn't stop them from leaving together.

"What are we going to do if the whole Galaxy Room empties out to follow them?" Kelly asked in dismay.

"Don't worry, we were prepared for this," Crute said. "As soon as your auctioneer noticed the ruckus our observers were making, my friend in facilities began projecting a holographic loop overlay showing our seating section during your keynote address. Nobody saw the observers leave, and now we can get up and move around without creating a disturbance."

"Doesn't that mean my chair is suddenly empty? What will Shaina think?"

"Oops," the Dollnick ambassador said. "Maybe the station librarian could help you out."

"Libby?" Kelly subvoced. "We're having a bit of a holographic emergency. Is there any chance you could paste me in so my seat doesn't look empty?"

"Done," the Stryx replied. "I'm sorry your auction got off to a rough start."

"I don't understand it myself. I thought the representatives from the sovereign human communities would jump at the chance to steer their own future."

"I'm going to assume the weak bidding on those last two seats for the agricultural working group was due to crop failure," the auctioneer said, glowering at her audience. "The next chairpersonship up for bid is for the Department of Manufacturing. Where's Bob from Floaters?"

"Here," the mayor who sat on the ad hoc committee replied reluctantly, raising his hand.

"I want to start the bidding at a thousand, Bob. You'll give me a thousand, won't you?"

"All of the money goes to the scholarship fund?"

"That's right, and I'm not charging an auctioneer's premium," Shaina said. "A thousand?"

"A thousand," the mayor of Floaters agreed.

"I know nobody is going to give me two thousand, but I have to ask. Two, two, two, tell me your answer true. Two? All right, I won't waste my time. One thousand going once. One thousand going twice. The chairpersonship of the manufacturing working group is sold to Bob from Chianga for one thousand creds."

As Shaina started over at a lower bid to sell the remaining seats on the working group, Kelly asked Bork, "What's the story with your observers? I thought they would be professionals, but they behave more like they're on vacation."

"The Drazen couple is on their honeymoon," Bork told her. "I should have picked the observers myself, but I followed the standard procedure and let it go to our home office, where they decided to hold a gourd-off."

"A what?"

"You know, where you sell a mountain of gourds for ten times what they're worth, but a few of them have prizes inside? It's how the home office raises money for team-building nights out."

"It seems a bit insulting, Bork. Does everybody think that humans deciding whether or not to establish an empire is a joke?"

"According to the odds, it is," the Thark ambassador said from his seat behind Bork. "None of the species sent serious diplomats as observers because they don't believe Humans are stupid enough to reject this chance. It's an incredible opportunity for your entire species. Once you get the empire set up, you can bring Earth onboard, and you'll finally be off probation."

"I don't think we're looking that far ahead," Kelly admitted. "But why would anybody buy a raffle ticket, I mean, a gourd, for a chance to attend a political event for another species?"

"Luxury hotel accommodations, open bars, a tradeshow with free samples," Bork enumerated. "They're all getting first-class treatment, and opportunities like this don't come up that often. If the observers are ambitious, they can go on the local talk-show circuit when they get home."

"Now that you mention it, why haven't I ever heard of humans being invited to observe a major event for another species?" the EarthCent ambassador asked.

"I doubt there's been a local observers-required event since you became an ambassador." Bork looked back towards the lectern where Shaina was calling out a sequence of rising numbers and pointing to where InstaSitters standing in the aisles were spotting the bidders. "I wonder which working group she's auctioning off now?"

"Entertainment," the Grenouthian ambassador answered him. "It appears that members of the nascent Human Empire have their priorities straight after all."

"Four, four, four. Gimme more," Shaina chanted. "Four thousand to chair the working group for entertainment. Thirty-five hundred is the bid, let's have—Four," she cried, seeing an excited Dollnick InstaSitter pointing at somebody with all four arms.

"But their votes are all worth the same in the end," Kelly protested. "If somebody wants to influence our future, a hundred-cred seat on the working group for trade carries the same weight in the voting as a four-thousand cred chair for the entertainment working group."

"That's an excellent observation," the Thark ambassador praised her. "My work teaching you about investments must be paying off because you've identified an inefficiency in your working group market."

"You're looking for investments?" the Grenouthian inquired. He showed remarkable agility for his bulk, slipping in between the Drazen and the Thark. "Why didn't you come to me? Investing is my middle name."

"Do Grenouthians even have names?" Kelly asked.

"It's just a saying. I know how your money must be piling up because my single point in the *Stone Soup* production is creating a river of cash. You have ten times that from the show, not to mention the cookbook royalties and all of the branding and certification money."

"I'm a little embarrassed about the whole certification thing," the EarthCent ambassador admitted. "I do try to sample the food products we certify, but they're piling up in the embassy kitchenette."

"If we all put our heads together, I'm sure we can find a worthy investing opportunity for your cash," the Grenouthian ambassador said, waggling his ears at the other ambassadors.

"You mean, a worthy investment opportunity for EarthCent's cash."

"Yes, of course. I know you to be far too intelligent of a sentient to get caught up in market fashions, so I assume you're looking for a long-term investment that will grow your capital while providing flexibility if you should need funds for important, er, Human stuff."

"You've read my mind exactly," Kelly enthused. "I don't understand why it should be so hard. Just a second," she said and fished her diary and the pencil out of her purse. "All right, go ahead."

"You're already working with the Dollnicks?" the Grenouthian ambassador demanded when he saw the cover of Kelly's paperback.

"No, it's just a notebook."

"May I?"

Kelly reluctantly handed over the paperback and the pencil, while in the background, Shaina sold the last seat for the entertainment working group and began the auction for the Department of Health.

"I've definitely seen this picture before," the Grenouthian ambassador mused, staring at the bare-chested Dollnick on the cover. "Could this be from a prospectus for a terraforming project, Crute?"

"I believe it's from a popular romance series, the Trillionaire Prince, or something of the sort," the Dollnick ambassador replied. "My secretary reads them."

"The cover is just to hold the pages together," Kelly protested. "Really. It doesn't mean anything."

"All right," the Grenouthian ambassador said, flipping to a blank page. He rested the spine of the paperback on the much-shorter Thark ambassador's shoulder and drew a five-pointed star with quick strokes. Then he labeled each point in fine alien printing.

"Nice hand," Bork commented.

"I won a penmanship award in school," the bunny replied, and then showed the page to Kelly without returning the book. "My clan follows a system known as Five Star Investing. In each—"

"There's only one star," Crute interrupted. "You should call it Five-Pointed-Star Investing."

"Semantics. Each point of the star carries equal weight in our decision-making process, and we don't invest in a new idea unless the total reaches a minimum of eighty points. For example, if each element of a new proposition scores fifteen out of twenty, which I believe is a solid passing grade by Human standards, the total is only seventy-five, and we keep our gold in our pouches."

The Verlock ambassador, who had been slow to his feet, now crowded in behind Kelly to look at the notebook. "But your system does not guaranty success," he observed. "If four elements of the business plan are scored at twenty, the fifth could be scored at zero, and your money would be lost."

"I'm sorry," Kelly apologized. "I can't read that script. What is it?"

"I thought it was Humanese," the Grenouthian ambassador said, clearly taken aback. "Srythlan?"

"It's Alt," the Verlock ambassador told him. "I picked it up myself because I was taken by the clean lines and compact expression. It's easy to confuse Humans with Alts if you don't pay close attention to the head size."

"So what does it say?" Kelly asked again.

"Let me see that," Bork said, claiming the paperback and the pencil from his colleague. "The point at the top is safety," he translated, printing the English word in the block letters of a draftsman, "moving clockwise we have required capital, return on investment, market dominance, and personnel."

"So you're talking about starting a business," Kelly surmised.

"Or participating in an existing business," the Grenouthian ambassador said. "I thought you were interested in investing."

"I am. I just hoped it would be more like opening a bank account."

"Investing in the right immersive production is better than money in a bank."

"You haven't refuted my point," Srythlan said. "What if a production scores twenty on four elements and zero for the last?"

"That's impossible," the Grenouthian retorted. "Try assigning points at random and see what happens."

"If safety is assigned zero points, meaning a one hundred percent chance you'll lose your capital—oh, I see."

"What do you see?" Kelly asked the Verlock ambassador.

"The elements balance each other. For safety to be zero in the eighty point scenario, required capital would score twenty, meaning there would be no money at risk."

"Exactly," the Grenouthian ambassador said. "Right now, *Stone Soup* is so popular that the network is looking under every rock for a spin-off, if you'll excuse the pun. Now, let's say we take it up a notch by creating a cooking show with chefs competing to make recipes from the All Species Cookbook ingredients."

"*Cookbook Wars*," Czeros suggested.

"Perfect," the Grenouthian said, recapturing Kelly's notebook from Bork. "I'm not going to claim it's a sure thing without testing the concept on focus groups, but I'd estimate eighteen points for safety. Srythlan?"

"Eighteen points sounds reasonable."

"For capital required, everything is already in place with our network except a dedicated set, so we'll call it nineteen points. Return on investment, well you've seen the results from *Stone Soup*, so that's a big two-oh. As for market dominance, is anybody aware of a current cross-culture cooking wars show?"

"There's something from off the tunnel network that's kind of interesting," the Fillinduck ambassador spoke up. "I've only seen smuggled copies, but it's from Floppsie space, and they use cooking tournaments to settle inter-species border disputes, so it's basically a substitute for war."

"Ouch," the Grenouthian ambassador said. "So if we make a big splash, all of a sudden we'll be up against tough competition from pirated content."

"Why would it matter?" Kelly asked. "It seems pretty unlikely that species from a section of the galaxy that doesn't even have relations with the tunnel network would share our food base."

"Nobody actually eats the stuff on competition cooking shows. It's all about the visuals, and they'll have interesting ingredients we've never seen before. Even though we could slot the new show in immediately following *Stone Soup*, I'm only going to score market dominance at ten, which leaves us with personnel."

"Celebrity Dollnick chefs are well paid," Crute pointed out.

"I suppose there's that. You see," the Grenouthian ambassador continued, addressing himself to Kelly, "we could use no-name chefs, but that would decrease our safety margin. So even though we'll have no trouble at all finding personnel, I'm going to score it at fifteen. Who's been keeping track?"

"Eighty-two," the Thark ambassador announced a split second before Srythlan.

"So it's a go," the bunny said, returning Kelly's notebook. "Tell me how much you want to invest and I'll take care of the details."

"Can I think about it?" she asked.

"Take as long as you want, but unlike a seat on the Human Empire's working group for health, a hot property like this won't be available forever."

Twelve

"The cooler will automatically ping us if the sandwiches start running out, but you'll have to judge the cookie demand for yourself," the Gem caterer told the EarthCent ambassador's son. She extended a tab. "Please swipe your acknowledgment."

"I can tell you based on the last two days that I'll be out of cookies by mid-afternoon," Samuel said after complying with the request. "This whole business with the Human Empire has really raised the profile of the tradeshow with all of the species."

"Then I'll send somebody by right after lunch to top you up."

"Didn't I deliver a gross of cubed mangos with raspberry sauce to you at the lounge for the observers last night?" the second Gem said to Samuel. "How can you be working for both the Humans and the Vergallians?"

"I have a full-time job at the Vergallian embassy, but we're mainly shutdown for Jubilee, so I'm on loan to EarthCent when I'm not working at this booth," Samuel explained.

"Ping us if you think of anything else," the first clone said. "We have lots of deliveries to make."

"I hope that doesn't mean everybody else is giving away free food. I count on the cookies and sandwiches to keep people here long enough for me to swipe their badges and make my pitch."

"Queens must be a hard sell to free peoples, though I hear the Alts are pretty happy with their results," the clone observed. "And don't worry about losing foot traffic. Everybody else on my list is just getting a few of this or that so it must be for their own lunch. You're lucky all the sales reps don't come here and eat your food."

"Good point," Samuel acknowledged. He double-checked that there were enough bottled drinks to last for a while in the ice tub and rearranged the glossy brochures for newly opened Vergallian worlds. "At least I have something concrete to promote this year," he muttered to himself.

"May I?" asked a woman in her mid-thirties, pointing at the tray of cookies that was still covered with cling film.

"Be my guest. And drop a card in the fishbowl to win a free trip to Aarden."

"And to end up on the Vergallian embassy's marketing list, no doubt," the woman said, but she dropped a plastic chit in the fishbowl. "Isn't Aarden a Fleet world? Your name tag indicates that you're representing the Empire of a Hundred Worlds."

"Relations have improved and Fleet agreed to co-promote," Samuel said. "I've never been to Aarden myself, but I understand they host one of the largest sovereign human communities. Now that the Empire of a Hundred Worlds is experimenting with the open world concept, we'll look to them as our model."

"Interesting. I'm here representing the Timble Documentary Performers Union—we have a booth where you can sign up for a vacation that includes work as an extra." There was a loud chime. "That's the opening bell so I better

148

get back," she said, and left without ever having told Samuel her name.

"Just like a Grenouthian," the EarthCent ambassador's son muttered to himself.

The first wave of tradeshow visitors surged down the aisle, shoveling freebies into their swag bags. Most of them glanced at the 'Vergallian Open Worlds' sign draped across the front of the booth and hurried past, but a serious-looking couple in their early twenties turned in.

"Help yourselves to a cookie," Samuel said. "We have Union Station Springs water on ice as well."

"Not - here - for - the - freebies," the woman replied slowly. "Seeking - new - open - world."

"The two of you grew up in a Verlock academy community?" Samuel guessed from the stocky woman's speech pattern.

"Academy - head - says - we're - ready - to - graduate," she confirmed.

"Looks - interesting," the man said, flipping through the Atien brochure. "Are - there - volcanoes?"

"I didn't see any in the brochure, but they wouldn't be considered an attraction for most people," Samuel said. "Vergallian worlds are tech-ban, you know, and volcanic activity tends to have a negative impact on agriculture."

"Thanks - anyway," the man said, and the couple shuffled off towards the next booth.

A pair of Sharf observers brandishing custom embroidered swag bags were the next visitors to the Vergallian embassy's booth.

"I'm not taking a metal splinter out of your thumb again," Samuel immediately said to the female. "You can go to the clinic."

149

"Why are you working here?" the male Sharf asked. "Did the Human Empire fire you?"

"I hope it wasn't because of my complaint," the female added.

"You complained about me?" Samuel asked in disbelief.

"If I'd known you were going to be so clumsy with the tweezers, I would have dug the splinter out myself."

"Nice looking world," the male said, flipping through the Atien brochure. "How many of us are you trying to recruit?"

"We're advertising for Human communities that want to establish—" Samuel began.

"You're discriminating against Sharf?" the observer interrupted, raising his voice and drawing looks from passersby.

"Since when do Sharf move to open worlds to work in agriculture? We're recruiting Humans because they don't have an inventory of livable worlds of their own to colonize."

While the male argued with Samuel, the female Sharf pulled the rest of the cling film off the cookie tray and used it to wrap a stack of a dozen chocolate chip cookies, which she deposited in her bespoke swag bag. "Stop teasing him, Hvadi," she said. "It's clear that the short-necked species don't have a sense of humor."

"Thanks for stopping in," Samuel called after their bony backs as they walked away. The rest of the morning went much the same, but he did harvest a good crop of business cards during the lunch hour when people crowded the booth for free sandwiches. Just as the traffic was slowing down again, a modestly dressed woman of indeterminate age approached.

"Excuse me," she said, looking Samuel up and down. "It appears to me that you're as human as I am."

"I'm employed by the Vergallian embassy. How may I help you?"

"My name is Lisbeth Townes and I'm here representing my community. We live in the Old Way, and it's becoming harder and harder to protect our youth from invasive technology on Earth. An itinerant blacksmith we sometimes employ reported that Vergallian tech-ban worlds are opening themselves to immigration."

"Yes, but how did you get here if you don't use technology?"

"We aren't Luddites, young man," she said, sweeping her white linen shawl back over her shoulder. "Followers of the Old Way farm without modern machinery and live without connection to the power grid. Manual labor for healthy lives is our motto."

"We have brochures from three worlds that would certainly meet your criteria, ma'am." Samuel picked up one of each and handed them over. "You should know that the Vergallian tech-ban isn't absolute, and human mercenaries taking work on those worlds are allowed to bring along teacher bots."

"We teach the old-fashioned way, in classrooms," Lisbeth said dismissively as she leafed through the brochures. "Very pretty. Would we have to swear fealty to the queen?"

"Not under the open world arrangement. Can I scan your badge?" he asked, pointing at her tradeshow pass.

"For my contact information? I don't imagine the Vergallians would know what to do with an Earth mailing address. We only get the post once a week as is."

"We have an, er, relationship with Astria's Academy of Dance, which has hundreds of locations on Earth," Samuel said, omitting the fact that the chain was a well-known front for Vergallian Intelligence. "I'm sure they'll be happy to act as middlemen for any correspondence. Could I ask if there are other communities like yours on Earth?"

"People who follow the Old Way? We have dozens of affiliates, and I'll be reporting at our annual convention after I return. If the Vergallians don't discriminate against religious people, there are hundreds more well-established communities that take a similar approach to life and farming, though their reasons are somewhat more spiritual than our own. I know that when somebody in my community needs a barn built, we always bring in an Amish framing crew."

After Lisbeth moved on, Samuel took the time to transcribe the highlights of their conversation on his tab and mark it for the highest priority follow-up. Then he took advantage of a lull to wolf down a few random sandwich halves left over from the lunch rush.

"Caught you red-handed," Aabina said as she entered the booth. "I knew there had to be a reason you were willing to do this job, other than loyalty to my mother."

Samuel swallowed the last bite of sandwich, and then asked, "Who's babysitting the observers?"

"Exactly," Aabina said with a mischievous grin.

"I don't understand."

"It was Shaina's idea. She suggested routing the observer requests for assistance through the station librarian, and if they're just asking for somebody to help carry packages or teach them how to use chopsticks, the call is reassigned to InstaSitter. I haven't gotten a ping in over three hours."

"That's great. It frees you up to help keep the working groups on track."

"They don't need any help. The only reason they're delaying a final vote is to take advantage of the meals and drinks our embassy is buying for their meetings." She pointed at one of the brochures. "Did you know that Atien is my homeworld?"

"Of course. Are you excited that your mom is going to open it up to alien immigration?"

"Somebody had to take the lead, but the funny thing is that as soon as my aunt made the announcement, two more worlds from the Imperial faction jumped on the ferry. Now that they've promised not to undermine humanity, the Empire of a Hundred Worlds is going to try to make a profit off Humans."

"I thought they'd be too busy making a profit off the Alts."

"The way my mother structured those agreements, the princesses who run things for the Alts all have a fiduciary duty to their contract subjects. It's good training for a queen-in-waiting, and there are some opportunities for profit-sharing, but I'll bet most of the princesses who take the job could earn more as fashion models. Of course, then they'd have to deal with the whole dieting thing."

"Can I get a bottle of Union Station Springs water, or are you too busy flirting with the princess?" a voice interrupted.

"Vivian!" Samuel hastened to dig a cold bottle out of the ice bath and passed it to his fiancée, who took it with her prosthetic tentacle. "When did you get back? Why are you all geared up for the tradeshow?"

"I got back twenty minutes ago, and I'm in disguise because I'm working," the girl replied, stifling a yawn.

"I've been assigned to check out the new line of floaters being produced by the factory on Chianga. It's just a busy-work assignment—I could get all the information by asking a sales rep. There's a demonstration in the Galaxy Room starting in five minutes."

"Shouldn't you go home and get some rest?"

"I went into stasis for the trip back to avoid Zero-G sickness and I'm still waking up," Vivian explained. "What are you doing here, Aabina?"

"The ambassador sent me to give Samuel a break since he's been doing so much for us lately. Why don't the two of you go check out the demonstration together? I'll cover the booth."

Samuel didn't need a second invitation and happily escorted Vivian out of the Nebulae room. "How was your trip?" he asked.

"If I never see another immersive starring Jeelop Huir it will be too soon. He's over four hundred years old and the Hortens keep casting him as a romantic lead."

"There's no law saying that middle-aged aliens can't have a love life."

"But he was playing across from a Horten actress who must have been Marilla's age," Vivian said. "It's creepy."

"Did you sit through the whole thing?"

"I had to, it was part of the assignment." She glanced around and lowered her voice. "The truth is, the Hortens have a pretty competitive lineup for the new season. I'm afraid we're going to lose ratings."

"You mean the Drazens are going to lose ratings."

"Who else would I be talking about?"

Samuel almost launched into a lecture about over-identifying with alien employers before recalling that she could level the same charges in his direction. Instead, he said, "I got a message from Jorb reminding me that I promised to give him a month's notice so he could come to our wedding and bring Rinka. How about picking a date?"

Vivian's prosthetic tentacle started twitching, and she had to reach up and grab it with her left hand to regain control. "I've been meaning to talk to you about that," she mumbled. "We may have to delay a little longer than I thought."

"What are you talking about?"

"If we wait until I have three years in at Drazen Intelligence, they'll foot the bill for everything."

"What bill?"

"For the wedding. You didn't think I was going to let an Elvis impersonator marry us, did you?"

"It was good enough for my parents. You're not planning on doing something like Dorothy's wedding, are you? Jeeves still complains about the cost, and that's after he got a commercial out of it. Besides, your mother already said she wants to pay, and she's one of the richest humans on the tunnel network."

"She didn't get rich turning down perks," Vivian said stubbornly.

The EarthCent ambassador's son came to an abrupt halt just outside the Galaxy Room and grabbed his fiancée's hand to stop her from entering. "What's this really about? I don't believe you."

"You don't? I was at the top of my training class in dissimulation at Drazen Intelligence. What part didn't you believe?"

"You admit you're lying to me?"

"I'm supposed to practice whenever I get the chance. It's part of being a spy."

"Put all of that aside for a minute and tell me what's really going on."

Vivian sighed and straightened the prosthetic extra thumb that had shifted when Samuel grabbed her. "We have to wait because of my job, but it's not the money. Okay?"

"Just tell me already."

"Drazen Intelligence has a minimum marriage age for agents. I guess it came about because they hire young females for undercover work, and then they get complaints from parents about girls falling in love with their handlers."

"How long are you talking?"

"They prorated my age for our life expectancy, so it's only another year and eight months."

"I'm really not okay with your agreeing to this," Samuel told her. "I've been ready to get married since the day I proposed. If Drazen Intelligence has a rule against it, quit and come to work for us."

"I'll never work for the Vergallians," Vivian said fiercely.

"I meant EarthCent Intelligence."

"Everybody will treat me weird because my father runs it."

"Hey, Viv," Jonah said, falling in beside the couple and giving his twin's prosthetic tentacle a playful tug. "Did you come to see Sephia's demonstration?"

"Who?" Vivian asked. She did a quick dance move to put her brother between herself and Samuel, effectively postponing the argument about her job interfering with wedding plans.

"My girlfriend," Jonah said. "You didn't watch *Stone Soup* while you were away?"

"I was too busy watching Horten sneak previews. Do you mean one of the InstaSitter assistants you have on the show as guests finally got her hooks in you?"

"Sephia is from Chianga, the Dollnick open world where they manufacture floaters, and she's been my guest assistant for three days already. Her father is the mayor and she's here doing all of the demonstration driving. Let's get in there before it starts."

As soon as they entered, a young woman wearing a racing uniform in factory colors approached and grabbed Jonah's arm. "Come on," she said. "You're riding with me."

"Sephia?" Vivian guessed.

"Who's the Drazen?" Sephia asked Jonah.

"My twin sister, she's in disguise."

"As long as it's not catching," Sephia said and offered Vivian a handshake. "Jojo didn't mention the costume fetish."

"Jojo?" Vivian asked in dismay. "You've known each other three days and you're already using pet names?"

"Pleased to meet you," Samuel said, grabbing Sephia's proffered hand. "I'm her fiancé."

"Do the two of you want to come with?" Sephia asked, apparently unbothered by Vivian's reaction. "It's just a demonstration, not a race, and the floater seats four."

"Come on, Viv," Jonah said. "It will be fun."

"You know that I get motion sick at the drop of a hat," Vivian said. "Flying around in fast circles isn't my idea of a good time, but I'll watch from here."

"You guys go ahead," Samuel told the other couple. "Vivian and I haven't seen each other in over a week, and we're actually in the middle of a discussion."

"Then again, when's the next chance I'll get to ride around in a floater on Union Station," Vivian said, and practically ran up the broad steps to the top seating section of the Galaxy Room. "Are you guys coming or what?"

The demonstration proved to be very low-key, with Sephia keeping the speed down so that the potential buyers who closely examined the stationary floaters on stage could appreciate the aesthetics of one in motion, rather than watching it blur past. Flying around the top tier of the stadium-style seating posed no challenge for the race-trained driver, and she quickly impressed Samuel with her direct speech.

"So when are you getting married?" Sephia asked a few minutes later.

"We haven't set a date yet, but we're working on it," Samuel replied.

"What's to work? Just pick a date and do it before you get old. I keep telling Jojo that living around so many aliens is dangerous for humans because you can start thinking in terms of their lifespans."

"I spend less time around aliens than either of those two," Jonah protested. "Vivian works for the Drazens and Sam works for the Vergallians."

"And living on Union Station, you probably don't make any decisions without checking with the Stryx first," Sephia continued. "When I want to do something, I just do it. I'd rather make my own mistakes than to go through life with a nanny."

"And you don't imitate the Dollnicks in everything?" Vivian challenged her.

"Only when it suits me. I can admit that our hosts are better at everything than we are, but what they don't know about being human would surprise you. It's true some of us go native—my older brother wears a prosthetic arm set and whistles fluent Dollnick. I'm more interested in figuring out better ways we can do things ourselves than copying aliens."

"I'm not trying to imitate the Drazens," Vivian retorted, her prosthetic tentacle standing up angrily.

"She's undercover," Samuel explained. "It's not like Vivian wears her Drazen gear when she's not working."

"Sometimes she forgets to take off the extra thumbs," Jonah put in.

"Well, they're useful," Vivian said.

"I think the two of you should get in on the ground floor of this Human Empire thing," Sephia advised Samuel. "You've obviously got the right connections, and it's not like anybody from the open worlds is going to want to get stuck doing all that diplomatic stuff. My dad says it's because Earth governments were so bad that everybody who emigrated equates politics with corruption, and they've passed that belief on to their children and their children's children. Dad's been the mayor of Floaters since before I was born, so he knows what he's talking about."

"We did have to offer perks to scare up enough bidders at the auction to fill all the working group seats," Samuel admitted. "I know that the human leadership on open worlds is usually selected in imitation of the way the host species operates, but I didn't realize the people were so anti-government."

"They're not anti-government, they're anti-human-government. Even the youngest tunnel network members have had at least a half-million years to work out stable systems that pretty much take care of themselves. Humans are still making it up as we go along, and we just aren't very good at it."

Thirteen

"What's the special occasion?" Dorothy asked her mother. She set Margie on the floor, and the two-year-old immediately toddled over to where Beowulf was relaxing on the rug in front of the couch and collapsed against the enormous Cayl hound's warm belly.

"Where's your husband?" Kelly asked in return.

"Dad caught us outside and drafted Kevin to help him move some kegs."

"I'm not going to ask your father to stop craft-brewing, but I wish he would stick with bottling for friends and let the keg business go. He doesn't want to give up supplying Pub Haggis for Ian's sake, but it's surprising how much beer they go through."

"Are Paul and Aisha eating with us?" Dorothy asked, observing the extra plates on the table.

"They'll stop over later. Come and help me put out the food."

"What's under that box?" Dorothy moved towards the table where an upside-down carton with the flaps folded out made for a strange centerpiece.

"No peeking," Kelly said, corralling her daughter and herding her into the kitchen. The pair of them brought out the food, and Dorothy was sure she smelled chocolate. Joe and Kevin came up from the craft brewery on the lower level, Alexander padding silently after them.

"Wolfie!" Margie scolded the older Cayl hound, who rose so suddenly that the toddler landed on her backside.

Beowulf stepped over her and raised his nose to sniff. Then he broke into a huge doggy smile and raced out of the ice harvester, Alexander right on his heels. A few seconds later, the Cayl hounds began to bark excitedly.

"That's his Myst bark," Dorothy cried and ran for the top of the ramp. "It's her. She's with Gwendolyn and some strange alien."

"I'll get the box," Joe volunteered, and carefully lifted the carton off of the chocolate fountain that Kelly was only allowed to put out for special occasions. "I turned it on a half hour ago so it should start flowing soon."

Dorothy met the clones at the bottom of the ramp and threw her arms around her childhood friend. "It's you! You haven't changed at all."

"But you're so old," Myst said in dismay. "What happened?"

"Time happened. You've been sleeping for a decade and I'm a married woman with a two-year-old daughter."

"I've been dying to see Margie ever since you sent the message. Does she look like you?"

"Everybody who knew me at that age says she could be my clone. And how are you, Ambassador Gem?"

"Gwendolyn," the older woman said, waving off her recently resumed diplomatic title. "And this is Lancelot."

"Lance," the alien said, performing a deep bow.

"From King Arthur's Round Table?" Dorothy turned back to Myst as the identity of the strange alien finally registered. "He's your boyfriend?"

"My betrothed," Myst said proudly. "I named him myself."

"But he's not Gem!"

"Of course he is, silly. You're just used to all of us being the same individual with different hairstyles and such. Does your husband look like you?"

"But it's obvious we're the same species."

"I'll be the judge of that when I see him," Myst said with a laugh. "Aren't you going to invite us in?"

"Yes, but listen," Dorothy said, lowering her voice. "If you think I look old, you're not going to believe my parents. Eleven years is a long time at their age, so don't say anything."

"I won't," Myst promised. "You just surprised me. You've really grown up."

When the introductions and reunions were all completed, everybody took their seats at the table, and Lancelot couldn't hide his excitement at the variety of food.

"Is this all safe for us?" he asked.

"One hundred percent," Kelly told him. "The recipes are from the All Species Cookbook, and I double-checked with the Gem caterers that handle our embassy events just to make sure it's safe for you."

"We haven't made much progress restoring our agricultural base," Gwendolyn explained. "Moving from dormitories into private housing was on the top of everybody's priority list, and most of the old farmlands of our homeworld have been overtaken by forest. There's still a debate about how much food we should grow locally versus importing, because nobody really wants to cut down all of the trees."

"Don't tell me you're still living on those factory-made nutrition drinks!"

"For the majority of us who grew up with them, it's not that big a deal, and everybody gets an imported chocolate ration."

"We had one solid meal a day in my school," Lancelot told them. "When I was little, my big sisters at home also saved the real food they earned and gave it to me."

"You have a family?" Dorothy asked in surprise.

"An adopted family. All of the new boys get assigned older sisters. I guess it's different than growing up with a mother and father like Humans, but we're learning."

"Lance is a first-generation HY2X variant," Myst said proudly. "He's a year older than I am."

"HY2X variant?"

"My sisters stuck with the names the Farlings used to label our DNA samples so we wouldn't get mixed up when it's time for our children to choose mates," Lance said without a hint of embarrassment. "I grew up as HY2X-891 until Myst gave me a real name."

"How did the two of you meet?" Dorothy asked.

"I picked him out of the male-order catalog," Myst said. "There was just something about the way his hair fell over his eyebrow ridge that made him stand out from all of the other HY2X's."

"It's called a bad hair day," Lance said. "I didn't know that I'd been chosen by the Hero of Union Station until the director of the pairing facility told me. It took me days to work up the courage just to speak in her presence."

"He's such a liar," Myst said. "Right from our introduction, Lance did most of the talking. It's all nanobots this, nanobots that. He was first in programming at his academy."

"You know about nano-stuff?" Dorothy asked excitedly. "I have an idea for using Gem nanofabric that I just know is going to be a huge hit if I can get Jeeves to go along with it."

The EarthCent ambassador shook her head as her daughter started regaling the young Gem with her plans for remaking the fashion world with programmable fabric. "So what have you been doing with yourself all these years?" Kelly asked Gwendolyn. "Are you looking forward to coming back to work as an ambassador?"

"Negotiating with aliens who look down on clones will feel like a vacation after my last job. When I got home, I thought I would take a nice quiet position teaching diplomacy at the university, but the head of the department insisted on resigning in my favor. The next thing I knew it was school politics around the clock."

"I suppose that your sisters must have had a lot of grievances saved up from their years under a military government," Joe said.

"And then some," the Gem ambassador said. "You'd think it would be easy for clones who share a form of limited telepathy to reach decisions, but take away the dictatorship and we couldn't agree on anything. At my very first meeting, there was an argument about how many different stylus colors instructors should be able to invoke while drawing on active blackboards, and they were still fighting over the same thing when I resigned a decade later. Every little decision turned into a debate. It's as if after growing up without choices, my sisters decided never to agree on anything if they could possibly avoid it."

"I can see that happening," Kelly said, twirling a cherry by the stem while she waited for the chocolate to start flowing. "Did you enjoy the teaching part?"

"It got better as the years passed. When I first started teaching it felt like I was lecturing younger versions of myself who were mainly differentiated by their clothes and grooming. But then we began getting students who had done all of their secondary education under the new system, and at least we argued about different things. The last couple of years I had an increasing number of young clones from the new male lines, and that made the discussions much more interesting."

"I can imagine. Is everybody satisfied with the compromise you reached to keep the empire together?"

"Everybody?" Gwendolyn laughed. "More like nobody, but the alternative is even worse so we're sticking it out. How about you? Gem Today ran a story before we left for Union Station about the possibility of a Human Empire, though it was pretty vague on the details. What have you decided?"

"It's not up to me or to EarthCent. The invitation to become an empire was tendered to our Conference of Sovereign Human Communities. CoSHC only represents a fraction of the people who have left Earth, or around a tenth of humanity overall, but it meets the empire criteria with a billion members spread over twenty star systems."

Gwendolyn swallowed a bite of vegetable quiche and sighed. "I almost forgot how good Human food is. So what has CoSHC decided?"

"We'll have an answer by the end of the tradeshow," Kelly said. "Most of the sovereign communities are in no hurry to make themselves subject to a new government, but turning it down would confirm the old prejudice that humans are Stryx charity cases."

"Other than a few business people, we don't have any Humans living on Gem worlds," Gwendolyn said. "There was a joke going around the university that you know you're succeeding as a species when the Humans start moving in." The clone paused and put her hand over her mouth. "I'm sorry, that didn't come out right."

165

"Humans have always been opportunistic settlers," Joe said. "It's in our DNA."

"I traded on a few Gem worlds after the old empire collapsed," Kevin said. "Everybody was so poor that I felt terrible I couldn't just give my goods away, but I had a ship mortgage payment to make."

"What did my sisters have to offer in trade?" Gwendolyn asked. "We're still having problems reintegrating with the tunnel network economy due to our lack of viable commercial products and services. If it wasn't for our nanotechnology, we'd be complete beggars."

"I mainly traded for curiosities that I thought would sell at fairs. Basically anything small that was empire-issued since I figured they would eventually become collectibles."

"Do you have any ID bracelets?" the clone asked. "Everybody rushed to destroy them when the empire fell, but now they're making a comeback as a fashion statement."

"I had boxes of them, but I lost it all when the pirates took my ship," Kevin said with a sigh. "I've seen them for sale since then, and I would have made a fortune."

"Still the best trade you ever made," Joe reminded him. "A ship for my daughter."

"Yes, sir."

Dorothy broke off her private conversation with the young Gem and announced, "Lance is coming to work for me at SBJ Fashions. It will just be part-time because he and Myst are starting at the Open University, but I need a nanobot programmer. Oh, and don't leave until I can talk to you about the nanofabric, Ambassador Gem. Did your old ambassador pass along my request?"

"So you're SBJ Fashions?" Gwendolyn asked. "I checked the embassy message log when we arrived on the station, and I did see something about nanofabric, but I haven't had a chance to read it all. I'm afraid that my predecessor decided to use up her saved vacation days when she learned I was returning, and she stopped coming in to work weeks ago."

Beowulf and Alexander abandoned their strategic posts near Margie's highchair, where food scraps had a way of descending like manna, and raced for the door to greet Samuel.

"Is that really your little brother?" Myst whispered in Dorothy's ear.

"Myst?" Samuel asked before his sister could respond. "Wow, you look exactly like I remember."

"You're all grown up," the young clone said in amazement. "You used to be half my size."

"I think I was ten or eleven when you left so I couldn't have been that small," he said, moving around the table. "And you must be Myst's, uh..."

"Betrothed," Lancelot said. "I've heard all about your family. Myst considered naming me after you, but she decided it would cause too much confusion."

"Ambassador Gem," Samuel greeted the older clone formally. "Before Ambassador Aainda left for Jubilee, she asked me to extend to you the welcome of our embassy."

"Samuel works for the Vergallians now," Kelly explained to Gwendolyn. "The Stryx have been using the co-op program at the Open University to encourage more cross-species diplomatic training, and the ambassador offered him a full-time position."

"It's very nice to see you again, Samuel," Gwendolyn said. "I'd be curious to hear what a young person like yourself thinks about the Vergallian system. To get out of my contract and return to Union Station, I had to promise my university that I'd write a diplomatic textbook."

"I should probably ask my ambassador's permission before making any promises," Samuel said cautiously. "But if you're writing a textbook about tunnel network diplomacy, don't forget to put in a big warning about alien observers."

"I think I saw an invitation for us to send observers for the Human Empire deliberative process in the message queue," Gwendolyn said. "I hope nobody was insulted that it went unanswered."

"You should send Myst and Lance," Dorothy said immediately. "I'll embroider the swag bags myself, and they'll get free rooms at the Empire Hotel and entry to the trade show."

"I'm not sure it would be ethical for me to choose Myst. Don't Humans have a special name for giving plum assignments to favored family members?"

"Nepotism," Kelly said, "but seeing that the Gem were comprised of a single individual until recently, I can't see how it would apply in this case."

"I wish you would sign up," Samuel said to the young clones. "At least I know you won't be demanding. Do you know what the Frunge honeymooners wanted last time I saw them?"

"Expensive wine?" his mother guessed.

"Two cases of pink grapefruits and a jar of tupelo honey. I never even heard of tupelo honey before, but it turns out that Drazen Foods exports it from Earth. A little jar was twelve creds!"

"It's a one-time affair, and it's twelve creds less that I'll have to worry about investing," Kelly said. "Have you had any trouble with the Horten observers? The male seemed to be very argumentative."

"You didn't hear about that? Aabina was worried it would end up on the Grenouthian news," Samuel said. "He and the Drazen observer went at it in the food court."

"They got into a fight?"

"An eating contest. You never saw anything so gross in your life. The Dollnick manager asked Libby to ping us, and we got there just as—I don't want to spoil your meal," he concluded. "Hey, the chocolate started running."

Kelly coated the cherry she'd been holding by the stem for the last ten minutes, and then surprised her family by feeding it to the Gem ambassador. The clone leaned back in her chair and thumped the table with both hands. "Oh," she moaned. "That was almost too good."

"Try it," Kelly said, pushing the bowl of cherries over to the young clones. "Where did Dorothy go?"

"She ran back to our house to get something," Kevin said.

"You don't live here with your in-laws?" Gwendolyn asked, looking from Dorothy's husband to Joe. "Is this one of the alpha-male issues that our sociologists are worried about?"

"Dorothy and Kevin were welcome to live in the ice harvester with us, the same with Paul and Aisha, but we have the room in Mac's Bones for them to have their own houses," Joe said.

"Private space is probably more important for women than men," Kelly told the clone. "We all have a nesting impulse. Didn't you just say that the main priority on the Gem homeworld was creating separate living spaces?"

"Yes, but I meant getting out of dormitory rooms with bunk beds. Standalone houses are unheard of in the cities and still rare in the countryside, though they're making a comeback where small farms are possible."

Dorothy pounded up the ramp and rushed back into the room brandishing a white T-shirt. She carried it around to Gwendolyn and said, "I want to buy all of this fabric that you can manufacture."

"I don't know anything about textiles," the Gem ambassador said. "Is this a nanofabric of some sort?"

"It's THE nanofabric," Dorothy said. "I got it from the lost-and-found. It's fully programmable for shape, color, and a bunch of other stuff. When I showed it to Jeeves, it was a black sash like a bunny would wear. He hacked into the nanobot programming interface and changed it to this."

"May I see it?" Lance asked, and Gwendolyn passed him the T-shirt across the table. The young clone took a tab from his belt and brushed it against the fabric. "It's just like you said," he told Dorothy. "I heard about this technology in school, but our instructor said it hasn't been manufactured in thousands of years. May I borrow this to do a complete scan and send the data home?"

"It's yours, or the ambassador's. The station librarian told me that the Stryx received a request from your government to check their lost-and-founds for forgotten Gem goods that might have commercial value. She let me borrow it to charge up the nanobots and see how it worked, but I'm officially returning it to you now."

"We must be pretty desperate if we're asking the Stryx to sort through their trash looking for something we can sell," Gwendolyn said sadly. "Are you sure that nanofabric will have a market?"

"Weren't you listening when I explained to Myst and Lance? It's going to be the biggest thing ever."

"There may be an issue with the pricing," Lancelot cautioned her. "I concentrated on nanobot programming rather than manufacturing, but the scan I just ran showed a lot of molecules that I've never even heard of."

"But we can make more, can't we?" Myst asked.

"With the data from a deep scan, it's just a matter of obtaining the feedstock and programming a nanobot factory to get to work, but who would buy a five-thousand-cred T-shirt, even one as heavy-duty as this?"

"Just don't repeat that when I introduce you to Jeeves," Dorothy said. "It's going to take a little coaxing, but I know we can bring him around. After all, it's for a good cause. And forget about coming to the convention as an observer. If you can figure out the programming, you're working with me in the SBJ Fashions booth. The show has three more days to run, and I have an idea that even Jeeves won't be able to reject by the time I'm through with him."

Fourteen

"I can't wait to try that pasta sauce," Kelly said to Donna. "It smells so good."

"Jonah started simmering it hours ago. The one he just made now was for the sake of the cameras, but you can't cook a good tomato sauce from scratch during a live broadcast," the proud grandmother explained. "What do you think of his assistant? I've never seen him so taken by a girl. Blythe told me that she's practically moved into his room this week."

"Sephia? You must have met her before. Her father is Bob, the mayor of Floaters."

"I knew she looked familiar," Donna said. "My memory must be getting as bad as yours."

"Libby says that my memory is above average for people our age," Kelly retorted. "Look, he's putting in the spaghetti to boil. I'm so glad you talked me into skipping lunch to participate in the audience. And here comes my favorite part of the show where he promotes an Earth product."

A Grenouthian cameraman maneuvered his floating camera closer to Donna's grandson. Jonah produced a medium-sized device that featured a metal mechanism mounted on a boxy wooden base with a drawer. The audience gathered in front of the temporary set in the Empire Convention Center food court consisted largely of aliens, many of whom were enamored with Earth's astounding variety of kitchen gadgets. They began guessing at the device's purpose, in some cases placing bets.

"My grandmother always told me that the longer you let the pasta sauce simmer, the better it will taste," Jonah said, winking in Donna's direction. "So let's take a minute to watch a short message from the Organic Coffee Growers Association, and then I'll show you how I like to start my mornings."

A holographic projection of a bearded man leading a donkey up a steep mountain path appeared, and Jonah began the voice-over from a script on his heads-up display. There was some groaning in the audience and creds exchanged hands as the aliens realized the kitchen gadget was a manual coffee grinder.

"Your special assistant is pinging you," the station librarian announced over the EarthCent ambassador's implant.

"I'll take it," Kelly subvoced. "Aabina?"

"The working group chairs have finally submitted all of the questions their committees want answered before taking a vote. Daniel is getting everybody together now for a discussion and I thought you'd want to be there."

The EarthCent ambassador cast a longing look at the temporary set and her promised pasta before replying. "Of course. Where are we meeting?"

"The center stage of the Galaxy Room. There was a break in the schedule and we're taking advantage."

Kelly dismissed the connection and whispered to Donna, "I have to go. Can you save me a plate to warm up at the embassy later?"

"Will do. Take this," the embassy manager added, producing something wrapped in a napkin. "You need to eat something."

"What is it?"

"Chocolate chunk cookie. I stopped by the Vergallian Embassy booth earlier to see how Samuel runs things."

Kelly slipped out of the audience and headed to the other side of the food court where one of the lower entrances to the Galaxy Room was located. She quickly navigated her way through the exhibitions of heavy equipment in the area under the stadium seating and emerged on the amphitheater stage.

"Sorry about the short notice," Daniel greeted her. "It's just going to be a small gathering with the chair from each of the working groups and whoever else shows up. I figured that by moving fast we could cut down on the number of alien observers and save ourselves the heckling. And if Aabina didn't mention, I'm hoping that you'll be able to answer the questions about tunnel network responsibilities and costs, since you're the one who goes to all of the required meetings with the alien ambassadors."

"I go to the meetings, but EarthCent is exempt from the contribution requirements due to our probationary status," Kelly said. "I can give examples of how these things are decided, but I never paid much attention to the costs."

"Don't worry. Wrylenth will be here and he'll have all the facts. And the Galactic Free Press sent us the editor who handles their freelancers since they do most of the special project reporting."

"Roland?"

"You know him?"

"We've met, and I remember his name because of Beowulf," Kelly said. "They're probably the two most famous heroes from medieval epics."

"Learn something new every day," Daniel said. "Aabina set out the place cards for everybody. Someday we need to invest in new active displays with voice programming for panel events."

Kelly took her place at the table that had been set up facing a seating section consisting of a couple of dozen folding chairs. She spotted an energy bar next to the water bottle behind her place card and scarfed that down, saving her cookie for later.

Aabina rushed over when she saw that her boss had arrived. "I'm sorry we didn't have any time to prepare," she apologized.

"Daniel filled me in on the details," Kelly told her, nodding to Roland as the editor took his seat. "Do you have a list of the questions we're going over, or will the working group chairs be posing them directly?"

"I have them on my tab and I'll read them."

The slow-footed Verlock employee of EarthCent Intelligence pulled out the carbon fiber chair on Kelly's right and settled in his bulk with a sigh. Then he saw the expensive bottle of Dead Sea mineral water Aabina had provided for him and he perked up noticeably.

"You look tired, Wrylenth," Kelly said. "Is Clive overworking you?"

"I slept over a hundred hours last cycle, I'll be fine," the young Verlock replied at the near-human speaking pace he'd achieved through constant practice. "How is Samuel managing? I saw him working the Vergallian booth in the tradeshow, and I know he's been helping Aabina with the observers. Is he taking Farling stimulants to remain awake?"

"I certainly hope not," Kelly said, pulling out her diary and making a note to ask her son if he was self-medicating. "Have you been sitting in on any of the working group meetings?"

"Finance," Wrylenth answered, and leaning closer to the EarthCent ambassador, he lowered his voice. "The representatives don't seem to understand the concept of government investment."

"I'm not sure I know what it means either. Are you saying they aren't willing to spend on infrastructure?"

"They aren't willing to spend on government. I'm beginning to suspect that Mrs. Cohan wouldn't have been successful in auctioning the working group seats if your embassy hadn't offered to pick up the food and drink tab for meetings in restaurants."

"The lack of interest at the auction probably had less to do with a reluctance to spend and more to do with an aversion to committees," Kelly said.

"Perhaps, but the working group members appear to be unwilling to commit to spending even the minor sums necessary to lease office space for the Human Empire."

"We don't pay rent for our embassy."

"That's because Earth is still a protectorate," Wrylenth reminded her. "An empire will be expected to foot its own bills from the inception."

"Ooh, that could be an issue," Kelly admitted.

"We came to the same conclusion," Roland contributed from Kelly's other side. "The working group members our reporters have interviewed don't want any part of building or operating an empire, especially if it costs money. The only reason they haven't rejected it outright is that they're afraid of losing face with the aliens."

"Humans can't remain probationary tunnel network members forever," Wrylenth cautioned them. "Either you'll establish some sort of governing body, or your people who leave Earth will eventually all end up as second-class citizens living in empires run by other species."

"It looks like everybody is here," Aabina announced to the two dozen or so audience members who were split between committee chairs, alien observers, and working press. "We won't be using microphones since it's just a small group. I have a list of the questions that your working groups need answered and I'll be routing them to the appropriate experts. EarthCent Intelligence has sent Wrylenth, their analyst responsible for the Human Empire portfolio, and I'm sure everybody recognizes Ambassador McAllister, who has over four decades of practical experience in tunnel network diplomacy."

"It can't be forty years already," Kelly said to herself as Aabina introduced Roland. She did a little quick math in her paperback diary, adding her time on Union Station to her early years working for EarthCent. Then she wrote herself a note to check with Donna about the retirement age again.

" —and Maker Dring, who is recording an official history," Aabina finished up the introductions just as Kelly started paying attention again. "I'll begin with a question about mandatory public works projects, namely, what sort of participation will be required on the part of the Human Empire. Roland?"

"Thank you, Aabina. I'd just like to remind everybody that the Galactic Free Press focuses our coverage on news that impacts humanity, and that defines the bounds of my knowledge of tunnel network activities. But given the popularity of human contract workers as a low-cost alternative to automation, we find ourselves publishing stories about most of the recent public works projects either mandated or encouraged by the Stryx."

"Public works projects for the benefit of the tunnel network members," Aabina prompted Roland.

"Yes. I'm afraid I'm more used to writing than speaking, so you'll be getting my thoughts without the editing," he said apologetically. "Some of the best-known projects involve historical preservation of lost civilizations, and keeping the space lanes around tunnel network exits clear of debris. The Stryx also enforce certain standards for self-preservation so that the member species don't become burdens upon each other."

"Could you give us some examples?"

"Well, let's take the Empire of a Hundred Worlds," Roland said. "Everybody knows that the majority of the imperial-controlled planets enforce tech-bans to varying degrees, but all tunnel network members are required to install asteroid protection systems so that they aren't crying for a Stryx science ship to save them every time a chunk of space rock threatens millions of lives."

"That's very interesting," Aabina said as if she hadn't already known about the requirement. "Defending a planet against asteroids involves a significant investment, but how about some less visible projects?"

"Well, the publication of the All Species Cookbook has led to a surge of interest in what makes so many Earth foods digestible by the other species, and whatever that mechanism is, it leads to the possibility of shared parasites as well. So there's an all-species project to collect and

178

analyze samples of, uh, post-digestion waste—I don't think I need to go into the details. But it's a good example of a required contribution that doesn't cost anything, in terms of creds, other than labeling and shipping small sample containers."

"I believe we all get the picture," Aabina concurred. "Ambassador McAllister. Many of the submitted questions deal with the diplomatic burden of running a Human Empire, such as opening and staffing embassies. But the various committee members are also concerned about humanity handling its own interspecies negotiations, from the interstellar ice-harvesting treaty to coordinating a tunnel network response to piracy. Everybody understands that the Stryx ban tunnel network members from warring on one another, but how much work goes on behind the scenes resolving disagreements over business and territory?"

"One of the greatest surprises for me when I became an ambassador was the number of mandated interspecies meetings the Stryx added to my calendar," Kelly said. "I even found myself attending a session on gaming tournament rules, one of many subjects about which I knew nothing. But the important thing is that the ambassadors on all of the Stryx stations are constantly sitting down with one another and getting their grievances out in the open before they can fester."

"So how are most problems settled?" Aabina prompted. "Do you take votes? Does money exchange hands? Do the Stryx always have the last word?"

"I'd be lying if I told you that I fully understood the process myself, but once we get together and start talking, things have a way of working themselves out," Kelly said. "The Stryx rarely even express an opinion, but representatives of the older species that have been tunnel network members for millions of years already know what's expected."

"Wrylenth," Aabina continued, spreading around the questions like a professional moderator. "Humanity has no interstellar navy of its own, and there were several questions about the costs of building the minimum required fleet for a Human Empire."

"One of the drawbacks to humanity's early admission to the tunnel network is that we, if you'll excuse my use of the pronoun to talk about all of you, lack the technological base to construct such a fleet," the Verlock said. "While the capabilities of warships vary greatly by species, Human manufacturers would have difficulty building a lifeboat that meets the minimum safety standard."

"So are you saying that a Human Empire isn't actually a possibility because we ultimately won't be able to fulfill our treaty obligations?"

"The Thousand Cycle option allows us to obtain a home fleet waiver until the empire's finances can support one," Wrylenth explained. "If we meet all of the other requirements, the Stryx will eventually help us finance the purchase of surplus ships from one of the less advanced species."

"The Stryx will help us buy military ships?" Kelly asked in surprise.

"Although it may sound counterintuitive, subsidizing the cost of purchasing alien warships by a responsible government will help remove hazardous equipment from the pre-owned market. The fleet requirement might also be met by purchasing support vessels to contribute to the mutual defense, such as armored tugs and hospital ships."

"A leaked intelligence estimate from one of the tunnel network species has estimated the GEP, or Gross Empire Productivity, for a Human Empire consisting of current CoSHC members at less than six trillion creds," Aabina said. "How much would we be expected to spend on a fleet?"

"One of the advantages of the Thousand Cycle option is that the two-percent of GEP requirement doesn't take effect until the end of the mentoring period," Wrylenth said. "After that, the build-up would be gradual, and of course, our productivity will be much higher by then."

"One question that was submitted by every working group asks whether we're insane to even be considering an empire. Perhaps you'd like to field this question, Ambassador?"

"I'll point out again that none of us on this panel are members of sovereign human communities or have a direct say in the process of accepting or rejecting empire status," Kelly said. "If you reject declaring a Human Empire through the transparent process that's been set up, the whole issue will go away without prejudice. That said, EarthCent, which I do represent, does feel that it's important for us all to begin thinking about the day that Earth is no longer a Stryx protectorate."

"And what do you believe will happen if humanity has failed to establish some sort of central government when that day arrives?" Aabina followed up.

"I'm not much of a prophet, but I've discussed this possibility many times with my colleagues. Our main worry is that the sovereign human communities will eventually become isolated and cease to identify as part of humanity. It's unclear what would happen to Earth itself if it fails to achieve full tunnel network membership on its own."

"And a related question asked by the vocal minority is, why doesn't EarthCent step up and handle this?"

"You have to remember that the diplomatic organization I serve is funded by the Stryx and was set up so that the other tunnel network members would have a single point of contact to deal with Earth," Kelly explained. "While all EarthCent employees take an oath to do our best for humanity, we try to keep in mind that we have no mandate from the people we are attempting to serve."

"Do you have something to add, Wrylenth?" Aabina asked.

"The Conference of Sovereign Human Communities has all of the makings of an empire but has yet to progress beyond a loose business organization. While the start-up costs for an empire are high, EarthCent Intelligence's contingency planning expert believes that the eventual advantages greatly outweigh the growing pains. Remember that all of the other tunnel network species made extraordinary sacrifices to achieve interstellar travel."

"Isn't Wrylenth the contingency planning expert?" Kelly subvoced to Libby.

"Yes," the station librarian replied. "It's impressive how working for EarthCent Intelligence has built up his confidence. Young Verlocks are usually far more reticent with their opinions."

"But the required sacrifice will be different for humanity," Roland pointed out. "The much larger investments you speak of the other species making were simply a matter of capital allocation since the money stayed at home. Purchasing warships from other species would lead to the Human Empire exporting Stryx creds."

"That's true," Wrylenth acknowledged, "but roughly half of humanity is currently working on alien worlds under contract, and they remit money to Earth in the form of Stryx creds to support family members who remained behind. Our most likely scenario will see the Human Empire expand over the next century to include Earth and all of the retirees from contract work, so by the time the Thousand Cycle period is up, we'll probably have excess monetary reserves."

"Yes?" Aabina said, pointing at the mayor of Floaters who had his hand raised.

"This is all way above my pay grade," Bob said. "I deal in financing for floaters, not trillion cred military build-ups and the balance of trade between civilizations. What we all want to know is if we accept this empire thing, what kind of cost are we looking at for the next fifty years?"

"Very far-sighted for a Human," the Verlock muttered to Kelly.

"The Thousand Cycle option is a process, not a switch that gets flipped," Aabina reassured the audience. "With the help of an alien mentor, the startup team will begin laying the groundwork for an empire, but we're talking about building institutional knowledge, not fleets and buildings. For the next fifty years, the investment required will likely come to little more than payroll, travel costs, and office space for the staff to do their work."

"Will EarthCent pay for it?" another member of the audience asked bluntly.

"Ambassador?" Aabina inquired.

"Just a moment," Kelly said, and subvoced, "Libby? Will the Stryx object to my using some cookbook money for this?"

"I think it would be a wise investment," the Stryx librarian replied.

"It sounds like we'll be able to foot the bill," the EarthCent ambassador continued out loud, "but my gut tells me it would be better to have some sort of cost-sharing arrangement with the sovereign human communities from the beginning, even if the amount is purely symbolic."

"I think we've covered all the questions, so we'll be expecting your decision soon," Aabina announced hastily, as some late-arriving alien observers stumbled out from one of the tunnels under the stadium seating. "And I won't name any names, but whoever held their last meeting in the red light district and charged their tips for dancers to the embassy, please don't do it again."

Fifteen

"Maybe we should have rented extra space for the un-veiling," Flazint said nervously, as the aisle on their side of the SBJ Fashions booth was beginning to jam up with women waiting for the big event. "Our neighbors are going to get angry about their booths being blocked."

"You've been to tradeshows before," Dorothy said. "Somebody is always going to have the popular booth, and right now it's us. Besides, the first three days of the show were slow for our side of the booth while Baa and Stick have been cleaning up out back. Have you checked on them recently?" she asked, gesturing at the curtain that separated their half of the booth from the half facing on the next aisle, where they were selling Baa's Bags and remedial dancing aids for men.

"You should have seen Baa's face when Stick wanted her to join him for the Shadow Dancer demonstrations," the Frunge girl said, breaking into a broad grin at the memory. "I thought she was going to turn him into an amphibian."

"Maybe she doesn't know how to dance," Dorothy said. "Baa would never admit to something like that."

"I still think we should have rented a side room. The people who are just arriving won't be able to see any-thing."

"I intentionally segmented our contact list into four equal parts so we'd get a good showing at the follow-up demonstrations this afternoon and tomorrow," Dorothy said. "Somebody must have blabbed to the Grenouthians because they have three cameras floating out there. I wasn't going to notify them until after we had the presentation down pat."

"I hope everything works," Lancelot spoke up. "I've never done anything like this before, and you only gave me one day to prepare. We don't have a retailing tradition on the Gem homeworld."

"The guys across the aisle from us recruiting mail-order-brides for asteroid miners just folded up one of their tables to let women stand inside their booth," the EarthCent ambassador's daughter reported. "We should be charging them commission for bringing in potential clients."

"You asked me to tell you when it's time to start," the station librarian informed Dorothy over her implant.

The EarthCent ambassador's daughter stepped up onto the box she was using in lieu of a stage and waited for the audience to stop talking. She smiled and waved to the women she recognized, and self-consciously noted the location of the closest floating immersive camera before beginning.

"Let's all be honest with ourselves," Dorothy said. "How many times have you bought a new outfit for a job interview or a date and worn it just once or twice before it disappeared into the back of your closet? Show of hands, please."

A few women in the audience raised a tentative hand, then a larger group, and in the end, almost two-thirds had their hands elevated.

"That's right," she continued, and brandished a tab that wasn't even turned on. "I have research here showing that clothes bought for special occasions are worn just three times on average. Think about the thousands of creds you'll waste over your lifetime."

"SBJ Fashions is one of the most expensive brands on the station," a woman in the front of the group pointed out.

"I'd like to believe that my designs never end up in the back of anybody's closet, and this market research doesn't apply to ball gowns or shoes, which are clearly an investment," Dorothy said. "But I wouldn't have brought the numbers up at all if I didn't have a solution, and that solution is FaaS."

"Fast?" somebody asked.

"F – a – a – S. Fashion as a Service."

"Is that what this is about? You want to rent us clothes? This presentation was supposed to be about something new under the sun."

"FaaS is a technology breakthrough made possible by our exclusive arrangement with the Gem, not some circular exchange that delivers poorly fitting dresses with mystery stains," Dorothy retorted. "Allow me to demonstrate. Lance?"

Myst's betrothed stepped forward to the clothing dummy that was sporting a black tube dress and touched the back with his programming device. The dress instantly turned fire-engine red, and the audience let out a collective, "Oooh."

"That's just the start of it," Dorothy told them. "The Gem nanofabric that makes FaaS possible is fully programmable, and unlike some previous attempts at chameleon clothing, it's protected by military-level encryption. Lance?"

The clone touched the dress with his programming device again, and the fabric flowed into an A-line pattern, at the same time changing colors to royal blue.

"It's an illusion," a Vergallian in the crowd cried out. "Whatever that fabric is, there wasn't enough of it to go from a tube dress to that A-line."

"I didn't see you there, Bavlah," Dorothy said, feigning surprise. "For anybody who doesn't already know, Bavlah owns the Courtier's Choice boutique on the Vergallian deck where they stock the latest fashions from the Empire of a Hundred Worlds. In answer to your question, Bavlah, the thickness and opacity of the fabric is also programmable, though the particular sample we're using today wouldn't be sufficient for a wedding gown with a train. Lance?"

Lancelot transmitted a new program, and the nanofabric flowed into a two-piece bathing suit, eliciting gasps.

"I'm particularly glad that Bavlah stopped by today because I might have forgotten an important part of my presentation otherwise. How many of you have visited a Vergallian fitting room?"

Ninety percent of the audience raised their hands.

"And how many of you have your avatar crystal with you right now?" Dorothy asked.

Approximately half of the women kept their hands up.

"Who wants to volunteer as a model?"

"Me," Chance cried, moving around the end of the table before any of the other women could react. The artificial person who worked as an EarthCent Intelligence trainer had willingly agreed to play a ringer, and she winked at

Dorothy as she handed over her avatar crystal. "Can I get something in a tango dress?"

"Let's start by going back to the tube dress in our volunteer's size so she can put it on and we can demonstrate hot-swapping," Dorothy said to Lancelot.

The clone inserted Chance's avatar crystal into a slot on the top of his programming device, and then touched it to both parts of the swimsuit, which flowed back together to reform the tube dress. Then he removed the dress from the dummy and handed it to Chance, who disappeared behind the curtain of the jury-rigged privacy booth.

"Are you saying that once you're wearing a FaaS dress, you can change it into something else without taking it off?" a girl asked.

"That's exactly what I'm saying," Dorothy replied. "We're filing for a patent on the custom erogenous zones filter which allows users of all species to map areas of their bodies they want to keep covered at all times. It's actually trickier if you're already wearing undergarments—"

"I'm not," Chance called from behind the curtain.

"—and in any case, some users will undoubtedly prefer to make wardrobe changes in the comfort of their homes. But the main feature of a FaaS subscription is access to the full SBJ Fashions line without having to return to a boutique or worrying that they might not stock your size. I can tell you from personal experience that becoming a mother changed my body, but a quick trip to a Vergallian fitting room to update your avatar and your FaaS fashion will adapt to your new measurements."

"Ready," Chance declared, coming out from behind the curtain in the slinky tube dress. The shapely artificial person moved with a dancer's grace, and the floating cameras belonging to the Grenouthian news service captured her from three angles to allow for an immersive holographic broadcast.

"Now for the moment you've all been waiting for," Dorothy said, finally turning on her tab and bringing up SBJ Fashion's full line catalog. "Who wants to pick a new look for our volunteer?"

Bavlah employed some sort of Vergallian martial arts move to elbow past the other women and snatch the tab from Dorothy's extended hand. She quickly scanned the options and picked a black tango dress that featured one lace sleeve, one solid sleeve, and large red frills or bustles on the opposing shoulder and hip.

"Number six-two-three," Dorothy called to Lance. The clone tapped the code into his device and touched it to the back of Chance's dress. For a few seconds, it looked as if the artificial person was being swarmed by hundreds of millions of nanobots, and then she executed a spin move to show off the newly formed dress. Pandemonium erupted as the audience surged against the table demanding to sign up for the new service.

"And how much does it all cost?" Bavlah shouted at the top of her lungs, silencing the crowd.

"We're waiting for the Gem to get back to us with the price for commercial quantities of the nanofabric. In the meantime, I'm gathering contact information, and when the FaaS service beta launches, we'll start with the women who signed up early."

"Ten thousand creds?" the Vergallian pursued the cost issue in a loud voice. "Twenty thousand?"

"Our initial analysis indicated that the subscription cost to apply new fashions from our catalog might be on the order of twenty creds a cycle," Dorothy deflected the question by pulling a figure out of the air. "We're looking into different business models for supplying the actual fabric, including the idea of fashion clubs, where a number of members could share a subscription. And for anybody who already pays a monthly fee to the Tharks for wardrobe insurance, we're planning a free fashion backup service that offers a superior solution for loss or damage."

"How would that work?" another woman called out.

"We would require you to create a high-resolution holographic image of yourself wearing each dress in your wardrobe as a backup. Tunnel network entertainment law allows us to use that imaging data to recreate the dress from our nanofabric should the original be lost or damaged."

"You'll be hearing from my lawyers," Bavlah snarled, and began fighting her way out of the crowd.

"I'll put your name on the list," Dorothy called after the angry Vergallian. The other women pressed forward, offering their tradeshow badges for scanning to reserve a spot in the queue. Flazint helped Dorothy capture everybody's information, while Chance and Myst's boyfriend continued reprogramming the nanofabric with different fashions from the catalog, all captured by the Grenouthian cameramen.

"Doesn't it feel icky when the nanobots are swarming all over you?" a younger girl asked Chance.

"Refreshing, actually. Like standing in a breeze," the artificial person replied.

"And how much is the programming device?" somebody else asked Lancelot.

"These are super cheap and we use them for everything," the clone said. "But we're also planning to add the programming function to the spare capacity of the adjustable ballroom shoes SBJ Fashions already sells."

"Though you'll have to stand on one foot and touch the fabric to the shoe for it to work," Chance added with a giggle.

Lancelot stepped up to the table to see if Dorothy needed help, and said, "You know that Myst felt really bad she couldn't be here, but she promised to help Gwendolyn with the embassy reopening this morning. The station Gem are throwing a welcome back party."

"You should have told me," Dorothy said as she scanned another tradeshow pass with her tab. "If I knew you had to be somewhere, I would have put off the unveiling until this afternoon."

"I wasn't invited to the party," Lancelot said. "I'm sort of the only male Gem on the station right now and Myst didn't want her sisters thinking she was showing off. She's going to take me around and make introductions later."

Stick stuck his head through the break in the curtain bisecting the SBJ Fashions booth. "Hey, if you're finishing up over there, I could use some support," he said.

"Be with you in a second," Lance told him, and tapped a few symbols on his programming device before offering it to the EarthCent ambassador's daughter. "If you plug in an avatar crystal and touch the end to the nanofabric, it will change sizes."

Dorothy snatched the device from Myst's boyfriend, eager to try it herself. "Go ahead and help Stick."

The aisle on the other side of the SBJ Fashions booth was mobbed by young men who had gathered for the Shadow Dancer demonstration, and now they were eagerly buying up all the stock of the add-on product that projected foot-placement patterns on linked heads-up displays to teach dance steps.

"We're selling the Shadow Dancer add-on for ten creds cash or five creds and their contact information," Stick informed his helper. "Everybody has been paying the ten creds."

"Why is contact information so valuable?" Lancelot asked after completing his first-ever sales transaction. "What else are these guys going to buy from SBJ Fashions?"

"We don't have much for males beyond the LARPing gear Baa enchants, but I'm pushing to expand the catalog," Stick explained. "I hope you can keep working for us because I'm tired of being the only guy."

"Is this the SBJ Fashions booth?" a vivacious young woman asked.

"The new product launch is around the other side," Stick replied, and then noticed Vivian's brother standing just behind the girl, carrying two swag bags. "Oh, hey, Jonah. You can sneak through from this side and jump the line if you want."

"We're here to look at bags of holding," Sephia answered in Jonah's place.

"Then you've come to the right mage," Baa said, uncurling from the giant beanbag chair she'd insisted on bringing to the booth. "I conceal the display during the Shadow Dancer demonstrations to keep grubby male hands off my purses." The Terragram mage snapped her fingers, and one of the two tables making up the booth's front on the aisle was suddenly covered with a selection of Baa's Bags. "What's your price range?"

"Something entry-level," the girl said. "I've never LARPed before so I don't know if I'll like it."

Behind her, Jonah caught Baa's eye and mouthed, "I'm treating." The mage grinned wickedly.

"Still, you don't want to start too low or you're just throwing away your money," Baa said, and another quick gesture reduced the inventory to just a dozen or so bags. "I see you as a five-feather girl."

"Five feathers?" Sephia asked, examining an elegant clutch finished with cultured pearls. "It looks very expensive."

"It's on me," Jonah insisted. "You bought lunch and paid for our tickets to Libbyland."

"But these bags..."

"Five-feather bags have the highest capacity for loot, and the weight reduction factor is a million-to-one," Baa said. "You could store enough sand in there to make your own beach."

"Something with a shoulder strap is better for LARPing because you want to keep your hands free," Jonah advised.

"Like this one?" Sephia asked, picking up a leather shoulder bag that looked like something an elf ranger might wear to carry extra food rations.

"It's kind of plain."

"I'm not really into glamorous clothes, you know. I just wore that two-piece the first day to get past the audition."

"But I want to give you something really nice," Jonah protested.

"I have the perfect gift idea," Baa said. "A unique bag from my signature line."

"Can we see it?" Sephia asked, replacing the leather shoulder bag on the table.

Baa held up her index finger, which began to glow a brilliant blue. Then she used her fingertip to draw an alien hieroglyph on one side of the plain bag. There was a faint odor of burning leather. "One of a kind," she declared. "As

194

my first signed piece, it will show up as epic status in your inventory when you enter the LARPing studio."

"How much does it cost?"

"I'll settle up with Jonah later," the mage said with a wink. "You can take it with you."

Business slacked off until the afternoon demonstration on the fashion side of the booth, where Affie arrived to take Chance's place as the ringer for the next demonstration of FaaS. Dorothy repeated her performance from the morning with similar results, but a few minutes before closing, Flazint's boyfriend arrived, looking grim.

"Is something wrong, Tzachan?" Dorothy asked. "I filled out the dating calendar the way you showed me, so your matchmaker shouldn't have a problem."

"I'm not here about that," the Frunge said. "As the attorney of record for SBJ Fashions, I was served a cease-and-desist order by Aaxina, Aleeytis, and Arriviya. They're the top Vergallian intellectual property firm on Union Station, and they're accusing us of intention to violate clothing design patents and trademarks. What have you been doing?"

"Bavlah!" Dorothy exploded. "I mentioned in our FaaS demonstration that the technology can be used for wardrobe backup. She must have run all the way to her lawyer's office. But since when is the intent to do something a crime?"

"We're not talking about criminal law, Dorothy. Intent to violate intellectual property law is a civil matter, and Triple-A must have a judge in their pocket on the Vergallian deck. The complaint states that you solicited dress owners to create holographic images of their wardrobes of sufficient resolution to produce exact copies, and furthermore, you offered an unlicensed means of creating those copies."

"I specifically said it should only be used if the original was lost or damaged. I know that Blythe offers subscribers to her romance book club a backup option for their entire collection as a perk, and she's never had any legal problems."

"Entertainment-related copyrights are different. Several species have laws allowing a single copy of digital works for backup purposes, though encryption may prevent the copy from working properly."

"But why should fashions be different from books and music?" Dorothy protested. "I wouldn't have any problem with some other company offering a wardrobe backup service that included our dresses."

"Are you sure about that? Do you really want to see the SBJ Fashions logo appear on dresses that weren't manufactured by SBJ Fashions? What if they're poorly made?"

"But the nanofabric can make perfect copies. The accuracy is only limited by the quality of the data."

"That may be true, I'll have to reserve judgment on the technology, but as a legal concept, wardrobe backup couldn't be limited to Gem nanofabric. It would have to apply to all methods of making copies from the original data."

"You mean..."

"Yes," Tzachan told her. "If you push ahead with this idea you'll be opening Pandora's box to services that will manufacture copies using the cheapest possible methods, perhaps selling them as ready-to-go backups. I've spoken with my partners and none of us can envision a scenario where this will end well for SBJ Fashions."

"So what do we do?" Flazint asked her boyfriend. "There must have been a thousand people between our two demonstrations today, and the Grenouthian News was here recording."

"Fortunately, the bunnies had no interest in broadcasting your sales pitch for free. They reported the nanofabric as a technology story, cutting between video of the dress morphing into new patterns on your model, and some stock footage of Gem nanobot manufacturing facilities. But no more talking about wardrobe backups."

"How about backups for dresses from our own catalog?" Dorothy asked. "We own all of the rights to those."

"Your FaaS subscribers will have no need for backups since you're already granting them the right to create any dress in the catalog," Tzachan reminded her. "And I hope you aren't making any implied promises about pricing."

"No, I explicitly said that it's in the works and that we're only taking names for a beta test."

"That's good," the Frunge attorney said, finally relaxing. "I'll draft a reply for the Vergallians saying that there was a misunderstanding and offer our apologies. I'm afraid that Bavlah is likely to send us a bill for whatever she paid Aaxina, Aleeytis, and Arriviya. Upper caste lawyers don't come cheap."

Sixteen

"Hey, Fenna. Hey, Mike," Samuel greeted the kids as they hurried past with buckets and brushes. "Are you going to stage another dog wash event to raise money for the Station Scouts?"

"Marilla hired us to help clean rental ships," Mike reported.

"That's what happens when you become a teenager. Everybody wants to put you to work."

"I'm a teenager," Fenna said. "Mike's only twelve."

The boy scowled at his best friend. "But I'm still taller than you are."

"I always thought you guys were the same age," Samuel said. "It's hard to keep track when Libby's school doesn't have grades."

"Marilla even asked her little sister to come help again," Fenna said. "We're really busy."

"Orsilla? The girl who was on *Let's Make Friends* with Mike?"

"Yeah," Mike said, somewhat mollified by the reminder of his fame as a child actor. "She's all happy because it means a break from doing homework. Hortens study too much."

"All of the alien kids study too much," Samuel said. He had meant to spend his first evening off in weeks with the

Vergallian meditation manual Aabina had loaned him, but he decided to find Marilla instead and offer his help.

"Aren't you busy keeping the observers happy?" the Horten girl asked when he finally tracked her down in one of the rental craft parked at the check-in area. She was trying to scrape something off the heavily padded chair without damaging the upholstery.

"Aabina hired InstaSitter to take care of the observers when it's nothing important," the EarthCent ambassador's son explained. "Mike and Fenna told me that you're so behind on cleaning that you even brought your little sister in to help."

"Orsilla is doing her behavioral psychology term paper on Humans, so I'm basically paying her to do her homework. My parents never would have let her out of the apartment otherwise. Sixth grade is such an important time in life."

"You couldn't get Mornich to come?" Samuel asked, referring to the Horten ambassador's son who was officially courting Marilla.

"I pinged him, but the band is playing a wedding. I'll do a better job planning next time I try a special promotion. And part of the problem is that the franchisees don't all clean ships to the same standard. I'd swear this gum has been stuck on the seat for at least a week."

"I guess I don't understand what's going on," Samuel confessed. "I thought you'd have the week off because all of your rentals were taken by sales reps coming for the tradeshow, and they'd return home in the same ships. Didn't Tunnel Trips offer a special discount in honor of the Human Empire or something?"

"Yes, but after Paul made me vice president, I decided to study up on the Human travel industry and I took an extension course at the Open University. Have you ever heard of double booking?"

"Isn't that Earth's version of accounting where they try to balance assets and liabilities? I've seen Grenouthian documentaries where they poke fun at it."

"This is something else, though the same potential for abuse is there. Suborbital flights on Earth always sell more seats than there are on the aircraft because they know that not every ticketholder will show up. There's a surprisingly sophisticated mathematical model behind it, and it gave me the idea to try something similar with rentals."

"You're re-renting ships that are already taken? Doesn't that violate the rental contract?" Samuel asked.

"Finally," Marilla said as the dried gum released from the seat without taking any fake leather with it. "No. Tunnel Trips accepts practically no responsibility for anything. I suspect that Jeeves wrote the rental contract for Paul."

"So what are you going to do when the sales reps who paid to rent a ship for the duration are ready to go home?"

"I got Aabina to share the data from last year, and it turns out that the reps who arrive early to set up for a tradeshow stay for the whole thing, plus at least one extra day to break down their booths and recover. The guests attending the show almost never stay the whole week, and since most open worlds don't have direct commercial service to Union Station, they're looking at days of travel time. We can offer them huge time savings for short-term rentals."

"So you're getting attendees to cash-out half of their round trip ticket on a liner and take a one-way rental home? Isn't there a big penalty for breaking a ticket?"

"A significant penalty, but these are mainly business travelers, and they're gaining at least a whole day. And I only offered the promotional price for destinations where there's an unfilled request for a rental to Union Station before the tradeshow wraps up."

"So you were able to get two extra one-way rental trips out of a ship that's already been rented for the duration of the show," Samuel surmised. "But wait a second. How are the people who come for the end of the tradeshow going to travel back when the convention wraps up and the original renters need the same ships to go home?"

"I guess you've been so busy that you haven't heard about the new ships," the Horten girl said. "Remember those Dollnick taxis we bought from the Sharf ship-carrier in the auction lot? The ones Paul and your father reconditioned and sold on to new franchises?"

"It was mainly cosmetic work since the taxis were extremely well maintained."

"The advance team for the ship-carrier visited Mac's Bones last week and offered us a deal on another lot from the same Dollnick taxi company. They even offered to swap out the seats and the Zero-G toilets for us. Paul agreed, and the Sharf will start delivering them on Saturday."

"So you're going to use the late renters returning home to distribute the new ships around the Tunnel Trips network," Samuel concluded. "That's pretty clever."

"If the other franchises want to buy more, Paul will sell them for an immediate profit, and otherwise they'll just become part of our home fleet. But it means that instead of those round trip rentals sitting here all week, we had to get them turned around and out again. Today we started getting in the final wave of ships from visitors arriving for the conclusion of the tradeshow, and they need to be ready to go out again by Friday evening."

"But if you already cleaned the ships once, why did this one have week-old gum stuck to the seat?"

"They aren't the same ships. All of the franchisees operate on a first-in, first-out basis, so even if we're keeping the numbers in balance for the booking system, the ship utilization is spread across the whole fleet. That's the way Tunnel Trips is set up."

"It sounds like you made a lot of extra work for yourself to earn money for the business. I hope Paul is paying you overtime."

"I'm very well compensated. My shares in Tunnel Trips vest in just another three cycles." She glanced around to make sure nobody else could hear, and added, "I'm going to be a ten percent owner, you know. That means Mornich and I will qualify as financially stable and we'll be able to move ahead with our relationship."

"You're finally tying the knot? Congratulations!"

"Knot? We get to start taking the advanced compatibility tests."

"Are you serious? You've been going out together for years."

"Hortens may not be as strict about dating as some of the other species, but we take marriage just as seriously as any of them," Marilla said proudly. "So, are you psyched to clean up some Zero-G vomit? I really don't understand why Humans have so much trouble using the bags."

"Beats me," Samuel said. "Maybe first-timers get carried away with floating around the cabin and then they can't get back to their seats quickly enough when their stomachs rebel. Have you ever considered giving out sick-bags with cords so that customers can hang them around their necks rather than storing them under the seats?"

"You don't think they'd be offended?"

"Humans have pretty thick skins about stuff like that. Where's my first job?"

"Kevin has been helping out by moving all of the really bad ships to the other side of the training camp field—the ones where people threw-up or didn't follow the Zero-G bathroom instructions. Your father said that he had an idea for getting them cleaned up quickly, and Paul is over there too. I have to stay near the kiosk to deal with any customers who come in and to keep an eye on the kids."

"All right. I'll see if they can use any more help." Samuel began jogging towards the training camp and Beowulf came out of nowhere and started trotting alongside. Then Alexander showed up and began running circles around both of them.

"Yeah, yeah, yeah," Samuel responded to the younger Cayl hound's implied criticism. "Four legs are better than two, I admit defeat."

"Just in time for the big show," Kevin called to his younger brother-in-law. "Don't trip over the hose."

"What are you guys doing with the power washer?" Samuel asked. "You can't use that on ship interiors, can you?"

"Have you already forgotten that we stopped by your Vergallian embassy booth for lunch today?"

"You ate the last roast beef sandwich and filled your swag bag with cookies."

"I put my card in the fishbowl and took one of each brochure," Kevin pointed out.

"But I sincerely doubt you and Dorothy have any intention of moving to a Vergallian open world, and I know Paul and Dad aren't going anywhere."

"Maybe I'll meet somebody looking for a new home and pass the information along. That's how word-of-mouth works. Anyway, there were some pretty interesting vendors at the tradeshow, and your father was so impressed by a start-up from a Dollnick open world selling retrofit wands for Horten power washers that he bought one on the spot."

"You mean the industrial type with high-pressure steam that the Hortens developed for cleaning restaurant kitchens? I know that Dad has one of those, but I thought he said it made too much of a mess to be used on interiors that aren't designed with a drainage system."

"That's where the new wand comes in. Some clever engineers figured out how to combine it with the containment technology from the standard Zero-G showers the Dollnicks sell for small trade vessels."

"Don't those require a special shower basin with a superconducting coil around the outside to form the containment field?" Samuel asked. "I remember reading about that technology in my intro to Space Engineering survey course."

"They sell the superconducting coil with the wand, and it's sealed in a rubber gasket with Verlock magnetic monopoles that don't interfere with the current. We tested it on a few hull sections and now your dad and Paul are setting up to try it in that rental."

"Why aren't you in there with them?"

"In case the containment field doesn't work. They both put on environmental suits, and there's not much room for maneuvering equipment in those rental ship cabins in any case. Don't forget there's no drain, so Paul has to operate the wet/dry vac while your dad does the wash."

"I'll take my chances," Samuel said. He climbed into the rental craft, staying close to the hatch. Joe and Paul had just finished arranging a large rubber loop around a spectacular stain spread over the deck and were stepping back to admire their work.

"Just in time, Sam," Joe said to his son. "We decided to start with a tough one, and I'm pretty sure whoever failed to seal that space-sickness bag properly was drinking red wine."

"How can you tell it was in a bag and not directly from the stomach?"

"From the way it's distributed," Paul said, pointing to the base of the fan-shaped mess. "Plus, the bag failures always happen when the ships come out of the tunnel and traffic control starts decelerating them to create weight. If the bag isn't secured, it goes flying against the bulkhead, and if it's not sealed properly, this is the result."

"I never realized that," Samuel said. "What's that container of blue stuff mounted on the wand? Some kind of solvent?"

"It's an optional tracer dye that shows the containment field's integrity," his father explained. "Plain water can be tough to judge. Why don't you double-check the seal for us?"

Samuel crouched down and examined the rubber outlet where Paul had attached the hose for the wet/dry vac, and as soon as he gave the thumbs-up, his father pressed the button on the power-washer wand. A well-shaped stream of blue-tinted water hit the stain, blasting away the solid matter. Joe swept the stream back and forth, rapidly removing all foreign matter from the deck, and Paul powered on the vacuum.

Samuel stepped back from the swirling mess, scanning for any leaks in the containment field, but the technology combination appeared to work perfectly.

"That looks pretty good, but I'm not going to be able to vacuum it dry as long as the field is in place," Paul said a minute later. "Want to try switching to steam?"

Joe nodded and used his foot to switch the power washer to steam mode. He gave it ten seconds, enough time for the containment field to fill with a blue cloud, and then shut down the flow. Paul kept the vacuum running until there was just the faintest tint of blue water vapor left. Then Joe thumbed the switch on the wand to kill the containment field.

"Uh oh," Paul said, examining the area inside the rubber loop containing the superconductor. "The cleaned spot looks just like new metal and the rest of the deck has a thousand-year-old patina."

Joe grinned and turned to Samuel. "I expected this would happen so I saved the hard job for the youngest knees. I thought it was going to be Kevin, but it looks like you volunteered."

"To do what?"

"The Horten power washer comes with a color-matching accessory kit," Joe explained, detaching a case from the side of the unit and handing it to his son. "There's a scanner in there that analyzes the light spectrum reflecting from the area surrounding the cleaned patch and then it mixes a new stain to match. Just rub it on with a rag and it dries almost instantly, but don't go over the same area too many times or it will end up darker than the rest."

"And wear these," Paul suggested, removing the gauntlets from his environmental suit. "If you get that Horten stain on your skin, it takes weeks to wear off."

"I guess I know why Kevin was really waiting outside," Samuel grumbled good-naturedly. "How many of these ships do we have to do?"

"Two dozen or so, and I'll leave you boys to it," Joe said. "I just wanted to see how the technology worked, but I promised your mother I'd sit down with her to talk about our estate planning this evening. Kevin can take over the power washing, and then all three of you should come to see us at the ice harvester when you're done because you're our beneficiaries."

By the time Samuel finished staining the first power-washed area, Paul and Kevin were two ships ahead of him. But it turned out that most of the digestive failures left behind by renters looked worse than they were, and the majority of them cleaned up so easily that the patina on the steel decks wasn't blasted off. Moving the equipment from ship to ship ended up taking more time than the cleaning process, and it was almost three hours before Paul shot a playful spray at the dogs and announced that they were finished.

"Do you think your mom will still be up?" Kevin asked Samuel. "Go and check. Between the tradeshow and the whole Human Empire thing, she must be running down by now."

"Ping Dorothy," Samuel suggested. "She may be there already if Margie is sleeping."

Kevin fell silent for a moment, and then without bothering to subvoc, said, "Where are you?" He nodded at the other two. "They're all waiting for us. Aisha is there too."

Before the three men even made it up the ice harvester ramp they could smell freshly popped popcorn.

"Did you skip dinner, Sam?" his mother asked as soon as he walked in the door. "Your father said you've been helping with the rentals since you got home."

"I ate all the lunch leftovers before I shut down my booth," Samuel said. "I'm going to put on weight this week, no question about it."

"Grab a seat at the table, there are glasses for anybody who wants a beer," Joe said. "We haven't had an official family meeting since—I don't know if we ever had one. Kel?"

"Not that I can recall," the EarthCent ambassador replied, and then looked down at her diary. "Before we start handing out the goodies, Sam, your father wants you to quit working for the Vergallians and sign up with the Human Empire. Now, I've purchased animal stickers—"

"What!" Samuel interrupted her, turning to his father. "You want me to quit my job?"

"First I'm hearing about it, though your mother has a point," Joe said. "You know that before the current Vergallian ambassador came along, none of them stayed on Union Station for more than two years. When she goes, your job is going to go with her. I know it's been a great experience for you, but even if the next ambassador is willing to keep you on, do you really want to spend the rest of your life working for the glory of the Empire of a Hundred Worlds?"

"You and Vivian are the only two humans on Union Station who passed the EarthCent civil service exam," Kelly reminded her son. "The working groups voted to move ahead with the Human Empire on the Thousand Cycle option, and it's going to be a real challenge keeping it on track when the timeline allows almost a century and a half for procrastination."

"But the Stryx sent me to work at the Vergallian embassy," Samuel protested.

"Years ago, for a co-op job. And then you stayed on and helped your ambassador with one of the greatest diplomatic coups of the last galactic rotation. But this could be your chance to contribute to the future of the entire human race. Would you honestly rather spend four hours a night dancing with aging Vergallian women, half of whom would dose you with pheromones if the ambassador wasn't there to protect you?"

"Affie had to go through Vergallian Intelligence vetting before she started handling the Alt affairs out of their embassy," Dorothy put in. "She told me that the officer who interviewed her asked a lot of questions about you and made it clear that they don't want you around. I didn't say anything then because I know how much you like your job, but you should at least think about the Human Empire thing. Besides, Vivian hates it that you work for the Vergallians."

"Well, I'd been dreading bringing that up, and now I feel a hundred percent better," Kelly said brightly and looked back down at her notes. "I should start by saying that your father and I aren't planning on dying anytime soon. We are both very proud of all of you and we're confident that you can secure your own futures without any help from us. But people do tend to accumulate material things as they go through their lives, and we want to make sure that our passing doesn't create any bad feelings."

"Feeling bad about our dying is fine," Joe interjected. "What your mother means is that we don't want to create any resentment among you over our estate."

"Right," Kelly said. "When my own mother passed, she divided her assets evenly among her grandchildren without taking into account your circumstances in life. Perhaps if we lived on Earth, your father and I would do the same, but to make a long story short, we feel it's more important to leave what we have where it will do the most good."

"Within the family," Joe added.

"Right," Kelly said again, wondering how she had ever gotten through a speech before Aabina started ghostwriting them for her. "Our most valuable asset turns out to be the lease on Mac's Bones, which we're leaving to Paul, along with all the equipment and the caveat that he and his heirs respect Dring's sublet as long as the Maker chooses to remain."

"But we need the money less than anybody," Aisha protested.

"Technically, a lease is an expense rather than an asset," Joe told her. "It's like leaving you a bill that repeats every cycle."

Kelly opened her mouth to object, and then scribbled a note to check her husband's definition with the Thark ambassador.

"It makes sense to me," Kevin said. "I'm fine with running the chandlery as long as Dorothy wants to keep working for SBJ Fashions, but someday I hope to convince her to get back to trading with me. I miss traveling, and I think it's a great way to bring up kids."

"If the Farlings ever create Zero-G sickness pills without side effects I'll think about it," Dorothy said. "Otherwise, it's Union Station or Flower for me."

"It turns out that my pension can only be inherited by Joe," Kelly picked up where she'd left off, "and EarthCent doesn't have any benefits for surviving adult children of diplomats. That means that our only other assets are the items in this ice harvester and our savings, the latter of which Libby will divide among you. So I bought these sheets of stickers and I want you each to pick your favorite animal. Then you can take turns using your stickers to label the items in the house you've always wanted." Kelly offered the sheets around the table, but nobody seemed in a hurry to begin claiming the mounds of books or old furniture. "Come on now," the EarthCent ambassador said. "Once we're gone, you're stuck with our stuff one way or another. What else are you going to do with it?"

"You're kind of famous, Mom," Samuel said. "If Paul doesn't need the space, maybe we could leave everything where it is and call it a museum."

Seventeen

"It's a bit early for me," Kelly said, politely rejecting the Frunge ambassador's offer.

"You don't have to drink the whole glass," Czeros told her. "Just breathe in the aroma and take a little sip."

The EarthCent ambassador didn't want to start the morning with a drink, especially when she was scheduled to spend the next several hours at the final day of the tradeshow before presiding over the embassy-sponsored farewell lunch for the observers, but she accepted the glass and gave it a sniff.

"Oh," Kelly said, and then practically stuck her nose in the glass. "It smells better than the flower market on the ag deck."

"Just a little taste," the Frunge ambassador coaxed her, pantomiming tipping back a glass.

"Mmmm," Kelly groaned as her taste buds were flooded. "This is almost as good as chocolate. What kind of wine is it?"

"The investing kind," Czeros said. "I paid just over a thousand creds a case for this vintage when I visited Earth a couple of decades ago to see the trees. I've arranged to sell ten bottles later today for eight hundred a bottle."

"This is the alternative investment on Earth you wanted to tell me about? For some reason, I thought you were talking about putting money in forests."

"How are forests an investment?" the Frunge asked.

"I forgot that you would never cut down trees," Kelly said, taking another sip of the wine. "This is really, really good. It seems a shame to open a bottle just for me."

"I invited my staff to a tasting after you leave. Besides, I know you'll return the favor if you decide to invest some of that cookbook money back into Earth. I understand that the vineyards are undergoing a renaissance, and I'd like to think that my humble efforts in spreading the word among Frunge connoisseurs has played a part."

The EarthCent ambassador forced herself to put down the glass, pulled out her paperback notebook, and flipped to her notes about investing. "It meets the definition," she said after reviewing the Thark ambassador's main points. Then she recalled something from her Victorian novels and asked, "Don't you need to store expensive wine in a cellar so it doesn't go bad?"

"It's important to control the temperature and humidity, but the climate controls available on Union Station are better than any hole in the ground you can find on Earth. I would advise you to stick with bottles, even though some wineries offer price breaks if you purchase by the barrel. The market for labeled bottles is much more liquid, and I'm convinced that the price appreciation is superior."

"Would you be willing to go in on an investment with me, just so I can get my feet wet?"

"You want to trample the grapes yourself?"

"I mean, I've never made an alternative investment before so I'd rather not do it alone. Rather than pestering you at every stage, if we split a purchase, I'd learn something about the process and, uh, give you ten percent of my wine as an advisory fee?"

"That's very generous of you, Ambassador," Czeros said. "I haven't yet decided what to do with the profits from this Bordeaux, so I'll contact my agent on Earth and have her look into the upcoming auctions. What's your budget?"

"I hadn't really thought about it," Kelly said. "It's a big number with lots of zeroes."

"Ah, the problems of wealth. You don't want to put too much in any particular alternative investment or you'll distort the market. Did I ever tell you the story about my uncle, the feather broker?"

"I didn't even know there was such a thing."

"A few centuries back there was a short-lived fad in Frunge society for decorating our hair vines with rare feathers. The red tail-plumes from an Osetruch were quite popular, but a subspecies of the bird had black tail-plumes that never caught on, likely due to the poor contrast with green. My uncle had one customer who was convinced that black plumes were the investment of the future, and year after year, he bought all of the available supply."

"So he cornered the market."

"He cornered the supply. There was no market, though fortunately, the feathers kept rather well in storage. But the reason I'm telling you the story is that every year, the price of black feathers rose. Nothing like a bubble, mind you, but a steady increase. At last the time came that the client decided to take his profits. He instructed my uncle to sell, but there were no other buyers to be found. The one customer had been the entire market."

"What happened?"

"Dumb luck happened," Czeros said. "On the very day my uncle was preparing to sell the whole lot for pillow stuffing, a Vergallian tourist who worked in the fashion industry bought every last feather for hatbands and the investor turned a nice profit."

"Oh, I'm glad it ended well," Kelly said. "I think I get the point, though. You're saying that even if I had the space to store millions of creds worth of wine, I'd be wiser to spread the money around."

"That much?" the Frunge ambassador asked. "How could our intelligence estimates be so far off?"

"Don't be too hard on them. It seems like we sign a new licensing deal for the All Species Cookbook brand every day, and dealing with alien print editions has been an eye-opener."

"Are the royalties that high?"

"It's the payment cycles," Kelly said. "We started with the English edition, of course, and aside from the initial batch that I ordered for embassy use, those books were printed and distributed for us by the Galactic Free Press. Blythe handled licensing the rights to alien publishers for us, but it turns out that everybody uses multi-cycle reporting periods, and then they're printing so many books that there was a huge reserve against returns. I think the only money we've seen from the alien editions so far is from contract-signing payments, but I'm getting buried alive in reports about the royalties we'll be receiving in the near future."

"You were wise not to sell the alien rights for a flat payment," Czeros complimented her. "I hope you will demonstrate equal insight when it comes to choosing a mentor for the Human Empire."

"I actually wanted to get the cash up front, but Blythe talked me out of it," Kelly said. "And I'm afraid the choice of a mentor won't be up to me." She took another sip of the wine and then realized that she had just finished a whole glass. "How do you decide when the time is right to sell?"

"It depends entirely on the vineyard and the vintage, but experience has taught me that prices on Bordeaux peak at around twenty-five Earth years, give or take a half a decade."

"Thank you, Czeros. I really appreciate your help, not to mention the wine," Kelly said, putting her notebook back in her purse. "Just let me know how much you'll need to make a purchase and we'll give it a try. I like the idea of alternative investments, but given your story about the feathers, it seems I should look into some more mainstream opportunities. Do you have any suggestions?"

"Talk to Crute," the Frunge ambassador suggested. "The Dollnicks are choosey about who they allow to invest alongside princes, and the minimum commitment may be more than you have, but infrastructure projects like space elevators provide a solid rate of return. I don't think you'll be interested in terraforming projects because the timeline is too long."

"Thank you again," Kelly said. "I'll check with him later today."

As soon as she entered the lift tube, the EarthCent ambassador pulled out her racy paperback again. "Libby? Can you tell me anything about the economics of space elevators, or is that competitive information?"

"The retail pricing is available through standard catalogs, though it's just a starting point for negotiations," the Stryx librarian said. "There's also a secondary market for used space elevators, but you have to be careful about the shipping and installation charges, which can run over half of the total cost for the project. The going rate for a new elevator installed on an Earth-type planet is roughly two trillion creds."

"That seems like an awful lot."

"Excluding certain military hardware, space elevators, and colony ships are the most expensive manufactured items for sale on the tunnel network. The advantage of space elevators is that once they're installed on busy worlds, they generate a continuous and predictable stream of revenue."

"Can you ping Donna and ask her to get me an appointment with Crute?" Kelly asked as the lift tube door opened on the Empire Convention Center.

"You can talk to the Dollnick Ambassador right now. He just entered the tradeshow, and it should be easy for you to spot him with his height."

"Thank you, Libby," Kelly said and hurried through the lobby to the Nebulae Room. The young women working the doors looked like they might have been hired from InstaSitter, but they recognized the ambassador and passed her through without requesting to see her badge. Kelly looked down each aisle in search of Crute, but she couldn't see over enough heads to get a good look.

"Here to visit your offspring?" a familiar voice at her shoulder inquired.

Kelly turned and frowned at the empty space, and then a Chert with an alien device mounted on his shoulder seemed to materialize out of thin air.

"Sorry," the alien ambassador said. "I still get a little nervous in crowds, which is why I waited for the last day of the tradeshow. Sometimes I activate my invisibility projector and forget I have it on. You must be proud to have two of your children here representing humanity."

"Thank you, but Samuel is actually here for the Vergallians," Kelly said. "You've been around the whole tradeshow already? I thought the doors just opened twenty minutes ago."

"I slipped in early and reconnoitered so I'd know which booths to stop at. I'm looking forward to your daughter's miracle fabric demonstration on the hour."

"Did you happen to see Crute come in?"

"Yes. We talked for a moment and he said he was going for the gold."

"Is that a sports thing?" Kelly asked.

"Gold, as in the metal," the Chert explained. "There are a number of your miners from open worlds selling forward contracts for production to reduce their risk. If I had the cash to invest I'd be tempted myself. Come, I'll show you where they are. And when you're choosing a mentor for your empire, keep in mind that we Cherts have held together a civilization with no worlds of our own for longer than we can remember."

Kelly followed her colleague through the crowd, keeping a close eye on the yellow alien in case he pulled a vanishing act. She didn't even notice the Dollnick ambassador until she heard him let out an untranslatable whistle of mirth just a few steps away.

"You want me to pay now for gold that's still in the ground?" Crute asked, shaking his head as one might express disapproval to a misbehaving child. "If I wanted to do that, I would open my own mine."

"The investment in equipment and mineral rights is appreciable, and I doubt you could match our production cost," the saleswoman said, tapping the top of a large monitor that faced towards the booth's visitors. "Just take a look at these figures. The graph shows our production ramping up against the cost per Princely Measure, and the numbers are straight from our Consortium Scales, and audited by the Drazen firm of Tork and Kurg."

"So why are the units in Dollnick?" Crute asked suspiciously.

"I saw you coming," the saleswoman said and tapped the top of the monitor. All of the numbers that weren't in Stryx creds cycled through different alien units with each tap of her finger, finally landing back on Princely Measures.

"It's not much of a discount, given the risk I'd be taking," the Dollnick ambassador said doubtfully.

"The risk is shared. If the price of gold has risen when the contract comes due, you'll have purchased our production at a discount on the current prices, and the additional gains will be pure profit."

"But if the price goes down..."

"Two options," the saleswoman said, tapping a different spot on the monitor. The screen shifted to showing something that reminded Kelly of the tote board in the off-world betting parlor, and then she realized that it was a real-time view of the Thark bookmaking operation. "You can hedge any risk by betting that the price will go down, and at the current odds, at worst you'll break even. Or, you can defer your contract delivery date by six cycles, and we allow up to three extensions."

"If the price of gold falls, you'll give me three more chances at six cycle intervals to take delivery at a higher price?"

"Correct," the saleswoman confirmed. "We can't predict the price of gold on the galactic market, but I do have a graph showing the last hundred thousand years, and as you can see, extended downturns are very rare."

"They'd have to be for the Tharks to charge so little for insurance. What's the minimum contract size?"

"One-thousandth of a Princely Measure," the saleswoman said.

This time the Dollnick let out a low whistle. "That's a bit more than I can afford. Can you do it in ten-thousandths?"

"The Thark bookmaking is based on one-thousandth and they'd charge another underwriting fee to change it."

"Maybe I can help," Kelly offered as she stepped forward. "I was hoping to get your advice on some alternative investments, Ambassador, and buying a little gold together seems like a reasonable confidence-building measure."

"You call a thousandth of a Princely Measure a little gold?" The Dollnick looked at the EarthCent ambassador with newfound respect.

"I remember reading some recipes from Dollnick open worlds and everything was in Princely Measures. I thought they were roughly equivalent to tablespoons."

"The measures used in cooking are unrelated to measures used in mining," Crute told her. "The price this fine young Human is offering for a thousandth of a measure delivered six cycles from now is—" he looked back to the screen.

"Twenty-one thousand Stryx creds," the saleswoman said.

"Well, I may have just committed to spending half that on wine with Czeros," Kelly said. "If you can come up with ten thousand, I'll put in eleven thousand, and we'll split fifty/fifty when the gold comes in."

"Done," Crute said immediately, grabbing her right hand in two of his own and shaking it effusively. "As your new partner in alternative investments, I advise you not to make any more deals like this. Even with the discount, you'll need the price of gold to rise appreciably just to break even."

"I'll write it off to education," the EarthCent ambassador said, pulling out her paperback and making a note of the transaction. "What I really wanted to talk to you about is space elevators."

"So which of you will be paying?" the saleswoman asked.

"Send the bill to my embassy," the Dollnick replied, and taking Kelly by the elbow with one of his lower arms, led her to the boundary between two booths where there was a little open space. "Before we talk about space elevators, Ambassador, let me ask you one other question. Have you ever before made such an expensive purchase on a whim?"

"You mean, other than my investment in wine this morning?" Kelly took a moment to think. "Well, there was the time I spent the six trillion creds from the Kasilian auction on discounted colony ships to bring them to their new home, but that was entirely a Stryx setup."

"Good. In the case of the gold we just purchased, can you tell me how you came to a decision so easily to spend an amount that, according to my information, represents more than half of your annual salary?"

"I never could have spent my own money that easily, it's all from the cookbook. I don't know if Joe and I are even worth that much in cash since he handles our finances."

"You feel so overburdened by your embassy's windfall from the cookbook that you're just trying to get rid of the money?"

Kelly stared up at the towering Dollnick. "I hope that's not what I'm doing. I guess I should have asked more questions. Why were those miners selling gold for future delivery at a discount anyway?"

"It's a relatively low-cost way for them to raise funds for operations and lock-in their required margins," Crute explained. "The novel part of the contract is the opportunity to defer delivery multiple times, but as the miners make their numbers in any case, they're only risking potential profit."

"And what made it an attractive investment for you?"

"I need the gold," the Dollnick ambassador said. "I have a niece who is apprenticed to a master goldsmith and she'll be ready to go out on her own in ten years or so. I want to commission formal tableware settings for my family to help get her launched, so that's where my half of the gold will be going."

"Oh. But I'll be able to find a customer for the gold, won't I?"

"There's always a market for gold, it's just a question of price. I'll talk to some of my relatives when the time comes and maybe they'll take it off your hands. Now why the sudden interest in space elevators?"

"Czeros explained that given the amount of money I need to invest, putting ten thousand here and fifty thousand there isn't going to get me very far," Kelly said. "He implied if I want to put millions of creds into alternative investments I should look into infrastructure projects."

"Typical tunnel network infrastructure projects cost from hundreds of billions to trillions of creds. While signing on as a backer for a project like a space elevator would give you an easy way to dispose of your capital, you would be a very junior partner with no control over the management."

"Then it doesn't meet the Thark ambassador's definition of an investment," Kelly said, nodding at Crute's point. "So either I need to find smaller infrastructure projects or abandon the idea of alternative investments. Do you have any suggestions?"

The Dollnick spread all four arms in an expansive gesture that took in the whole room. "Planetary-scale infrastructure is necessarily large." He brought his hands together. "Community-scale infrastructure is necessarily small. Why not invest in your sovereign human communities?"

"Because the money is actually EarthCent's. If we start funding projects for the sovereign communities, it might be misunderstood as an attempt to interfere with the Human Empire through soft power," the ambassador explained. "Even though my associate ambassador dedicates most of his time to CoSHC, we try to maintain a degree of separation."

"I don't understand why that is, nor do you seem to be doing a very good job of it," Crute commented. "Have the Stryx placed some limitations on EarthCent that my intelligence people aren't aware of?"

"No," Kelly said. "Maybe I'm overthinking it. But to your point about community investment, the host species on the open worlds provide the basic infrastructure. Perhaps we need to focus on institutions."

"I suggest you talk to Ambassador Srythlan. The Verlocks have forgotten more about running academy systems than most species ever knew."

"But what kind of return on investment can schools offer?"

"Educated children," the Dollnick replied.

"I know that," Kelly said in exasperation. "EarthCent is already spending the cookbook money as fast as we can find worthy projects that fit into our mission."

"Educating children isn't a worthy project? If you choose me as the mentor to the Human Empire, I'll stress civic education as the key element to building for the future."

"I appreciate your willingness to help us, Crute, but it's not my decision. The ad hoc committee is going to discuss mentors with Daniel, and don't forget whoever they choose will require Stryx approval."

"Suit yourself, but if you offer the mentorship to the Vergallians, I'm keeping your half of the gold," the Dollnick ambassador huffed.

Eighteen

"One more demonstration and we're out of here," Dorothy told Flazint and Lancelot, glancing around as if she was expecting somebody who hadn't shown up yet.

"Myst hated leaving early, but it was the last chance she had to take the ASATs before the next semester," Lancelot said.

"ASATs?"

"All Species Aptitude Test," he told her. "I guess the Stryx waive them for Humans."

"She's going to kill me if you skipped the test just to work with us," Dorothy said. "Myst keeps talking about how you're going to take the same courses and do your homework together."

"How romantic," Flazint said. "I almost wish I was back in school."

"I already took the ASATs on the Gem homeworld," Lancelot told them. "Myst said my scores were the second best thing about me in my catalog description."

"After your hair," Dorothy recalled with a laugh. "Anyway, we made it through three demonstrations, and Jeeves is going to be impressed by how many potential customers we lined up. I never thought I could get tired of talking about fashion, but I'm close."

"You kept it interesting by changing what you said every time," the Frunge girl said. "I've lost track of all the promises you've made."

"They weren't promises, they were ideas. I was just thinking out loud."

"I hope all of the customers who gave us their contact information realize that. While we have a few minutes to breathe, I'm going to stick my head through the curtain and see if Baa and Stick need any help packing up."

"Don't be too long," Dorothy said. "We're up again in ten minutes and the crowd is already starting to gather."

Flazint slipped through the curtain to the other side of the booth and found Baa absorbed with arranging Stryx creds in stacks according to the denominations. "Another good day?" the Frunge girl asked.

"Sold out," the Terragram mage replied. "I should have thought of charging to sign my name two years ago. Easiest money I've ever earned."

"Didn't you used to collect tithes directly from your worshippers when you were in a pantheon?"

"Do you think it's easy being a goddess?" Baa demanded, and dropped to her knees in front of the shocked Frunge. "Oh, Great and Mighty Flazint. Make it rain upon my crops, but smite my neighbor's field with hail. Freeze the river so I can cross without getting wet, and see if you can do something about the hole in my roof. Oh yes, and make the chieftain's son fall in love with me."

"Get up," Stick said irritably. "You're scaring away the customers with your dramatics. If I can sell the last four units I won't have to bring anything back to the office."

"Wow, both of you have done phenomenally well," Flazint said as Baa got to her feet. "We don't have any sales to speak of on our side, just contact information we're collecting."

"And we didn't get a fraction of the crowd you and Dorothy drew with the nanofabric demonstrations, but the people we did attract were all buyers," the Vergallian sales manager said. He gave her an intense look. "Dorothy didn't accept any money for the promises she was handing out, did she?"

"No, Tzachan was very clear about that. Taking money is like making a contract. All we took were names and contact information."

"I don't think anybody else is coming," Baa said, looking up and down the aisle. "Some of the other vendors are already folding up their tables."

"We have a final demonstration scheduled on our side," Flazint told them. "The numbers of casual drop-bys have been way down since lunch, though. I guess most people who are attending a tradeshow don't leave it for the last afternoon."

"That's because the vendors have run out of freebies by the last day," Stick said. "I haven't seen any of those Human Empire observers come through since Wednesday. They stuffed their swag bags a few times and then found somewhere more interesting to be."

"As the acting manager of SBJ Fashions, I declare this side of our booth closed," Baa announced. "Flazint, hold my bag for me."

"Where did you get this one?" the Frunge girl asked. "The clasp isn't mine, and I don't recognize the design."

"It's experimental. Just hold it open."

"Are there six feathers embroidered on the side? I thought five was the limit."

"For bags we sell, not for prototypes." The Terragram mage started by dumping stacks of coins into the purse, and then began feeding in her beanbag chair a handful at a time.

"Baa," Flazint whispered. "The weight isn't changing and the bag should have been full with just the coins."

"Don't mention it to Dorothy or she'll start telling people that we'll have them for sale any day," the mage said, following the beanbag chair with an improbably large thermos. "I doubt the Stryx would allow me to sell real interdimensional storage bags to the great unwashed, but while Jeeves is away..."

There was a loud 'pop' and the young Stryx appeared in the booth. "What did you do now?" he demanded. A tendril of visible energy spun off the end of his pincer and touched the six-feather purse. "You've created a real bag of holding," Jeeves said accusingly.

"I don't recall anybody telling me that I couldn't," Baa retorted, taking the purse back from Flazint. "And I'm keeping the creds I earned signing bags. I checked with counsel and autograph fees fall under the 'personal appearances' clause in my contract."

"Did your legal consultation have anything to do with the three-thousand-cred invoice I received from the law firm of Aaxina, Aleeytis, and Arriviya?"

"I just remembered I have to help Dorothy with something," Flazint said and ducked back through the curtain.

"That has nothing to do with me," Baa said. "And the acting manager of SBJ Fashions gave me the rest of the day off just before you arrived, so I'll be on my way."

"I'll finish cleaning up and be on my way as well," Stick said, but when he moved towards the table, Jeeves stuck out his pincer and stopped the Vergallian.

"I want to know what's going on around here," the young Stryx said. "I caught Dorothy's demonstration of the Gem nanofabric on the Grenouthian news and hurried back, but I didn't see anything in it that would explain why a Vergallian law firm is demanding I compensate them for fifteen hours of billable time."

"It was all a misunderstanding and Tzachan took care of it," Stick said. "I guess the party of the first part wants us to pay their legal bill, but it all happened within the space of an afternoon, so I don't see how they could charge us for fifteen hours."

"Us? Are you offering to pick up part of the tab?"

"I meant SBJ Fashions."

"The invoice shows three partners at four hours each, so apparently they discussed the merits of Dorothy's crimes over a long lunch. The three hours billed for obtaining a court order is obviously padding, but you have to expect that." Jeeves lifted his pincer like a turnstile to allow Stick to proceed with cleaning up, and then the young Stryx slipped through the curtain to the other side of the booth. Even though it was still a minute before the hour, the EarthCent ambassador's daughter launched into her final demonstration the moment her boss appeared.

"I've been talking about our miraculous new fabric for two days now, and in just a minute, I'll ask Lance to put the nanobots through their paces," Dorothy began. "But first, I want to ask a question. How many of you enjoy ordering expensive dresses from a catalog, and then hoping that you won't split a seam the first time you turn around to look at the back in the mirror?"

"That's kind of a leading question," a woman wearing the Drazen version of a power suit responded.

"Sustained," Dorothy said and pounded her fist on the table like a gavel. "Here on Union Station, we're blessed with dozens of boutiques that carry all the sizes for our respective species, but how many of you are from open worlds?"

Around three-quarters of the women, primarily sales reps from other booths who had heard about the SBJ Fashions demonstration and had been waiting for the tradeshow to wind down, raised their hands.

"Perfect. How many fashion boutiques are there in your community?" Dorothy asked, pointing at a woman whose raised hand displayed a prosthetic second thumb.

"None, actually," the Drazenphile replied. "I update my avatar crystal whenever I'm somewhere with a Vergallian fitting room and order my clothes from catalogs, but most of the women in our mining consortium don't have an avatar."

"And you?" Dorothy pointed at a woman whose hair was dyed green and wound around a trellis in imitation of vines.

"There aren't enough humans in our factory town to support any high-end retailers, but I got this dress in a Frunge boutique and did the alterations myself," she said.

"Nice job," the EarthCent ambassador's daughter complimented her. "But what if there was a better option than avatar crystals for mail-ordering clothes? What if there was a magical way you could try on any dress in a fashion house's catalog before placing the order?"

"Are you talking about building an alternative to Vergallian fitting rooms on open worlds?" the woman with the avatar crystal asked. "As good as they are, it's still just holographic projections. You can't actually feel the clothes."

"But with our breakthrough technology, you can," Dorothy proclaimed and turned to her Gem assistant. "Show them, Lance."

The young clone touched his programming device to the tube dress on the dummy and cycled it through several styles. Jeeves remained at the back of the booth, simultaneously watching the demonstration and reviewing Union Station's security imaging of the booth from the last two days.

"Now I have an admission to make," Dorothy announced dramatically. "During our three previous demonstrations, when I asked for a volunteer from the audience, I actually chose ringers who have worked for us as fashion models."

"Everybody does that," said a middle-aged woman who was either an amateur bodybuilder or from a high-gravity world.

"That's because you never know when somebody might be capturing video, but in this case, a model with a perfect dress size wouldn't prove anything," Dorothy said. She read the name off of the stocky vendor's nametag and asked, "Can I draft you as our volunteer, Sandra?"

"If you think it will stretch to my size," Sandra said. "I'm not responsible if it rips."

"It would take advanced weaponry to damage the nanofabric," Lancelot assured the woman as she squeezed through the gap between the table and the curtain dividing the space from the next booth. "I'll just need to know your rough size to start."

Sandra whispered a number in the clone's ear.

"Just step behind our changing curtain and we'll test the wisdom of crowds to pick out something nice for you," Dorothy told her. "Tell us when you're ready." Then she brought up the SBJ catalog on her tab and set it to start cycling through the different styles in full-screen mode so she could hold it up for the audience to see. "Let's do a show of hands. Vote as often as you see something you think will suit our volunteer."

Some styles received near-unanimous approval, but every hand went up for a calf-length tea dress in a floral pattern. Dorothy reported the catalog number to Lance, who reprogrammed the nanofabric just as Sandra called out, "Ready." The young clone pulled the now-loose dress from the clothing dummy and gave it to Flazint to deliver to the woman. A minute later, the volunteer model stepped out from behind the curtain, drawing a round of applause.

"That's just for starters," Dorothy said and examined the fit critically. "Normally, I'd do this with pins, but— Lance, take the waist down a full size and let out the hips."

Lancelot entered the new settings on his programming device and touched the dress, which quickly adjusted, causing Sandra to let out a squeak of surprise.

"I think you're being conservative with your bosom, Sandra," Dorothy continued. "Let the chest out a half-size, Lance, and run a gradient to the waist."

"A what?" the volunteer model asked.

"It's just technical talk for spreading the difference over a measured distance," the fashion designer said and nodded in approval after the clone made the changes. "How does it feel, Sandra?"

"Like the best fit I've had in years."

"Now we can really have some fun," Dorothy said and winked at the audience. "Let's see an A-line with the same settings."

Lancelot tapped a single icon and touched his device to the dress, which reformed itself in a matter of seconds.

Sandra looked down like she couldn't believe what was happening, and the women in the audience broke into applause.

"The tube dress," Dorothy said, and the nanofabric re-made itself again at a touch from the device. "Can you match it to her eyes?"

"Just look at the blinking light," Lancelot requested, holding the device in front of the woman's face. "Got it."

Some of the women in the audience actually began cheering as the dress re-colored itself aquamarine, and Sandra grabbed the clone's wrist to stop him from making another change. "This is it," she said. "I want to buy this one. I don't care what it costs."

"Save the parameters, Lance," Dorothy said. "I'll have to get the exact price to you since it's a special order with the fabric color and modifications, but I'm guessing it will be within twenty percent of the catalog price." She glanced at Jeeves for the first time before continuing. "I don't want to sound like I'm headhunting any of you from your current jobs, but SBJ Fashions is now taking names for potential, er, direct sales franchisees on open worlds. We don't know the exact fee structure yet, and the majority of your cost will be the nanofabric fitting technology. If any of you want to sign up..."

"I'll sign up," Sandra said immediately. "Are you going to offer financing for new franchisees? I can't even imagine what this nanofabric must cost. I live on a Verlock open world and I've never seen anything like it."

"We haven't finished crunching the numbers yet, but we are hoping to launch within the next few cycles," Dorothy said, looking over at Jeeves again. "Everybody who is interested should leave their contact information.

We'll get you a, uh, prospectus as soon as we finish the fine print."

Practically every sales rep in the audience stayed behind to register for the franchisee contact list. There was still a crowd at the SBJ Fashions booth when the Dollnicks sounded the chime announcing the end of the tradeshow, but eventually Dorothy realized that she couldn't avoid Jeeves for the rest of her life, and allowed the last woman to depart.

"Are you going to keep staring at me?" Dorothy confronted her boss. "You told me not to buy any nanofabric and I didn't. We borrowed this sample from the Gem ambassador."

"And how many different people did you promise it to?"

"None, I mean, not in so many words. We told everybody that it was all very beta, and we got a ton of free publicity from the Grenouthians."

"Three thousand creds worth?"

"That was a misunderstanding," Dorothy said stubbornly. "I was sure I knew from somewhere that buyers can always make one backup copy of anything."

"I've reviewed all of your presentations from the security system. While I admit to being impressed with your final concept, its evolution was messy, and I won't be surprised if we hear from more lawyers."

"You liked my franchise idea?" The EarthCent ambassador's daughter flipped from defensive to triumphant like somebody had thrown a switch. "Of course you did, it's brilliant. I knew you'd go for the franchise model because it means we get a sales force equipped with nanofabric universal fitting dresses for a minimal investment in training."

"We still have to buy the nanofabric from the Gem," Jeeves pointed out.

"But the franchisees will buy it from us," Dorothy countered. "We'll have to offer financing if it's really expensive, but you'll make a profit on that. Maybe my mom will invest some of the cookbook money."

"I can't tell the Gem how much to charge for manufacturing, but I'm estimating that a piece of nanofabric sufficient for all of the styles in our catalog will sell for more than most of our customers earn in a year," Jeeves said. "I spent my few off-hours the last three weeks scouring the galaxy for low-cost feedstock wholesalers to supply the nanobot factory."

"But our franchisees won't need anything else," Dorothy pointed out. "No inventory means no stockroom—they can even skip a storefront and make house calls." Then the second part of what Jeeves had said sank in, and she asked, "Why would you be trying to find cheap raw materials for the Gem after I promised not to buy any nanofabric?"

"Because I know you better than you know yourself, and it was clear that you were going to find a way to make the nanofabric part of our business. As my elders are taking an interest in helping the Gem rebuild their economy, I have some extra leeway to work with, so I decided to get out ahead of you for a change."

"You mean—"

"I mean that your intentionally starting with a terrible idea and bringing the wrath of the Vergallian legal system down on my head was totally unnecessary," Jeeves said. "You can't out-Stryx a Stryx, and I know perfectly well that you wasted the first three demonstrations presenting bad business models so that I would jump at the only one that made sense. Have you forgotten who used to troubleshoot the tough matches for Eemas dating service?"

Myst's betrothed took advantage of Dorothy's momentary speechlessness to step forward and bow formally to the Stryx. "I'm Lancelot, Sir Jeeves."

"I take it Dorothy hired you, though I can't imagine under what authority," Jeeves responded. The twinkling lights on his casing made it clear that he was tickled to be addressed as 'Sir.'

"It's just part-time to do the nanofabric programming," Dorothy hastened to explain. "Lance is starting at the Open University next semester, and I did get Baa to approve the hire. Myst too."

"I heard that Myst returned with Gwendolyn, but I didn't realize she had joined SBJ Fashions management," Jeeves said.

"I didn't mean that she agreed to hire Lance, I meant that I hired her part-time as well."

"And what is Myst's particular specialty in the field of spending my money?" Jeeves asked.

"Jewelry," Dorothy told him. "We had an idea for a whole line of matching necklaces, bracelets and tiaras when we were kids, and since she's been mostly sleeping since then, she never forgot. We're going to call it the Princess—where did he go?" she asked, blinking at the empty space that the Stryx had occupied a second before.

"I can't believe you tried to trick Jeeves," Flazint said. "You're even crazier than Tzachan thinks you are."

"Imitation is the sincerest form of flattery," the EarthCent ambassador's daughter replied lightly. "Jeeves can't be angry because I tried to manipulate him for a change, other than the bit about the Vergallian lawyer's bill, I mean."

Nineteen

"—and adding free drinks did the trick," Kelly explained to the members of the intelligence steering committee on the holoconference.

"So the observers were all basically there on vacation?" Ambassador Oshi asked.

"Some of them filled their swag bags the first day and then we never saw them again. I couldn't get our station librarian to tell me why observers are even required."

"I've come to believe that most of the rules related to the tunnel network treaty are anachronisms that the Stryx stick to because they're resistant to change," Ambassador Zerakova said.

"You think the Stryx are hidebound traditionalists?" the president asked. "I've always been impressed by their willingness to play it by ear."

"I don't mean they aren't accepting of new ideas, though it may be a mistake to assume that anything is actually new to first-generation Stryx who have been around for nearly a hundred million years. What I mean is that once they put a system in place, they aren't in any hurry to make changes to accommodate those of us who think that a century is a long time."

"Perhaps, but let's hear the remainder of Ambassador McAllister's update," the president said. "Kelly?"

"Ultimately, the working groups voted unanimously for the Thousand Cycle option, and Daniel was delegated to officially notify the Stryx," Kelly continued her recap of the week's events on Union Station. "Then they voted on disbanding and designating the working group chairs as points of contact for whoever gets stuck trying to launch the empire. Not surprisingly, that vote tally in every working group was four in favor, one against, but majority rules."

"So a small group of civic-minded people learned too late never to be the high bidder at a government auction," Ambassador Fu said with a chuckle. "But will Earth qualify to join the Human Empire?"

"I don't see why not," EarthCent's president replied. "Are you worried that our current status as a Stryx protectorate would interfere?"

"There's a Verlock tunnel treaty expert on Union Station I can check with once everything else is settled," Kelly said. "My own take is that this Thousand Cycle option is equivalent to what my daughter would call a 'soft launch' in the fashion business. At some point in the future, when all the criteria are met and the Human Empire becomes more than a new name for the Conference of Sovereign Human Communities, I believe the Stryx will be ready to let Earth out from under their wing."

"At which point EarthCent will become obsolete."

"If we do this right, our embassies and employees will be rebranded for the Human Empire and none of our institutional knowledge or working relationships with alien diplomats will be lost. That's why I think it's important that we start actively promoting our civil service exam to draw applicants for both organizations."

"So a century and a half from now, or whatever the math works out to, EarthCent and the Human Empire will be prepared to function as a single entity, without a sharp transition period," the president concluded. "How about recruiting your girls, Svetlana?"

"I suppose I'll have to fill out applications for them," Ambassador Zerakova said. "When the co-op jobs with aliens that I signed them up for were completed, they both transitioned to full-time employees, but ultimately, I don't see a career path for humans working in alien diplomatic or intelligence services."

"That's exactly what I've told my son and his fiancée," Kelly said. "I'm counting on the Vergallian ambassador to ease Samuel out if he can't make the decision for himself."

"So we're all comfortable with spending the cookbook windfall to help launch the Human Empire?" Ambassador White asked.

There was a chorus of half-hearted assents from the members of the intelligence steering committee.

"The money is still coming in faster than I can invest it, so there will be plenty left over to finance other worthy projects," Kelly told them. "We're already subsidizing the Twenty-Second Century Bazaar program that Hildy set up to train Earthers in alien relations and to keep expatriate humans connected to the homeworld. But I have a sneaking suspicion that the Stryx timing in awarding us the new edition of the All Species Cookbook wasn't a matter of chance after all. The sovereign human communities never would have gone ahead with the Human Empire if it had meant instituting a new tax."

"You can't argue with education and institution building," the president said. "Still, I'd recommend choosing a mentor before you start shoveling money out the door."

239

"Any progress on that yet?" Ambassador Oshi inquired.

"The ad hoc committee members are arguing about it as we speak," Kelly said. "I was in the meeting right up until I excused myself to get on this holoconference. Every committee member wants to offer the mentorship to the Union Station ambassador corresponding to their host species back home. It's really put me in an awkward position since the alien ambassadors have turned it into a competition."

"The aliens turn everything into a competition," the president said. "I have faith you'll work something out. Right now I have to get to a business lunch where I'm the guest speaker, and that means the rest of you must be getting hungry as well. At least we got Universal Human Time right."

The holographic images of the other ambassadors on the intelligence steering committee began winking out, and Kelly realized that nobody had a miracle cure to offer for her mentor problem. One thought led to another, and she wrote in her open notebook, "M793qK?"

"I have to run out, family emergency," Donna's voice announced from Kelly's display desk. "I asked Libby to deliver this message when you got off your conference call. And Aabina needs to ping the management of the Empire Convention Center."

"That doesn't sound good," the Vergallian girl muttered.

"Aabina!" Kelly exclaimed. "You're so quiet that I forgot you were standing right behind me."

"Part of my early training was attending all of my mother's royal audiences. My tutor impressed on me that the role of a princess in the presence of a queen is to listen attentively and never interrupt."

"Are you casting me as the queen?"

"Officially, you remain the Carnival Queen until the next time Union Station holds an election for the job," the Vergallian girl told her. "I couldn't help noticing what you wrote in your notebook, and although asking the Farling doctor to become the Human Empire's mentor would eliminate the problem of choosing one of the local ambassadors over the others, my mother warned me that she's never negotiated with anybody so deep."

"You mean she's unsure of the doctor's intentions?"

"There's no doubt that his ultimate aim is to rise to the top of the Farling hierarchy. Apparently, he made his move too early and got exiled, though he passes it off as a difference in opinion. What my mother meant is that M793qK was always at least one step ahead of her, and that means he'll be—" Aabina hesitated.

"At least two steps ahead of us, if not a country mile," Kelly said.

"The Farlings have been around longer than any of the tunnel network species, and they never saw the need to join because they're powerful enough on their own. I'm afraid that M793qK would find the position of mentor to a new empire just too tempting not to take advantage."

"It could be moot if Daniel and his ad hoc committee have already decided on somebody else," Kelly said. "Let's get back to the meeting and see what they ordered for lunch."

The Vergallian girl waited at the door for the EarthCent ambassador to wave open the security lock, and then the two of them crossed the lobby and entered the conference room. Daniel was talking quietly with Dring, who was adding some decorative artwork to the margins of his scroll as he listened, and Shaina was reading something on her tab.

"Where did everybody go?" Kelly asked.

"For starters, Samuel got a ping from Vivian and ran off," Shaina told Kelly. "It sounded like she wasn't happy about her twin brother getting married before her."

"What!"

"Kelly hasn't heard yet," Daniel observed. "I'll let you explain, Shaina, because I'm not sure I understand what happened myself."

"You missed quite the drama in the last half-hour," Shaina said. "Jonah has eloped with Sephia, the Mayor of Floater's daughter. Donna grabbed the mayor for an emergency meeting with Blythe and Clive, and the rest of the ad hoc committee members took it as an excuse to call it a day."

"We were just going around in circles anyway," Daniel said. "The only thing everybody agreed on is that the mentor can't be from one of the tunnel network species and that the final choice is up to me."

"That gets us off the hook with the alien ambassadors," Kelly said with a sigh of relief. "But how could Jonah just run off? Doesn't he have a show to do today?"

"Ambassador Crute stopped in," Shaina continued. "We told him you were in a meeting, but he was looking for Donna. It turns out that Jonah and Sephia spent the night at a nest-and-breakfast on the Dollnick deck, and then they convinced a Dolly tour-ship captain to take them on a loop around the station and marry them."

"They eloped to the Dollnick deck?"

"Sephia's father was relieved when he heard. Spending the night before the wedding in a nest is required for the Dollnicks to recognize a marriage on Chianga. She races floaters for the factory, you know, and there's a moral turpitude clause in her contract that would have been violated if she hadn't followed tradition."

"Several of the tour ship passengers recognized Jonah from his cooking show," Daniel chipped in. "The captain thought he'd better report it to the Dollnick embassy to clear any liability with the Grenouthians."

"What do the Grenouthians have to do with it?" Kelly asked.

"The bunnies have Jonah under contract. For all the ship captain knew, he might have stepped in it by performing the marriage."

"How did Blythe and Clive take the news?"

"Better than Vivian," Shaina said. "Blythe was younger than Jonah when she got married, as was Donna, and you remember that Chastity eloped. There's a pretty extensive write-up in the Galactic Free Press gossip column."

"I suppose Samuel will give me all of the details when I see him," Kelly said. "Assuming that Donna never ordered lunch, why don't I treat everybody to a meal out? Maybe a change of scenery will help us think outside the box on the mentor issue."

"We've been thinking outside the box since everybody ran off," Daniel told her. "I even considered asking Libby if M793qK would be acceptable, but then I remembered the way he cleaned us all out when we played poker."

"No, I don't imagine he would be the best choice," Kelly said, glancing at Aabina.

The doors to the corridor slid open, and Daniel and Shaina's daughter entered, accompanied by a little Stryx with a twitchy pincer, and a Cayl hound who towered over the pair of them.

"There's my princess," Daniel said. "What are you doing out with Queenie?"

"Mikey couldn't take Queenie for her late morning walk because he went with Grandpa to sell kitchen gadgets at a fair on the Drazen deck," Grace explained. "Twitchy came with me to the park deck, but now we have to get ready for *Let's Make Friends,* and the bunnies won't let Queenie in the studio."

"I'll take her," Shaina said. "I should really stop in at work now that the tradeshow is over. There's nothing I can do to help you choose a mentor for the Human Empire."

"Dring," Kelly said suddenly. "How about it?"

"Are you suggesting me as a mentor for the Human Empire?" the Maker asked. He shook his head slowly. "Tempting as your offer is, that would be unfair to the Stryx. They would end up approving of whatever you did simply because I was involved."

The Cayl hound jumped up and put her front paws on the table, and then she stretched upwards until her nose almost touched Dring's globe. She cocked her head sideways, studied the sculpture, and then gave the exposed part of the North Pole a tentative lick.

"Down, Queenie," Daniel scolded. "I'm sorry, Dring. She's never done that before."

"Perhaps she's trying to tell you something," the Maker insinuated.

"But what's on the North Pole?" Kelly asked.

"Santa Claus," Grace suggested.

"Polar bears," Shaina put in.

"Brynt!" Kelly exclaimed, the mental image of a polar bear bringing the Cayl emperor to mind. "When he stayed in Mac's Bones, he said that if there was anything he could

244

ever do to repay us for reuniting the Cayl Empire with their lost columns, we only had to ask."

"The Cayl do run one of the most successful empires in the galaxy, and the tunnel network species look up to them for their scientific achievements and military might," Daniel mused. "Libby?"

"A mentor from the Cayl imperial family would certainly be acceptable to us, and Vrine happens to be heading back in that direction. Do you wish me to have your request passed along?"

"Can we have the afternoon to write up an explanation of the situation and extend a formal invitation?" Kelly asked, looking significantly at Aabina to make clear her help with the exact wording would be appreciated.

"Vrine wasn't intending to depart immediately," Libby said. "Just let me know when you're ready."

Shaina left with Queenie, Grace, and Twitchy. Kelly decided to check the kitchenette for leftovers since nobody seemed to be in a hurry to take her up on the lunch invitation. She found a new box of product samples certified by the All Species Cookbook and pieced together a meal. When she stepped back out to ask if anybody else was hungry, both the associate ambassador and Aabina were gone.

"What happened?" Kelly asked Dring, who was rolling up his scroll.

"Your special assistant told Daniel that the management of the Empire Convention Center was very upset over the condition of the special suites that were vacated this morning. It appears that some of the observers harvested more of the furnishings than is normally considered acceptable for hotel guests, and they've already departed

Union Station. Daniel asked me to tell you not to wait lunch."

"Oh. Will you join me?"

"I have to catch up with my gardening, Ambassador, and I believe your visitor would like some privacy."

"Visitor?" Kelly looked up where the Maker was pointing and saw Jeeves floating near the ceiling. "What are you doing up there?"

"Readjusting the rotational speed on Dring's globe and cleaning the spittle off the Arctic," the young Stryx replied. He sank back down to his normal floating height. "Thank you for notifying me, Maker. And while you're correct that I want to speak to the ambassador, there's no need for secrecy."

"What is it, Jeeves?" Kelly asked. "Is my daughter spending all of your money again?"

"She has a very good idea this time, and I'm happy to invest. The problem is getting the nanofabric from the Gem."

"You want me to negotiate with the Gem for you? I'm sure Gwendolyn and I—"

"I've already completed the negotiations," Jeeves interrupted. "The obstacle is that the Gem manufacturing concern can't afford the feedstock to begin producing nanofabric. I would advance them the capital myself, but that would be a Mari'tayin."

"A what?"

"It's a Vergallian legal concept," Dring informed Kelly. "Mari'tayin prescribes otherwise legal actions that may be misinterpreted by onlookers. For example, one should not produce vegan products that are indistinguishable substitutes for non-vegan products lest those following a vegan diet become confused about the food served in a restaurant."

"So, you're worried that if you pay the Gem in advance to buy the feedstock to start nanofabric production, the other species might interpret it as Stryx interference, even though it's smart business for SBJ Fashions," Kelly said to Jeeves. She fished her notebook out of her purse and flipped to an open page. "How much do they need?"

"It's a sure thing because SBJ Fashions will sign a contract to purchase all of the nanofabric produced. You'll have your investment back long before you can figure out how to start spending it on the Human Empire," Jeeves said.

"How much?"

"Did I mention that you'll be doing a good deed, and further cementing humanity's connection with the Gem by aiding their return to a viable economy?"

"How much?" Kelly repeated a third time.

"How much do you have?" Jeeves asked.

"You don't know?"

"I would never check the balance of your programmable cred without permission."

Kelly took the embassy's programmable cred from her purse, shielding the amount with her fingers, and carefully examined it as if she were checking a poker hand. "We have eight digits," she said.

"Twenty million would get the Gem started."

"Twenty million! But I only have—" she paused to mentally insert commas every three numbers on the programmable cred display to figure out the balance, "—that's more than I realized. I guess I can do twenty. What's the rate of return?"

"I can't negotiate on behalf of the Gem, but I'm sure you'll come to a mutually beneficial agreement," Jeeves said. "SBJ Fashions thanks you."

"How are Myst and Lancelot working out as employees?"

"Lancelot reminds me of Paul at his age, and I'm hoping he generates enough profit to offset Myst."

"I take it Myst reminds you of Dorothy."

"I'll put it this way," Jeeves said. "If I didn't know several low-cost methods for synthesizing diamonds, I'd be in trouble."

Twenty

"You may as well give those estate planning animal stickers to Fenna for her collection," Joe said to Kelly as they entered the lift tube capsule in the corridor outside Mac's Bones. "It's been over a month now and the kids haven't touched them. I can understand their not wanting to stick their names on our furniture while we're still alive."

"It seemed like such a good idea when I read it in *Estate Planning For Humans*," Kelly said mournfully. "I'd hate for the kids to fight over my Love-U massaging recliner when I'm gone."

"Better it should happen when we aren't around to see it," Joe said philosophically. "I usually stay away from those *For Humans* books myself, but I would have taken a look at that one if I'd known you bought it."

"Oh, I just flipped through the pages in the bookstore. They repeat all of the important bits in the margins, and I copied a few things into my diary."

"I think you just enjoy pulling your diary out all over the station for the attention that bare-chested Dollnick draws. I'm sure you could get Blythe to print you one with any image you want."

"I didn't want to make trouble for her," Kelly said disingenuously as the capsule doors slid open. "The Grenouthians are so lucky to have their embassy right across from a lift tube. I wonder if the Human Empire can find a location like this. Has Samuel said anything to you?"

"About their hunt for office space? I know he and Vivian have started looking at places, but he's putting off the final decision until the Cayl emperor's granddaughter arrives, and that's a couple of cycles away since she's waiting to hitch a ride back with Stryx Vrine. But who would have thought that the emperor would insist that Samuel be the Human Empire's first hire as a condition on the mentoring deal?"

"Brynt probably assumed that's what I wanted, but I have to admit it worked out for the best. The timing was perfect with Aainda deciding not to return to Union Station. I'm just thankful she didn't call Aabina home."

"I wouldn't be surprised if Aainda arranged the whole thing with the Cayl behind our backs," Joe said, nodding to the ceremonial guard at the entrance of the Grenouthian embassy. "I've noticed that your alien diplomat friends take liberties that way."

"Well, I'll miss having Aainda as a friend, and I don't expect to have the same relationship with her replacement," Kelly said.

"The new Vergallian ambassador has arrived?"

"Returned home is more like it. The Empire of a Hundred Worlds decided they needed somebody who was already up to speed on Union Station. They chose a local lawyer who abdicated her throne in favor of a younger sister around a century ago to pursue the law. Aleeytis is her name."

"Kelly, Joe," Gwendolyn greeted them. "It's a relief to see some friendly faces. I don't know if everybody is ignoring me because I'm a clone, or because I don't have the kind of money to invest in a big production."

Joe pulled his pockets inside out and said, "Twins."

"It's not like any of the cookbook money is mine," Kelly protested guiltily. "I almost wish that the Human Empire needed more funding right now, but according to our intelligence people, it will be decades before they start spending significant amounts. Besides, the Grenouthian ambassador invited everybody he knows with a new business idea to present tonight. I think he called it a 'seed capital' round." She paused to check her memory against her diary, and nodded in satisfaction before adding, "Is there any news from the nanofabric factory, Gwen? Could they use another loan?"

"Sorry, but they've already purchased all the feedstock material they needed to get started, and they expect to be able to ship the first experimental batch by the end of the cycle," the Gem ambassador replied. "Myst brought home one of the draft prospectuses that SBJ Fashions is preparing for franchisees and it looks like an exciting business. It's too bad they haven't worked out the pricing yet, or Dorothy could have presented here tonight."

"Can I get you a glass of wine, Ambassador?" Joe asked the clone.

"Yes, thank you."

"I think Dorothy's business model for the nanofabric is much farther along than the seed capital round," Kelly told the Gem after consulting her business funding notes again. "Maybe financing their expansion into franchises would be the venture capital or mezzanine stage?"

"It's all new to me," Gwendolyn said with a sigh. "Back home, a sister selling apples from a pushcart is our idea of big business." She glanced at the latest ambassador to arrive and did a double-take. "What's that thing on Crute's vest?"

"It looks familiar," the EarthCent ambassador said. "Joe has an old photograph of the control room from Earth's first moon landing and I think the scientists all had those, though I'm not sure what they are. I can ask when he gets back with our drinks."

"Ambassador Crute?" Gwendolyn addressed the towering Dollnick. "Could you tell us what you're wearing on your vest?"

"It's a pocket protector," the four-armed alien explained. "If you're going to carry scribal gear, it's practically a must. I have a nephew setting up in the business if you're interested."

"Is he looking for seed capital?" Kelly asked.

"An order would suffice at this point," Crute said, pulling a paperback with a colony ship on the cover from his back pocket and flipping through to a blank page. "How many can I put you down for?"

The Drazen ambassador stepped up to Kelly's side before she could answer, and asked the Dollnick, "You're selling pocket protectors? Will they work with this?" He produced a small tube that might have been a case for an expensive cigar and removed a fat pen with a single point. "My cousin's daughter is starting to manufacture these multi-color pens, but the prototypes have an unfortunate tendency to leave ink spots on clothes."

"Let me see that," Crute said, accepting the pen from the Drazen and sliding it into his pocket protector. "The plasteel envelope stretches and is impervious to damage, but how does it look?" He turned his profile to Kelly and Gwendolyn, puffing out his chest at the same time. The pen did make an unfortunate lump.

"Maybe not," Bork said. "Give the pen a try while you have it. I think that with a few tweaks to the mechanics, the multi-color technology is ripe for a comeback, and my cousin's daughter is looking for angel investors."

Kelly and Gwendolyn exchanged a look, and then the EarthCent ambassador opened her notebook once again to check the funding phases for startups to get an idea of how much the Drazen might need.

Crute accepted the pen from Bork, selected a color, and began doodling in his order book as the Frunge ambassador approached. "Try this," the Dollnick ambassador said to the new arrival without looking up. He extended the pocket protector to Czeros with one of his lower arms, while he continued holding the order book and drawing with his remaining three hands.

"Clever," Czeros said. "Would you mind?" he asked Bork, handing his wine glass to the Drazen. Then he pulled out his thermal stylus, placed it in the pocket protector, and slipped the whole unit into a horizontal pocket in his suit-coat that Kelly had never even noticed. "Seems to work well. Is it a gift?"

"Crute is selling them for a nephew," Gwendolyn told the Frunge.

"Is that why he keeps looking up every few seconds?"

"Ambassador Aleeytis," Kelly greeted the Vergallian who had just taken over from Aainda. "I've heard so much about you."

"From your daughter?" the new ambassador asked.

"From my special assistant, Aabina. I wasn't aware you knew Dorothy."

"Her name appeared prominently in the last injunction I filed before returning to the empire to interview for the ambassadorship," Aleeytis said. "And now I suppose you'll hold me responsible for your son losing his position at our embassy as well. How awkward."

"Everything worked out for the best with Samuel, and it's not the first time Dorothy has caused trouble," Kelly told her. "Would you really have fired my son if he hadn't resigned?"

"I would have assigned him to a rubber room."

"You would have tried to get Samuel committed?"

"A rubber room is what we call a chair in a closet without any job duties or even the most basic display desk. It's how the diplomatic service encourages unwanted personnel to move on."

"Why wouldn't they just fire him?" Gwendolyn asked.

"The diplomatic service of the Empire of a Hundred Worlds never fires anybody," Aleeytis explained. "That would be equivalent to admitting a flaw in the hiring process."

"Done," the Dollnick ambassador declared and held up his order book for their inspection. The sketch of Kelly and the Gem ambassador was executed in full color and looked like it should have taken at least fifteen minutes to draw.

"That's fantastic, Crute," Kelly exclaimed. "Were you an artist before you became a diplomat?"

"I only took up drawing when I was posted to Union Station," Crute said modestly. "An artist should have a few hundred years of work experience in another profession to gain perspective before attempting to produce serious works."

"Put me down for a dozen of these," Czeros said, handing the pocket protector back to the artist.

"Ambassadors," a handsome man said, stepping confidently into their ever-expanding circle.

"Dewey," Kelly greeted the artificial person. "Is Flower back already?"

"She won't be here for another week, but she sent me ahead to negotiate with the launch team for the Human Empire. Now that Flower has been accepted as a sovereign human community, we're offering the empire custom-built office space at a steep discount, and we feel we can make a strong argument for locating the headquarters on board."

"That's very interesting, Dewey, but you'll have to take it up with my son, Samuel. He's postponing any major decisions until our Cayl mentor arrives, and that's still three or four months off."

"Flower also wanted me to inform you that she's available as a backup mentor should the Cayl bow out," the artificial person said. "But I'm officially here to meet the Grenouthian ambassador about doing an anime version of *Cookbook Wars*."

"Your son has pushed aside your associate ambassador to head up the Human Empire?" Aleeytis asked Kelly. "It sounds like Aainda did a good job training him."

"That's not it at all," the EarthCent ambassador protested. "Daniel wants to keep his focus on building up current trade and relations between the sovereign human communities, while the Thousand Cycle plan is focused on creating a template for the future."

The Vergallian ambassador reached in her purse and pulled out a paperback with the scantily-clad hero of an imperial drama on the cover. "May I?" she inquired and borrowed Bork's multi-colored pen. "I realize that most diplomats put great faith in their memories, but the habits of a century of practicing law are hard to break," Aleeytis explained while carefully writing down Kelly's explanation.

"Interesting notebook," Gwendolyn said. "I suspect they would sell very well in Gem space, as my sisters have all become addicted to Vergallian dramas since the fall of the empire."

"Retro paper notebooks and day planners with covers from the print adaptations of popular dramas were all the rage in the Empire of a Hundred Worlds when I returned for vetting," Aleeytis replied. "Somebody is getting rich quick."

The Thark ambassador sidled up to Kelly and said, "Spotting the next big trend in retail before it happens is the philosopher's stone of investing. There are rumors that the Stryx have sufficient data to figure it out, but I don't credit them."

"Spotting the next big trend in retail is next to impossible," Kelly wrote in her own diary, and added in capital letters, "Check with Jeeves."

"May I have everyone's attention for just a moment," the Grenouthian ambassador requested in a loud voice. The groups of ambassadors and businessmen invited to the event all turned to the small platform where the giant bunny was standing next to what appeared to be an easel displaying the top sheet of an enormous tablet of paper that must have come from an art supplies store.

"More paper," Czeros grumbled. "Why does the galaxy have to be so weird?"

"Thank you all for attending my investment party and I hope you're finding attractive opportunities for your capital," the Grenouthian ambassador continued. "I regret to inform you that I will not be accepting partners in Cookbook Wars after all. I've sold the concept for a finder's fee to a packager working for a network affiliate on Echo Station and my involvement is at an end."

"You're going into competition with Flower in the packaged food business?" Dewey asked, sounding rather alarmed.

"A show-packager, somebody who takes a concept, puts it together with scripts, actors, and sponsors, and presents it to the studio," the Grenouthian explained. "It turns out our studios here on Union Station are currently operating at full capacity, and adding another cooking show would have meant bumping an existing show from the schedule, which completely changes the economics."

"And you gave up the chance to have points in the new show?" Kelly asked.

"I can't keep a close eye on the production due to the distance involved so I preferred to cash out."

"Sound thinking," the Thark ambassador said approvingly.

"So I thank you all for coming, and I hope those of you with uncomfortably high balances on your programmable creds find an alternative investment opportunity while you enjoy the catering," the Grenouthian ambassador said. "I'll be looking for a good place to put this finder's fee to work myself."

"Here you go," Joe said, extending one glass of wine to Gwendolyn and the other to his wife.

"Where have you been all this time?" Kelly asked.

"Talking to Ambassador Srythlan about the kids. He wanted ideas for what to give Samuel and Vivian for their wedding when Flower gets here."

"I was thinking about a multi-colored pen," Bork said.

"Aren't they registered?" Aleeytis asked.

"Srythlan wanted to get them something with a personal touch," Joe explained.

"That's a mistake," the Thark ambassador observed. "If the couple is registered, they may be counting on a cash kickback from the retailer to finance the wedding."

"Oh, Blythe is paying for everything and handling the arrangements," Kelly said. "I think the only decision she and Vivian let Sam make was to choose the band."

"And a very good choice he made," the Horten ambassador said, working his way in between the EarthCent and Gem ambassadors. "You're just lucky that Universal Human Time is so out of sync with our clock, because my son's band was booked solid for the next two years on our calendar."

"What's that you've got there, Ortha?" Czeros asked, indicating the glowing pair of rods in the Horten ambassador's hand.

"A little investing opportunity my uncle asked me to promote." Ortha fumbled a moment to separate the rods, and then drew them apart to reveal a holographic illuminated scroll packed with dense alien hieroglyphs. "It's in the Maker's language, so good luck reading it, but this is for you, Ambassador," he said, passing the open scroll to Kelly.

"Did you copy this from his history of the birth of the Human Empire?" Kelly asked. "It's beautiful."

"I've never seen a holographic scroll," the Dollnick ambassador commented. "It's an interesting juxtaposition of the new and the old. How much are you selling them for?"

"The scroll-style projection handles will be less than twenty creds when we go into mass-production. They include a scanner function, of course, so you just pass the rod over the scroll you're copying. It only took me two minutes to duplicate Maker Dring's history once he rolled it all out on the deck. In addition to saving on wear-and-

258

tear for rare scrolls, you can advance through the holo-gram without actually having to wind a roll of parchment onto the handles."

"I can see where that would be useful for religious texts," Aleeytis said.

"My uncle is a follower of Gortunda," Ortha told them. "It's where he got the idea of creating holographic scrolls. But it turns out that the scribes of the Old Tongue were granted an eternal monopoly on Horten religious scrolls over a half-million years ago, so he has to look elsewhere for a market."

"Have you asked Maker Dring if you can use his name in promotions?" the Thark ambassador inquired.

"He offered a testimonial to the accuracy of the repro-duction," Ortha replied with a grin, and produced a handful of thin holo-chits from his pocket. "I brought copies of the prospectus if anybody is interested."

As the ambassadors mobbed the Horten, Kelly felt a gentle tug on her sleeve and turned to find Jeeves floating behind her. "I had a message that you were looking for me," the young Stryx said.

"I have a couple of questions," the EarthCent ambassa-dor said, following Jeeves out of the scrum. "First, has Dorothy told you that she's expecting?"

"She hasn't informed me yet, but I'm sure I noticed be-fore she did."

"Oh, I forget who I'm talking to sometimes. I don't want to tell you how to run your business, but I was wondering if you could grant her a longer maternity leave this time around."

"Grant her? I practically begged her to stay home long-er than six months when she had Margie, but she insisted on coming back to work. I even threatened to revoke her family-adjustment raise if she came back sooner than a year after giving birth, but my sentient resources officer told me it would violate our employee guidelines. That's what I get for not writing them myself."

"Sometimes I wish I could stay home all day and watch the children for her, but Donna just checked EarthCent's retirement age for ambassadors, and it's still seventy-five."

"Don't tell Dorothy, but when we moved to the office, I set aside a room for a nursery," Jeeves said.

"Why can't I tell her?" Kelly asked.

"Because if she knows, she might try coming back to work in three months instead of six," the young Stryx explained. "I'm hoping that between her maternity leave and Myst starting at the Open University, I might be able to keep SBJ Fashions out of the jewelry business until the franchises are producing an income stream."

"I guess all of this investing I've been doing has started to sink in because I actually understand your logic," Kelly said. "I had another question for you. Can the Stryx spot retail trends before they start?"

"You know better than to think I can answer that," Jeeves said. He deftly deployed his pincer to turn her back towards where the ambassadors were still clustered together, trying to interest each other in new business ventures. "I just heard Bork telling Aleeytis that you might know something about that yourself."

Kelly returned to the group and addressed the Drazen ambassador. "Did you have a question for me?"

"We've been putting our heads together trying to figure out where this new craze for all things related to writing started, and I seem to recall your racy notebook being the first one I saw," Bork said.

"I remember commenting on it myself when you came to the off-world betting parlor to talk with me about investing," the Thark ambassador added.

"Do you remember where you got the idea to start taking notes that way?" Aleeytis asked her.

Kelly thought for a moment, shook her head, and then pulling her notebook out of her purse, flipped to the first page. "Sorry," she said. "I guess I didn't think it was important enough to write it down."

From the Author

The next EarthCent book will be Space Living, the fourth book of the EarthCent Universe spinoff taking place on the circuit ship Flower. For notifications of new releases, sign up for the mailing list at www.ifitbreaks.com. You can find me on Facebook at facebook.com/E.M.Foner, if they haven't banned my account for my not owning a smartphone, and my e-mail is e_foner@yahoo.com.

Also by the author:

CPSIA information can be obtained
at www.ICGtesting.com
Printed in the USA
BVHW040203150720
583771BV00015B/426